I0527671

LESLIE O'SULLIVAN

NOT TO SCALE

BEHIND THE SCENES 💚 BOOK 3

NOT TO SCALE

LESLIE O'SULLIVAN

CITY OWL
PRESS

This book is a work of fiction. Names, characters, places, and incidents either are products of the author's imagination or are used fictitiously. Any resemblance to actual events or locales or persons, living or dead, is entirely coincidental and not intended by the author.

NOT TO SCALE
Behind the Scenes, Book 3

CITY OWL PRESS
www.cityowlpress.com

All Rights reserved. Except as permitted under the U.S. Copyright Act of 1976, no part of this publication may be reproduced, distributed, or transmitted in any form or by any means, or stored in a database or retrieval system, without the prior consent and permission of the publisher.

Copyright © 2023 by Leslie O'Sullivan.

Cover Design by MiblArt. All stock photos licensed appropriately.

Edited by Lisa Green.

For information on subsidiary rights, please contact the publisher at info@cityowlpress.com.

Print Edition ISBN: 978-1-64898-423-5

Digital Edition ISBN: 978-1-64898-422-8

Printed in the United States of America

ALSO BY LESLIE O'SULLIVAN

Rockin Fairy Tales:

Pink Guitars and Falling Stars

Gilded Butterfly

Wild Azure Waves

Crimson Melodies

Emerald Spire (Winter 2024)

***

Behind the Scenes:

Hot Set

Press Release

Not to Scale

PRAISE FOR LESLIE O'SULLIVAN

"*Hot Set,* by Leslie O'Sullivan, is a contemporary love story that creatively infuses modern concerns with the nostalgia generated by a period television show. The Irish setting was fantastically romantic, and I thought the cast of characters was refreshingly practical for a group involved in show business." — *Reader's Favorite 5-star review*

"As full of heart and soul as the music it describes, *Crimson Melodies* drew me in with a fresh take on a classic tale, masterfully combining celebrity and monster romance vibes to give me everything I wanted and more!" — S.C. Grayson, author of *Beauty and the Blade*

"Submerging readers into a fantastical world, *Wild Azure Waves* is a love story swimming with music, mysticism, and magic." — *InD'tale*

"*Pink Guitars and Falling Stars* is a fast paced and very engaging read, with a constantly evolving main character and a colorful cast. The adventure wraps up nicely, and ends with a hint of what is next in the Rockin' Fairy Tales series. This is a great read if you are looking for an action-packed modern fairy tale with aspiring rock stars who fall from the sky." — *Paranormal Romance Guild*

"*Gilded Butterfly* is a unique and magical mashup of fairy tales, Shakespeare, and lore, unlike anything I've read before. At its heart, is a beautiful story about family, the destructive power of chasing fame and money, and the healing power of love. The twists, turns, and magic sprinkled throughout create an engaging story that brings a new kind of fairy tale to modern Hollywood." — *Megan Van Dyke, author of Second Star to the Left*

"*Pink Guitars and Falling Stars* is an interesting take on the story of Rapunzel...O'Sullivan has definitely nailed the initial animosity between Justin and Zeli. As they become closer, the relationship jumps off the page and morphs beautifully. There are awesome love scenes with a lot of description which pull the reader right in and keep a tight grip... A fascinating remix of a popular fairy tale with some very sexy differences. One to add to the e-reader and to be read list!" — *InD'tale*

"With wickedly clever wordplay, fresh and lovable characters, and an utterly unique take on a classic fairytale, *Pink Guitars and Falling Stars* is one of the swooniest romances I've ever read. You'll be cheering for B.A.S.E. jumper Justin to help Zeli escape her tower in the heart of Hollywood's twisted music industry and fall equally hard for their chosen family on the Boulevard. A romantic, heart-in-your-throat read!" — *Sarah Skilton, author of Fame Adjacent*

"Leslie O'Sullivan's narrative style in *Gilded Butterfly* celebrates truth, love, and heritage, and reads as pure poetry from the opening line until the end." — *InD'tale*

"*Pink Guitars and Falling Stars* reads like glitter and stardust, like a song of the heart set free and realizing every dream." —*Fairrryprose*

Pink Guitars and Falling Stars is a winner of a 2023 Gold Author Shout Reader Ready Awards "Top Pick."

Hot Set is a 2023 Holt Medallion Winner for Mid-Length Contemporary

To everyone living with bipolar disorder and the mental health professionals and families who support them.

AUTHOR'S NOTE

Bipolar disorder looks different in every person who faces the challenges of this mental illness. In *Not to Scale,* Elodie's relationship with her diagnosis is directly modeled after my own personal journey. I have been fortunate to be well taken care of by open-hearted psychiatrists, psychologists, therapists, and beloved friends and family who help me navigate life with this reality. My gratitude to them is limitless, and it is my wish that all who live with bipolar disorder will find a team as beautiful as the one I have been gifted with.

CHAPTER 1
BAGGAGE CLAIM

The tall blond Irishman on the morning shift behind the rent-a-car counter at Shannon Airport pins me with a knowing stare. "Ms. Pettipas, are you certain a stick shift is the way to go? It'll be your off-hand doing the work."

I treat him to a casual wave while my insides organize an uprising. Twirling the silver birthstone ring on my right ring finger with my thumb calms the insurgence. "I'm always up for a challenge."

Five minutes later, I'm loath to admit tall, blond, and Irish was right. I should have opted for an automatic rental. It's been ten years since I last drove a stick, and that was with my right "on-hand." There's a serious communication breakdown at present between my brain and left extremity as I attempt to work the gear shift. I'm not even close to leaving the rent-a-car parking lot when sticky third gear growls an unhealthy grinding noise. I half expect the cheery rental car attendant to throw himself in my path, waving his arms to insist I stop torturing his car. Adding to the miserable experience, I look over my right shoulder instead of my left to back up and stare at the car door.

A wise woman would head inside to the counter and insist on an automatic with a backup camera. Stubborn and determined me refuses to give in to my perpetual fear of failure until I stall for the third time in a row. Crawling back to the original parking place in second gear, I kill the engine and drop my head onto the steering wheel. Seeds of panic sprout in my chest.

I can't do this.

I punch my thighs. "Stop it, Elodie. You're thirty-two. At your age, panic is a choice."

At far too many points in my life, in my career, I've let anxiety drive me into hiding. It's set me back and made it harder on the next job to convince myself I'm not a fraud. Today it will not be anxiety for the win. I've landed my dream job, heading the art department of a crazy popular TV show with resources that would make most production designers moan with contentment. Even better, *The Chieftain's Son* is a time-hopping period piece begging for the very research deep-dives that set me on the road to my career in the first place.

I point a finger between my eyes. "You will not cocoon because of a stick shift." Determination to seize the gift of reconstructing history my new job promises bubbles inside me.

After fourteen hours in the air and a lost suitcase, I wish this moment was history. Years of travel working in film taught me to pack my carry-on as if I'll be stranded on a deserted island with only the contents of two zipper compartments for survival. My current deserted island is Ireland.

"Elodie Pettipas, you are a self-sufficient and capable woman."

My therapist, Kevin, is a huge proponent of positive self-talk. Still, the vise constricting my chest converts breaths into gasps.

"Correction, you are a self-sufficient and capable hot mess."

The bright yellow sticker on the sun visor screams at me to drive on the left side of the road. My whole life has veered onto the left side of the road. I will be living in Ireland for the foreseeable future. I barely know the sum total of one person here, Bobby Provost, the showrunner who hired me from video chats and phone calls. Rich and Amethyst Bettencourt, the angel mentors who took me under their wings in my early days of TV art direction, plunked me onto Bobby's radar and vetted me to the showrunner. I respect their faith in my talent more than my waning confidence. The Bettencourts would never recommend me if they doubted I could handle this monumental opportunity. Screw imposter syndrome, I will not let them down.

Their daughter, Gillian, is a writer on *The Chieftain's Son* and married to its star Jack O'Leary, a union I've sworn not to blab about. I suppose that increases my total to knowing one person virtually and two others by association. Three people in Ireland I almost know.

The cell buzzes in my pocket. It's Bobby Provost. "Hey Bobby."

"Welcome to Ireland, Elodie. Are you still at Shannon? The airline said your plane landed an hour ago."

I'm surprised how quickly his voice grounds me. We've already planted the seeds of our working relationship long distance. Bobby is easy to laugh with. We're both guilty of bird walking off work topics, then stretching conversations by sharing the horror stories from previous shows we worked on, disagreements over movies and other TV shows, and regaling each other with theater major shenanigans from our mutual but separate days at the same Hollywood adjacent college. I enjoyed talking to Bobby at the end of his days when mine were just beginning in LA and felt a little guilty keeping him chatting into his wee hours. Not guilty enough to end the call. I wonder how much opportunity we'll have for these talks when we're both buried in the demands of a brutal production schedule.

"It did. The short customs line was the stuff of dreams."

"Our driver, Patrick, can't find you."

"You sent me a driver for a three-hour trip?" Am I offended he discounted my ability to drive from County Clare to Kerry or touched at the gesture? I settle on relieved I'll dodge baptism by fire on Irish highways while jet lagged.

"Didn't you get my text?"

I scan my phone screen. "No text."

He's quiet for a second. "Damn, I emailed. Sorry, meant to text." Bobby pauses. "I wish I'd had time to call before you took off, but my schedule was nuts today." There's a definite charm running through the scattered tone of his voice, reminding me why I'm always eager for his calls. "Anyway, Patrick's camped out at baggage claim."

Judging from the small crowd at the single terminal airport, Patrick's probably the only person still at baggage claim.

"Look for a retired footballer type in a *Chieftain's Son* baseball cap."

The long trip and lost luggage tip my attitude from *relieved* to *touched* by Bobby's gesture. "A guy who will save me from driving an off-hand stick shift on the left side of the road? Yes, I'll go find St. Patrick in a baseball cap."

Bobby laughs. A surge of warmth dissolves my rising panic. I'm getting very used to that laugh. I wouldn't mind getting even more used to it.

My phone buzzes with an incoming call from the airline. "I've got another call. Talk with you soon, Bobby."

"Looking forward to it, Elodie Pettipas."

The man's voice is the sunny equivalent of a smile. I answer with my own smile as I click over. My heretofore jumpy stomach is infused with a dose of Bobby Provost honey for a moment before my nerves fire up again. Am I leaning too far into the connection I've forged with Bobby over our transatlantic chats? Damn, I know my therapist would push play on his familiar tune that I tend to attach to authority figures and hunger for their approval. Bobby probably already has an Irish girlfriend. The good ones usually do. I hard swallow the lump of disappointment taking up residence in my throat as my phone pesters me with a reminder someone is waiting for me to answer. "Elodie Pettipas here."

"Ms. Pettipas, good news, we've found your luggage. It should be arriving at Shannon Airport within the hour."

Luggage, a driver, and only a few hours until I meet Bobby face-to-face. Looks like Ireland is not my deserted island after all.

CHAPTER 2
THE CLAN

I point out the window with my slice of take-out pizza. Not take-out, take-away. I've been schooled by Patrick, my driver, to use the correct Irish term for to-go orders. "There's another one. Can we stop? I want to take pictures."

Patrick chuckles but doesn't slow as we soar past the long-dilapidated stone tower near the roadside that screams *castle*.

I accidentally slap the window with my pizza as I strain my neck to keep my prize in sight. "Hey, we're going to miss it." Wiping the smudge with my napkin only makes it smear more.

"You've already used up your pull-over quota taking pictures of the last five stacks of stone." He raises a finger. "And a food stop. If we don't push on to Waterville, I'll miss my own dinner at home."

After setting my slice on the grease-soaked paper plate in my lap, I turn to Patrick. It's weird having the driver to my right. He offered me the back seat, but I insisted on joining him in the front. As far as I'm concerned, we're equal players on the same team. I won't act hoity-toity by succumbing to any front-seat/back-seat societal pyramid.

"I don't have it in me to pass honest-to-God castles. It's the perfect research opportunity to touch the stones, close my eyes, and soak in their story."

Patrick glances my way to answer but frowns when he sees my pizza art on the window.

"Sorry. I'll clean that up."

He waves a hand. "No need. I suspect I'm just as handy with a spray bottle as you."

"The smudge blew my chance to convince you to increase my castle stop quota, didn't it?"

St. Patrick pats my arm. "Stop your worrying, darlin'. You'll have plenty of chances. You can't swing a wet cat in a circle without hitting a castle in Ireland."

After one castle-free stop to dump the pizza box, which Patrick claimed was stinking up his fine car, we finally turned onto the famous Ring of Kerry, the road that loops around the scenic Iveragh Peninsula. Despite the chill outside, my new pal, Pat, insists we crack the windows to chase the pizza smell away. As we near our destination of Waterville, we bond over our love of *Star Wars* and the root beer barrel hard candies I brought from home.

"I'm to deliver you straight away to The Clan so you can catch folks before the day's over."

I'm itching to explore The Clan, a self-contained production facility repurposed exclusively for *The Chieftain's Son* TV show. I've been in touch with most of my department leads and am excessively impressed with the production design playground at my disposal.

As we turn down a lane so narrow, I'm surprised the car fits, Pat jerks an elbow toward the road we'd been travelling on. "I'll drop your gear off at Water Villa in town. You'll be staying in the same flat our Gilly once claimed." He winks. "Maybe the place has a bit of magic, and you'll be as lucky in love as our Mrs. Jack O'Leary."

The car wobbles sharply as Pat's hands slip off the wheel. He recovers control, but his face flames. "Och, there I go running off at the mouth about things I shouldn't." Pat wipes a hand over his chin. "Our publicity boss, Meg McGrath, will have my head on a platter."

I lay a hand on his arm. "It's okay, Pat. I've signed my NDA concerning Gilly and Jack. I also know her parents. The O'Leary marital status is old news to me."

His upper body sags in relief. "Brilliant."

"And I'm good at playing dumb, so this Meg will never know you busted out state secrets."

Pat turns to look at me. "You're a keeper, Ms. Elodie."

I lean back in the seat, enjoying the lush country around us. "The only love I'm on the lookout for is with history and making Ireland's visual past come alive."

After one unfortunate liaison with a lighting director who was so persnickety, he ironed a crease into his jeans, I've avoided show relationships. There's beauty and danger to attachments that form when people make stories together. Existing inside a creative cocoon fosters closeness replicating true love but inevitably falls apart after the show wraps and common purpose fizzles. The fact Gilly and Jack took the marriage step signals a level of commitment I hope for their sake will defy the odds and stick after the end of *The Chieftain's Son*.

My self-preservation, avoidance policy certainly doesn't support the hints of a mini-crush I have on Bobby Provost. I rub my hands over the thighs of my denim overalls, replaying some of our longer conversations. His friendliness was probably nothing more than making me feel at ease and welcome in my new position. I might as well be crushing on Jack O'Leary. An echo of Bobby's laughter bops around in my head. What if my attraction is not one sided?

Pat slaps the steering wheel. "Oh, now you've gone and done it."

I shoot a glance around me for additional pizza damage. "Done what?"

"Said you're not looking for love." There's a twinkle in Pat's eye and a grin that says trouble. "You've given the Good People permission to find it for you. Watch yourself. Next thing you know, a cat'll give you the eye after it washes its face, a sure sign you're in for a marriage."

I pause for him to go on with his tease. Our talk of the Good People and respecting Irish superstition is one more appealing layer to help me truly understand this country from the inside out. "Do people here really believe in them, Pat, the fairies?"

"Some more than others."

"And you?"

"Let's leave it with I'd never mess with a fairy mound or a hawthorn tree." We pull up to a guard station and Pat hails its occupant. "Yo, Dev."

I'm introduced to Dev, the guard who could easily pass for a bouncer. He exchanges outrage with Pat over a football match. This Irishism I know. Football here is soccer to Americans.

While Dev and Pat harangue about *Fucking useless strikers,* I take an opportunity to soak in my surroundings. Sheep dot a palette of deep-green, sprawling fields like white paint spatter. The land is idyllic, timeless. My heart aches a bit for the generations of Irish who had to leave their verdant treasure because of famine or violence. Vistas from Shannon Airport to here in Kerry, the jovial company of Pat, and of course castles already have me falling a little in love with my temporary home.

We blow by a gravel parking lot, oops, car park, in front of the warehouse-looking headquarters of The Clan.

Pat drives a block down the road and stops the car. He points at a small rise in the near distance. "They're shooting Jack and Gilly's travel show on that bitty hill. I don't want to get any closer and spoil the sound." He opens the glove box and hands me a yellow wrist band. "This'll tell the lot you're one of us." Looking off across the field, he sighs. "The show's gotten so big, we've had to up our security. Lots of snoopers make their way onto the property." Pat fans a hand over the hazy landscape. "This late in the year, it's not so bad. In summer, poor Dev needs backup from the Gardái."

"The Guards?" I picture American National Guards riding in on tanks with Jack O'Leary, hero of *The Chieftain's Son,* Donal Cam, on his white horse, Streaker, in the lead.

"Gardaí—police." Pat snorts. "You need to set yourself down in front of Irish TV for some education."

"That's probably the best advice for acclimating I've gotten yet." I shrug into the flannel-lined, waterproof down jacket recommended to me for Irish weather and grab my backpack. Before I close the door, I lean in and give Pat a peck on the cheek. "Thanks for the lift and the unplanned castle stops."

A slight blush makes his cheeks rosy. "Follow the curve in the road around to the far side of the hill, and you'll see the main path to the top. Be seeing you, new girl."

Being called a girl from Pat doesn't feel demeaning at all. It's sweet and brings the same flattering rush I get from being carded at bars. Barely being able to claim five feet and the youthful genetics gifted to me by my parents does allow me to still pass for *girl*. Being dismissed because of my youthful vibe or getting called kid pisses me off, but I'll take a well-intended *girl* until the day under-eye wrinkles rob me of the title.

As soon as I shut the door Pat, or Paddy as Dev called him, rolls the car in reverse down the road a way before he starts the engine and disappears. Turning, I face the hill and my future. I giggle as my inner Bilbo Baggins plays in my head. I always recite a slight variation of his iconic "Stepping onto the road" quote every time I start a new gig. Now's as good a time as any to bust it out.

I whisper Bilbo's words, since I'm not sure how close I am to the shoot and mics.

My heart pounds as I come abreast of the hill and hear the faint murmur of voices from the top. The quiet of the surroundings allows sound to travel unimpeded. There are a handful of well-placed boulders on the slope, and the climb doesn't look too steep. My stomach flipflops at the thought of trudging up the main path while everyone stares at me. If I approach from here, it will give me a chance to peek at my new work family before they see me. First impressions matter, and I want to make a good one. Once I get the lay of the land, I can step out from behind a boulder and enter the scene with a prepared witty comment or surprise them with my sense of fun.

My trek is successful until I hit the halfway point. The damn hill is much steeper than I figured, and the ground has turned into sticky muck. I pause, calculating the difference between the distance to bail and go back or to forge on. It's not much further to follow through on my hill-climbing commitment. If only I had the waterproof hiking shoes tucked away in one of my suitcases instead of airplane-comfy slip-on sneakers.

I silently swear, sloshing and sliding another few feet toward the top. This is not exactly the entrance I envisioned to introduce myself to seasoned members of my new crew. Pat's affectionate title of *girl* is about to take a derogatory turn once I slurp onto the scene. Shit, I need these people's respect.

Get over yourself, Elodie.

I can spin my arrival on the scene as daring and adventurous, not the idiot who ignored the smart way up the hill. On my next step, my sneaker sinks into a mud patch. Before I have a shot at fighting the suction, Ireland attempts to swallow me whole. Calf, knee, and thigh follow my foot as I grab hold of the ropy root of a nearby tree. I list sideways as my right leg disappears into the soupy hole. Tragic imbalance pitches my body forward, the reward—a face full of Irish soil.

Every Irish folk tale I read in preparation for this job zips through my brain. Am I being pulled into the underworld to be mocked by the fae? Is the ancient spirit of an Irish king claiming me as his vassal?

From the hilltop, I hear a clapperboard and the announcement of a take. Instinct takes over. I don't dare move and spoil the shot. As I lay shivering like a half-dipped chocolate-covered strawberry, I'm treated to a beautiful narrative of the marriage proposal Jack O'Leary gave Gillian Bettencourt on this very hill. Bobby told me they squeeze in shooting segments whenever they can for Jack's companion show, *My Two Loves*, the two being Ireland and Gilly. The filler to air between *The Chieftain's Son* seasons will arrive on the heels of the public announcement of Jack and Gilly's marriage. They're banking a true-life romance will temper the disappointment of Jack O'Leary fans who harbor dreams of snagging him as the star in their own love stories. Rich and Amethyst Bettencourt filled me in on the PR nightmare their son-in-law endures preserving the ruse of his single status. The insanity is a strain on the whole family.

I conquer nature's forces with minimal maneuvering and free my leg from the hole with a muted suction *pop*. As silently as possible, I slink behind a boulder. I'm glad to be in Ireland, but I never intended to give it a literal hello kiss. Thankfully, my water bottle is easily accessible so I can rinse the grit from my teeth. Attempts to slough the mud off my jacket only smears it. This is a disaster.

Mud bath me will absolutely not be meeting anyone today. As soon as the company leaves the location, I'll pick my way to the road and take Patrick up on his offer to call if I need *toting about*. He seems the generous sort to be all in for a rescue mission to sneak me into my apartment in Waterville for a thorough de-mudding. Poor man. His car will never be the same after meeting me.

A simultaneous drop in light and temperature cues the end of the afternoon. The cuff of my jacket protected my smartwatch, and I see it's after four p.m. The hustle on the hilltop suggests they got their shot and are wrapping the day.

I wait out the familiar sounds of a crew packing up. As the October nightfall gets serious, the chatter from walkie-talkies dies. I hug the shadow of the boulder so cold it may as well be a block of ice until a van and equipment truck amble down the road toward The Clan's facility.

Carefully regaining my feet, I decide continuing the short distance to the top of the hill is the safer risk than navigating merciless mudholes on the downslope. Pat told me to take the honest to goodness path to the hilltop. I should have listened instead of attempting this ill-advised jaunt to appear spontaneous. How big a bribe will it cost me for Pat to agree to a pinky-promise NDA to keep silent about my regrettable mud slog?

Time to climb. After gingerly testing the ground in front of me with the muddy toe of my sneaker, I slide around the boulder and get smacked in the face by a blinding beam of light.

CHAPTER 3
IMPRESSIONS IN MUD

T he momentum of shielding my eyes works in tandem with the
steep slope to send me face-planting for the second time onto
the soggy ground.

The light drops as a man calls out, "Jeez, sorry. Stay there. Let me
help you."

Between the growing darkness and retina burn, I can't see a damn
thing. Fingers grip my upper arm to help me to stand.

"Elodie?"

In the glow of the flashlight, I see the outline of a familiar face in 3D
for the first time.

Bobby Provost.

This is the mother of horrible first impressions. Nothing to do but
make light of it. "No one here by that name."

"It's me, Bobby." His grip becomes gentle as he helps me up the few
feet to the flat top of the hill. "Patrick said he dropped you off. When
you didn't show, I semi-freaked out."

I pretend to scan the area in alarm. "Why? Are there lurking alpha
predators you've re-introduced here on studio land?"

"Not unless you count irritable sheep." Bobby sweeps the flashlight
over me, assessing the damage. "Patrick should have shown you the easy

way up." He bends to wipe the mud stuck to his hand from my jacket on a patch of grass.

"He might have mentioned it. Let's leave it at I opted for the bigger challenge." I take a step away and attempt to slough mud off my sleeves. Bobby will brand me the biggest idiot he's ever met. What sane person ignores a nice well-trod path in favor of a steep sloppy slope?

I brace myself to endure the extreme awkwardness of the moment, mentally preparing a speech to defend my capabilities to be the new production designer of *The Chieftain's Son*.

Hey Bobby. Don't you prefer a bold and daring person to head your art department? Risk taking—the path less traveled and all that. You're looking at her.

"Elodie, I can safely say you look…" Bobby attempts to swallow a chuckle and fails miserably. "Shorter in person."

I stretch my arms wide, inviting a hug. "Great to meet you too, Bobby. Bring it in."

He jumps backward so quickly, it's my turn to giggle. In moments, we're sharing a laugh at our ridiculous rendezvous, and my tension eases up.

"I'm more accustomed to being covered in paint," I say, taking a breath and shaking out the bottom of my jacket. The snap of a frigid breeze throws me into a shiver.

"We need to get you dry. I'll drive you to The Clan." He gestures toward the official path down the hill. "My car's at the bottom." Eyeing my muddy coating, he adds, "I've got a blanket in the trunk you can sit on."

As we make our way to the road, I stare down at the me-mess he sees. "It's not far. I'd cause less damage walking behind your car."

"Not going to happen. I won't have you dying of exposure your first day on site." Bobby opens his trunk and retrieves a plaid blanket followed by a large garbage bag. "Do you mind stowing your jacket and shoes in here?" He flashes a dubious eye at my overalls but doesn't add them to the inventory.

"Bobby, I refuse to walk into The Clan like…" I fan a hand down my body. "I've already blown a year's embarrassment quota with you. This melted fudgesicle look will not be the eyeful on which my team will form their initial impression."

Bobby raises a fist to his lips to hide a laugh then drops it. "Fair point."

"If you'd be so kind as to give me a lift to my flat in Waterville, I'll transform and meet my people tomorrow as a competent and loveable boss." A clipped "Oh" escapes my lips as another blast of frigid air lowers my core body temperature.

Bobby scampers around to the passenger door of his black Hyundai. I lower my head to hide a smile. His high energy bled through the internet, but I didn't take him for a scamperer. It's charming, an entertaining addition to my overall positive opinion of the showrunner. I decide to add *Scamper-Bobby* to the list of attributes I already find appealing about him.

"I'm not going to make you marinate in mud for half an hour." He spreads the blanket over the seat. "My place is close. I'll take you there for a preliminary rinse and dry before we hit town. I promise my shower is not single guy grungy."

Single guy—so noted.

I scan my surroundings, which are devoid of any building apart from The Clan complex. "Do you live under a tree in a Peter Pan and Lost Boys situation?"

He laughs. "Actually, that was a childhood dream of mine."

I cock my head to the side. "Only childhood?"

He holds up hands in surrender. "You got me. I'm still in search of a well-appointed underground hideout."

"If your dream has a shot at coming true anywhere, it's going to happen in Ireland," I say, scooting, not scampering to the passenger side. Are scooters and scamperers compatible?

"Truth," he says and shuts my door. He slips behind the wheel, starts the car, and without my even having to ask, cranks the heater. "I stay in a very small house that's not much more than a glorified trailer we had put on the property down the road from The Clan. Jack and Gilly are my only neighbors in a matching mini domicile. Our low-key pair of addresses gives them privacy and me the convenience of short travel time to a bed given my ridiculous work hours."

A vision of Bobby in bed wearing a come-hither look warms my insides. When he accelerates, I nearly bite my tongue the road is so bumpy.

Bobby whips his gaze to me. "I mean, if you're okay with it." He runs a hand through his hair. "I'm not trying to make you uncomfortable, taking you home the minute we meet in person." He gives a nervous laugh.

I add *Nervous-Bobby* to my catalogue of moods he wears adorably. The urge to cup the side of his face and tell him it's cool dies quickly. That brand of touching within moments of meeting is a recipe for awkward. As if my mud romp hasn't achieved full awkward.

In the bluish light from the dashboard, I see his lip crinkle. "It's just after all our late-night conversations, I feel comfortable with you, as if you're already a friend."

Friend zone warning lights flash in my psyche. Ugh, such a zone has killed many a possibility between two consenting hearts. Shoot, is that what I have, a consenting heart? Is my resistance to cross the crime scene tape into Friendlandia with Bobby cranking up my crush?

While my mind races, my mouth stays conversational. "Your late night, my early morning."

"Right, right," he says, nodding while he studies the road illuminated by headlights alone. It's bizarre driving into pitch darkness. In a few moments we're alongside The Clan buildings, which lend a little light to the situation. "I can take you into Waterville if you prefer."

My preference is to spend more time with Bobby. The warmth I've felt through our chats carries over into real life. My curiosity about this fine fun fellow is something I may be interested in exploring. Besides, a chance to clean up ASAP and remove mud from places it has no right to linger is too good to pass up.

I twist in the seat to face him, careful to stay on the blanket. "Am I keeping you from work? If you want to drop me at your place, I can call Pat to haul me into Waterville once I'm presentable."

The combination of blue dash light and Bobby's blush turn his face a delicate lavender. "I actually granted myself a night off to welcome you."

"And cleaned your shower for me. How thoughtful." I'd bump his shoulder with mine if it wouldn't unleash an avalanche of quickly drying mud flakes. I throw mud to the wind and crank up my flirting. "Do I want to know what else you've planned for our getting to know you night?"

"Hmm, if the shower went well. I considered a personal..." He winks at me.

I love he dishes the flirt right back.

"Tour of The Clan and a good ole Irish pub dinner."

Is this legit flirting or is it friendly banter? What do I want it to be? Mini therapist sitting on my shoulder screams the warning *please the authority figure* in my ear. I'd better make the shower nice and cold.

Bobby pulls next to a metallic pre-fab house the size of a three-car garage. A motion sensor light blasts across the gravel drive. The place is no frills except for the wooden flower boxes bursting with pansies and daisies on the ground along the front of the compact house. It's a nice touch. I wonder if Bobby does the gardening or a greensman from the crew does it for him. He jumps out the driver's side and as I suspected, scampers around to open my door.

"Elodie Pettipas, you are very welcome to my humble Hobbit hole of a house."

Taking care not to shed any more mud than I already have in his car, I swivel and stand. He hands me the trash bag of my muddy duds. "I'm honored to heave my happy heft henceforth."

"Hereafter a heartfelt happenstance to..." He waves me off. "I'm H'd out."

"A head writer with no words? Did I break you?"

"Just my H's."

I can think of a few more when it comes to him: handsome, heavenly, hot... I sneak a peek to the front of his slacks, but it's too dark to satisfy my wonderings of if hung, horny, and hard will ever be on the table.

Thirsty much, Elodie? Slow down. No matter how many lingering convos you've clocked together, don't consider jumping him two seconds after you've met.

Bobby is not someone you swiped right on a dating app. You have to work together.

My stomach rumbles, and my H theme shifts to hungry, hamburger, hash browns. This afternoon's takeaway pizza buzz has long since worn off.

Bobby folds the blanket into a plaid envelope and slides it out of the car. Stepping over to the fringe of what appears to be wild grasses, he shakes the mud clots free and calls over his shoulder. "Door's open."

Wow. There is still a place in the world where you can leave your door unlocked. Twenty Pettipas points for The Clan land.

I smile at the memory of the silly point system between my dad and me. He used to award me points for just about anything: cleaning my room, finishing my homework without being nagged, making him smile. Being a tragic pleaser, I stored up a dragon's hoard of virtual Pettipas points. Rarely, I'd squander a couple for a trip to the ice cream place on the corner for a chocolate dip cone or a ride on the carousel at the mall. If I'd only known dad wouldn't be in my life long enough to cash them in.

I stop on the collection of pavers at the front door fitted together to create a small entry area and stare down at my still muddy overalls. "I think I should add a few things to the dirt bag."

He scans me in a decidedly non-sexy way. "I'll turn around."

Ouch. Loss of Pettipas points for that disappointing vibe. I am a head case. Visions of dancing naked in the Irish moonlight with Bobby is so un-PC as to be ridiculous. While he gazes into the Irish night, I strip off my overalls and socks, leaving me in t-shirt, bra, and underwear, the only survivors of muddagedon. Damn it's cold.

I reach for a nonexistent knob. Instead, there's a latch higher on the door. I step inside and use the door as a shield. "You can turn around."

"Leave the dirt bag on the stoop. I'll have wardrobe perform their magic on it tomorrow. Bathroom is the door to the right. Use whatever you need. I'll dig up some clothes for you."

Blindly patting the wall inside the door, I locate a switch and turn on the lights. He's right, the place is Hobbit scale without the charm. No architectural detail. Furniture that would take first prize in a contest for bland. I stand in a main living space, hugging my shivers to take in a small functional kitchen to my right and an electric fireplace to my left. It may be a vanilla space, but since I'm basically the size of a Hobbit, Bobby's house feels perfectly to scale for me. He gets points for a handful of pictures on the wall I plan to inspect later, and a collegial theater/film department pennant push-pinned between the two side-by-side doors on the back wall. We touched on the subject of college. Knowing we share an alma mater makes my heart glow with a little slice of home.

Through the open door on the left, I spy a bedroom. The queen bed covered in a generic beige comforter claims most of the space. The sight of it triggers exhaustion from both travel and my travail up the hill. I ache to get clean and collapse in this potentially cozy with some added personal touches, house. Maybe Bobby will let me take a run at decorating for him.

Sweet warmth restores my core temp when I step under a balmy spray compliments of a tankless water heater. I wash airplane miasma and Irish earth off my weary body. There's one towel hanging from a hook and a second on a rack on the back of the door, which I claim guest rights to. From my trusty *be prepared* backpack I grab toothbrush, clean undies, and a sports bra. I'm dealing with my hair when a knock at the door makes me jump. As if I don't know who it is.

"Shorts or sweatpants?"

Shorts? Is he kidding? Yoga pants and a long-sleeved tee are stashed in the bottom of my backpack, but borrowing Bobby's clothes has a sensual appeal I'm not going to pass up. Is it the fresh Irish air that sends me straight to the naughty place?

"Which has a drawstring?"

"Sweats."

"Ding, ding. We have a winner." With the towel wrapped around me, I crack the door and look up at Bobby. He looks taller in the light. I reach for the clothes and get a little thrill as his gaze sweeps down the towel with more heat than his previously non-sexy assessment. Maybe I'm not the only one harboring a little bit of naughty.

Or maybe he's in shock his new production designer is basically naked, wrapped in his one guest towel. I pull the door shut.

After taming my hair and my libido, which I decide to categorize as going too far in appreciating a friendly face in new surroundings, I step out of the bathroom. Bobby's *Chieftain's Son* sweatshirt is so long, it hits my knees. With cinching and rolling, the sweatpants are baggy but workable.

Bobby hunches at the small table for two in his kitchen with his nose buried in a laptop. I sidle up beside him, probably closer than I need to be. "You're working."

He turns his head to smile at me. "You know me. I'm always working."

I do know several outer layers of this man, but does that mean I really know him?

Bobby side-eyes his screen as a message beeps in. "Ready to go?"

"Kicking me out already?"

Bobby snaps the laptop shut, refocusing on me, flustered. "I thought you'd be anxious to get to your flat and get settled after—"

"My mudtastic debut?" I stroll over to the college pennant and run my finger over the felt. "Remind me... Class of?"

"2008."

I lay a hand over my heart. "2013."

He leans back in his chair. "We just missed crossing paths."

I raise a fist and sing the opening lines of our alma mater.

Bobby jumps to his feet, joining in.

Together we bust out the rest of the song in the middle of his living room. Laughing after our mutual final flourish, Bobby hugs me.

Oh, damn. This is nice. He's a squeezer. The initial contact stretches a few counts past the standard grab and go. I'm first to retreat, despite how yummy it feels. Perspective and pace, I tell myself.

Bobby practically jumps away, increasing the distance even more. "Elodie, I'm sorry. Meg is always at me to dial down the physical." His nervous laugh makes another appearance. "She's worried I'll be too touchy with the wrong person and well, misinterpretation could lead to unpleasant legal consequences."

Again, the urge rises to rest my hand against that handsome cheek, sprouting the beginning of brownish-black stubble. Maybe smooth a stray cowlick of his mostly straight-with-a-few-sneaky-waves hair back into place. I twist my ring to fight temptation. "We've been chatting for weeks. I just used your shower and am wearing your clothes. A simple hug between theater alums is not an issue for me." My words sound casual enough, but a burn in my belly drifts to the possibility of a less simple hug in the future.

"Thanks for letting me off the hook, Elodie."

A yawn escapes before I can quench it. "It's probably a good idea for me to get settled. I have studying to do before I meet my peeps tomorrow."

He raises eyebrows. It makes his gray-green eyes the color of my jade earrings look rounder and puppy cute. "Studying?"

"You'll see tomorrow."

"Will I?" He grabs his keys. "Might this have something to do with all the personnel pictures and bios you had me send?"

"Hey Bobby," I say, not taking the bait.

"Yes?"

"Do you know a good place to get decent takeaway fish and chips in these parts?"

"I might," he says, throwing the door open wide. "I could insist you answer my question before I feed you." He laughs. "But I'm not the dealing kind of guy."

It's my turn to laugh. "Yes, you are, Mr. Showrunner."

"Okay, yes, I am, but you get a first-night pass. Good for one time only."

As I step through, my shoulder brushes his side. The heat rising off his body is as warm as his personality.

Ms. PR Meg may soon bust me for being too touchy. Ah, but what delightful consequences too touchy might offer.

CHAPTER 4

HAMMERS VS. LATTES

ello crispy Irish morning and renewed perspective. What the hell was I thinking bringing on the flirt so strong with Bobby the first time we met in person yesterday? That's a sure-fire way to send him running for cover. Except I didn't see any signs he was lacing up his track shoes. I'd like to blame jet lag, but *Elodie the Needy* is the prime suspect. I crave a friend, a comrade, and most of all approval in this new lifescape of mine. Bobby Provost is the candidate I'd like to throw my vote behind, given he's been my most steady contact thus far with *The Chieftain's Son's* production team. I've had minimal contact with my new team since my predecessor, Jeff Palmer, has still been handling loose ends, leading up to the big hand off to me. I'm glad I can finally stop going through him and dial direct with my people.

Ugh, *approval*. The word sticks in my brain. Craving Bobby's approval could be a slippery slope for me. Given my penchant for crushing on authority figures to validate me, common sense says he'd best be a romantic red light. The problem is, I want to blow through that red light. Bobby's contrast of sweetness and sharp wit are powerful lures.

Reality check. *The Chieftain's Son* is my shot to accomplish a challenge and elevate my status in the film, TV design world. I've got decent professional momentum going for my age, and I intend for that train to stay on the track. Examining the tiny upsweep of Bobby's smiling lips and jewelry-worthy eyes at close range will have to get in line behind that.

My Irish language practice app prompts me to type in the phrase for *the seal wears orange pajamas*. I'm swiftly losing faith my oddball knowledge of Irish phrases is going to impress Doolin, the strict Irish tutor Bobby's warned me of. Part of the requirements for this job is to take Irish lessons. It's one of the factors of the full-immersion deal with *The Chieftain's Son*. I'm already anxious to meet the language task master who likely will never ask me if seals wear orange pajamas.

The one humanizing factor Bobby shared about Doolin is they golf together. Golf is a big subject with Bobby. Maybe I should consider taking it up to spend more time with him.

Whoops. So much for newfound perspective on easing back on my tendency to crush hard and fast on authority figures. Maybe I just need to meet a hot, single Irish dude in a pub for a rousing one-night stand to take my focus off Bobby in *that* way.

Even across thousands of miles, I hear the faint echo of my therapist grinding his teeth. When my bipolar disorder takes an upward swing toward manic, I tend to oversexualize. Thanks to kickass meds and having the best therapist on the planet, my manic is usually controlled. I'm more prone to the anxiety that flips the switch in the direction of depressive downswings of crippling self-doubt. Thank goodness for the past ten years since I was diagnosed, except for a few bad episodes, I've become very adept at using my mental and emotional tools to avoid that pit of hell. I am not my disorder. I think of it as a needy passenger in my brain who misbehaves if I don't offer it snacks and beverage service.

I hook the straps of my olive-green painter's overalls. Hopefully the layers of thermal shirt and flannel button-down will be enough. My MO is to dress like I'm ready to grab a hammer and work side-by-side with my crew. I refuse to show up for a first meet in business casual and lord my authority over anyone. I'm one of the guys who can cuss and wield power tools with the best of them. I discovered early cultivating a potty mouth gave crews permission not to hold back around good ole Elodie.

Given my lack of height and being a woman, I've had to grab at any inroad to get art departments to accept me as a lead.

I cringe at memories of the handful of sexist, misogynistic assholes I've endured along the way, but for the most part, I've always been able to earn respect with my work ethic of never ask someone to do something I wasn't willing to do myself. Thus, years of paint in the hair and hopeless fingernails. Truth is, a tool or paintbrush in my hand will always give me a rush of confidence. Honoring union rules, I'm not always able to be as hands on as I'd like, but my willingness alone to get down and dirty with enthusiasm has always served me well even if it means just being on site to cheer my people on.

Bottom line, despite my ungrizzled age and barely past newbie status in the industry, my reputation as a damn good designer is my cornerstone. Twisting my ring, I dig deep for confidence that shouldn't be so damn hard to summon as I head downstairs to meet Pat in front of Water Villa.

On the drive, he schools me with the rules of football so I'll know when to be righteously angry if a referee makes a shit call. Pat promises to take me to a match of his favorite club, Cork City over in Turner's Cross, and wants me to be prepared. I try to pay attention, but my mind sticks on meeting my own team.

"You're quiet over there, Ms. Elodie," says Pat. "Do you harbor a secret dislike of football or are you not yet on Kerry time?"

"I happen to like football, and time is of no concern when one is scared shitless, Pat. You may quote me."

He laughs. "I promise no one on *The Chieftain's Son* bites. You'll do fine."

"From your lips to the Good Peoples' ears."

"I'm a Catholic. I'll loan you God's ear on my behalf."

I relax into the seat. "I'll take every ear I can get." Nerves make the ride from Waterville to The Clan facility feel infinitely shorter than going from Bobby's place to my new borrowed flat. I furiously swipe through the files on my phone as if cramming for an exam. Pat's piña colada air freshener starts me craving something sweet. Smuggling extra donuts from craft service ought to calm my nerves and give me enough of a sugar high to survive the first meeting with my team. As if I could eat anything this morning.

The crunch of tires over gravel shakes the car and my phone plops into my lap.

Pat pulls up to the front entrance. "Chin up, Ms. Elodie. You charmed me, you'll charm them."

I gather my backpack and a wool cardigan from the back seat. "You're not coming in?"

"I'm due in a spell to drive Miss Tellefson."

"Shoot. I'm sorry. We could have carpooled to save you the trip." I feel bad making Pat do a double loop into town, even though by Los Angeles standards the trip is the snap of a finger.

He waves me off. "You're fine. I'm off for breakfast with the wife first."

"Hot date, huh?"

"Scorching. Luck to you."

I shut the passenger door, and Pat is off. Digging into the bib pocket of my overalls, I free the lanyard with my ID and key fob. There's a high front counter in the lobby of The Clan backed with a museum quality painting of the two stars as their counterparts, Donal Cam and Nieve, *The Chieftain's Son's* lovers. I'd be hard pressed to find prettier people. Intimidating.

"Are you, Elodie Pettipas then?" asks a college-age looking guy in a button-down shirt with *The Chieftain's Son* logo on the breast pocket.

"Yeah, hi," I say, raising my ID for him to see. Can you aim me toward the scene shop?"

He smiles. "I'll do you one better." Something beeps behind the desk. "She's here." He refocuses his attention on me. "I'm Michael by the way."

I raise my hand to reach his. "Elodie. Nice to meet you."

Double doors to the left of the desk crash open and a woman I recognize as Gillian Bettencourt O'Leary from the phone pics her parents shared with me jets over. "Elodie." She grabs me in a hug. "You're very welcome to The Clan." Releasing me quickly, she blushes.

"Hey, I'm Gilly. Sorry if I came on strong. I've heard so much about you from my parents. It's as if I know you."

"Same, and I'd expect no less given the attack style hugs of your mom and dad." We share a laugh, and I appreciate this tiny bud of familiarity with her.

"You've got us pegged. Bettencourts are huggers. I'm pretty sure they want to adopt you." Gilly reaches for the door. "Come on in. I'll take you back." Before swinging it open, she turns to the desk. "Thanks, Michael. Oh, and Jack wants me to ask if your dad has an ETA on his new golf clubs."

"He's finishing the grips today, so you should have them by late afternoon."

"Awesome," says Gilly and nods at Michael. "If you want custom golf clubs, Michael's dad is your man."

"I don't golf."

"Yet," says Michael with a laugh.

Gilly nudges me as Michael buzzes us in. "We'll fix that."

A huge red light on the wall would be bright and spinning if a shoot was in progress. The soundstage is on the other side of the door. Adrenaline shoots through me as I take my first step into my new kingdom—chiefdom. It's massive. There must be at least five finished sets up and camera ready. A medieval banquet hall off to my right is cordoned off with *Hot Set* signs. Bobby mentioned shooting pickups, those extra shots needed to add texture to a scene and allow for multiple POVs.

I love sound stages. Like theaters they speak a universal language. I'm immediately at home here. I belong. I know this world, and it knows me. There's comradery in the spaces where visual stories are told. The people who inhabit these realms of creation understand one another on a gut level.

Gilly grumbles as she leads me past sets in various stages of being struck or built. "We've got zero breathing room between writing seasons three and four if we're to have any lead time on production."

The only hesitation I had over committing to the series was its ball-busting pace. Season two started airing last month, and they're still feverishly finishing principal production on its last few episodes. I'm taking over in time to finish the lingering bits of the second season and get season three up and running ASAP. At my interview, Bobby warned *The Chieftain's Son* has brutal turnarounds between seasons and a non-stop shooting schedule that make other TV drama productions look languorous. Apparently, True Time Network is hellbent on using *The Chieftain's Son* to test a rapid release model of two seasons within a twelve-month period instead of the traditional season per year offering.

"Aren't we sliding a spectacular Skellig Michael destination wedding in season three as well?"

Gilly chews her bottom lip, delaying her response. "So they tell me."

I almost jump into questions concerning her obvious lack of enthusiasm for the PR-spectacular wedding True Time Network is staging for the O'Learys. Her mom, Amethyst, told me Gilly is not fond of the spotlight. Good luck with that, being married to the hottest guy in the known universe. The couple agreed with PR to a wedding with all the bells and whistles if it could be protected from a press and fan mob scene. Getting hitched on a barely accessible island is as isolated as it gets.

I play the sunny-and-light card. "At least the ceremony will dovetail with the last location shoot next season. Two for one deal."

Gilly chews on the end of the pencil she rescues from behind her ear. "Initially I thought I'd be jazzed for an over-the-top storybook wedding." She lets out a sour laugh. "Joke's on me. All I needed was Jack and family to make it the perfect day."

She guides me through another set of doors at the far end of this football field-sized soundstage into a long hallway. We pass the wardrobe beehive that appears to be in the throes of outfitting a small country. My head spins as she names off other places on our route in rapid succession, like the armory and training room. I need a floor plan of the complex so I can visualize and internalize its layout.

We pass through more double doors at the end of the corridor. The smell of freshly cut wood and the faint buzz of a table saw off to my left instantly ground me.

"If you go to the right, you'll get to the writer's room, publicity, and Doolin's classroom."

Before she continues, I point left and inhale deeply. "And this way to paradise."

Gilly laughs. "Yep. Scenic construction and beyond, the horse arena."

The doors we just passed through crash open. We both jump out of the way as Bobby bursts through. "Here you are. Good morning, ladies."

Gilly gives me quick hug. "We'll catch up later. I leave you in Bobby's capable hands."

The phrase *Bobby's capable hands* gives me a low belly clench. When he snaps his fingers, focusing on Gilly, I feel left out.

"Where are we on episode 310, G?"

"Waiting for location confirmation, and then we'll know which way to go with the last scene."

"Dennis doesn't have confirmation?" The edge in Bobby's voice gives me a glimpse into the flip side of his affability. Showrunners don't become big cheeses by shying away from power and control. I wonder if seeing *Full Throttle-Bobby* will be a turn off or a turn on.

Gilly nods at me as if reminding Bobby I'm there.

He lays a careless hand on my shoulder. "Sorry. Didn't mean to exclude you."

I aim for levity. "I'm damn glad I'm not Dennis."

Bobby presses his lips together. "He's our third location coordinator this season. The turnover is a pain in my ass. Especially with the tight timeline on your build schedule for season three."

Given *The Chieftain's Son* is infamous for the location fire they caused in season one, I'll bet there's not a lot of warm fuzzies from folks at potential shoot sites. I make a mental note to get involved quickly in scouting locations. Since coercion is one of my superpowers, I may be able to score us some prime real estate that Dennis-the-Third hasn't locked in.

Bobby waves hands in front of his face like he's shooing gnats. "Tell the team I'll be over after the art department meeting. We need to finesse the arcs for the final episodes."

"Gotcha, Boss," says Gilly. "Catch up with your later, Elodie." She retreats through the doors on the right.

"Give me a sec," says Bobby, whipping out his cell and practically swallowing it. "Danna, can you cover for me in editing for a spell? I'll be with the art department." Without a goodbye, he ends the call.

I'm a bit irked to be labeled *the art department,* even if it is accurate. Worse is his apparent need to babysit me through the meeting. "Bobby, introduce me then scram. I got this."

As he studies my face, creases fan across his forehead. "I didn't mean to imply…I intended to come off supportive."

"I'm a big girl, Bobby." I fan an arm down my body. "Not a tall one, but puny can pack a punch. I'm well versed in being a woman in a man's job. No hand holding necessary." It occurs to me my journey through the mud did not illicit a heaping helping of confidence from Bobby in my leadership abilities. Well, watch and learn, Mr. Provost.

I stroll before him to the door of the scene shop, striving for poise while entertaining a whim he's checking out my ass. Sadly, overalls do not show off my attributes to their best advantage, but today it's all about the uniform.

The drone of the table saw cuts off when Bobby and I enter a construction shop the size of two generous high school gyms. A group of men and women, with decidedly more men than women, gather in this cathedral of wood, hardware, paint, and plaster. The aroma of coffee and sawdust saturate the air as people from every facet of the art department, from builders to CG artists mill around, forming cliques. I requested everyone congregate in the shop instead of having to reintroduce myself to every department individually. Team spirit, baby!

A very tall, very built man with sandy blond hair and laugh lines strides over to meet us. "Well, now, a hearty good morning to you, Bobby." He sticks a meaty hand in my direction. "And if I'm not mistaken, Ms. Pettipas. I'm—"

"Mac MacDonald, lead carpenter, my new best friend."

His look of surprise quickly fades into one of good humor. "Can't have too many friends." We shake, and he calls over his shoulder. "Bring it in, folks. Our new chieftess is on the floor."

"Someone get Miss Boss an apple box," calls a voice from the crowd.

Being the shortest person in the room does not for a strong first impression make. A quick scan reveals a three-step, faux stone stair unit off to the side. After a glance at its exposed undercarriage to confirm stability, I skip to the top. "I think this'll do." A smattering of applause ripples through the group.

"Good morning, all," says *Perky-Bobby*. "Jeff Palmer sends his best from California and thanks for the well wishes on the occasion of his new hip."

"Too bad his non-Irish bones didn't take to our rain." I spot the speaker. Pictures and bios stream through my mind. It's Tim Martin, the head scenic artist.

"Then it's lucky for me, Tim, that I take my calcium seriously." There's surprise on his face that I've called him out by name. Before Bobby creates any more of a buffer between the crew and me, I've rattled off names and greetings to a majority of the team. I hit the department leads and many others Bobby was able to rustle up ID pictures for. I may not have the most efficiently functioning emotional brain, but my memory is impeccable.

When I catch his eye, Bobby is incandescent with appreciation. It's a look I'd like to see repeated in a very different circumstance.

In my prematurely overactive dreams.

"I can't wait to get started on the centerpiece for next season, the recreation of the OG Rock of Cashel. Are you with me for the challenge?"

The light friendly cheer and few raised fists encourage me. There are skeptics in the crowd for sure. I make a mental note to woo them harder than the rest.

"I'll be scheduling confabs with each department to get completely up to speed and layout the updates on the season three prep and build. Jeff Palmer schooled me well on where we're at. I promise a transition as smooth as a well-planed plank."

A particular throng near the back of the gathering appears grumpy. My guts drop to my shoelaces. Fuck. I totally forgot to ask Bobby last night for intel on the one department missing from my prep, the plasterers. Judging from the dried residue on the front of their shirts, that's the very group giving me the stink eye.

My careless slight chips away at my forced veneer of authority. "Cool. Let's do this." My muscles clench at the quaver in my voice. The call to arms I planned to be strong and authoritative fumbles a bit. I try to cover by calling over the leads and requesting a tour of the rest of our department.

As they gather, Bobby pulls me aside for a boss chat. The proximity of his lips to the shell of my ear strips the moment of pure professionalism. "Impressive."

I take a turn with my lips at his ear. "I screwed up. Didn't mention the plasterers."

He locks a pensive stare at me. "You'll fix it. I think you've got the group pointed toward warm and squishy. More than I've ever managed."

I give him a sly smile. "That's because you bring a latte to the table, and I bring a hammer."

Bobby barks a laugh, then fans an arm across the scene shop. "Have at it, Elodie Pettipas." *Man-on-a Mission-Bobby* darts away at a brisk clip.

I miss the warmth of his presence at my side. The gravity of what I'm undertaking slams into me. Every neural highway in my body flickers with the threat of panic. The voice of Kevin, my far-away therapist, takes up arms against my internal foe.

Focus—Calm—Balance. You were hired for this job for a reason.

Earworm Kevin makes a good point. Bobby Provost and the Bettencourts believe I can do this. I've prepped like crazy so our season three environments will sing their songs of the distant past. My track record, albeit on smaller palettes is proof I'm the right person for the job. I've been out-of-my-mind thrilled to face the challenge. So, after making what I consider a decent first impression with a minor bobble, why the hell did anxiety choose this moment to throw a party in my gut?

I blame it on the plasterers.

CHAPTER 5
PRE-VĪZ

"Y̶ou took the door off," says Bobby, poking his head into my office on day three of claiming my new domain. "And you're working on a Sunday."

I spin the chair to face him, snug in my newly cleaned jacket thanks to wardrobe. "So are you. I saw a parade of writers heading in when Pat dropped me off."

He rubs a hand over his chin. "I want to bang out the rest of season three scripts so I can give them a shot at some time off while you literally world build."

"Task master."

"Door destroyer."

"Technically, a friendly grip named Mick I met at craft service on Friday offered to remove the offending barrier for me." I stand, gesturing to the remaining wall separating me from the beehive of my department. "This is my next target. During the walk-through on my first day, I kept thinking a walled office is too me vs. the rest of you. I also want to lose these cubicles and go for a more open plan to make a fluid space. Everyone should be encouraged to circulate between departments. Less corporate, more artsy."

I breeze past him into the warren of divided workspaces and pass through an arch to the next room that looks like a twin of the first. "If we pull individual stations away from the walls, we'll create floor-to-ceiling community spaces to display the visuals." I walk the length of the room, gesturing at a collection of computer monitors. "Everything on Maya, AutoCad, Vectorworks, Blender, 3D Studio, yadda yadda will live right here in real time." I snap my fingers. "Hey, will you spring for a couple of huge flatscreens so we can cast from computers for grander look-sees?"

I lead him through the next doorway into a larger space. Motion sensor lights click on to reveal worktables covered with plans and models. There are a few shallow niches in the walls with desks, but no doors or walls separating them from the main room.

I stretch my arms wide. "See, more like what's happening here. I feel artistic energy pulsing, feeding into a central nexus of creativity. If we transform the whole department to embrace this vibe—"

Bobby squeezes my shoulder. "Whoa, Chieftess." The inherent power in the *Chieftess* title works for me, and his touch sends a yummy thrill down my arm.

"Whoa?"

"Allow me to share a cautionary tale." He settles onto a stool near the closest worktable. "You know I took over as showrunner for the final season on *Clash of Empires* as my first big gig."

With the assist of a small step stool, I hop up to sit on the table next to him, swinging my legs. "Epic show. No wonder they snatched you for another epic."

He nods. "I'm an epic kind of guy."

Beside epic, Bobby is a highly intelligent, driven kind of guy. His intensity speaks to me.

"*Clash* was already a fine-tuned machine, but instead of appreciating that, Mr. Upstart—" He slaps his chest. "Dove in with what in hindsight were unnecessary changes in order to smack my mark on the show." Bobby squeezes his eyes shut for a second. "Ugh, it still gives me indigestion to think about it."

The catalogue of changes floating through my head begins to blur. "What's wrong with making something your own?"

He eyes me. "If it ain't broke…"

I cross my arms over my chest, feeling a bit called out over my vision of a sweeping departmental layout update.

Bobby stands to face me, his chest inches from my knees. Oh, the possibilities of our position with a juicier brand of tension. I picture his hands resting on my thighs as he tips forward, lips seeking mine. My daydream takes precedence over answering him.

He tries to be patient, but my reply doesn't come fast enough. "Elodie, I'm not trying to piss you off or discourage you from taking charge in a way that works for you. This is meant as friend to friend advice. We are friends, right?"

All those phone and video chats as well as our first night at his place play through my head. In reality—friends. In my imagination… I register the heat blazing across my cheeks. Our gazes lock and my throat completely dries up. I'd jump to the floor to diffuse the moment if he wasn't basically pinning me to the table.

My silence makes Bobby jittery. He reads my discomfort and backs off. "All I'm saying is don't be me. Observe the department a bit before you call in heavy machinery and knock shit down."

I push off the table onto my feet and start back toward my office. "Downshift. Got it." What he's saying makes sense, and I'm sure I'll appreciate it once I shed the humiliation of my boss not exactly signing off on my initial plan to improve *The Chieftain's Son's* art department.

Bobby catches up with me. "Elodie, wait."

I stop. My snitty walk out is a complete overreaction. Bobby's eyes are slightly squinty in what I assume is a stress tell for him. He's being helpful, and I'm internalizing instead of having a conversation. Shit, my response is petty *you didn't take the trash out* level angst. What the hell am I doing? Point—insecurity. I perform an immediate attitude adjustment my therapist would applaud. "If by wait, you mean, hey let me show you where to get coffee, I'm all ears."

"Did I just fuck something up here?"

I go for a casual shoulder bump. "Nah. I'm a real prize before I have caffeine."

His eyes relax. Yep, the squint is his definite stress tell. Thank goodness he laughs. "Aren't we all?"

I go one step further with damage control. "Got a minute?" Based on our previous conversations, I've learned Bobby never has a minute unless it's late at night. Even then, he pulls serious editing all-nighters. "I want to show you the updated renderings for the Rock of Cashel."

"Didn't I already sign off on it?"

"Yes, but after forcing Pat to let me run my hands over some ancient stones on the drive from the airport, I've got new insight."

"Sure," he says with an edge. Crap. He's being *Nice-Bobby* for me when *Tense-Bobby* knows the writers are waiting for him.

I fall into nervous narration as I lead the way to my doorless office. "As I told you before, there's almost nothing left of the original structure to duplicate, but I think I've gotten closer to period authentic with minimal fudging." It was so much easier to connect with Bobby before we met in the flesh. He didn't feel like my boss then. He sure as hell does now.

That labels him an authority figure my emotions are programmed to cozy up to. I shake off the tendency. This is Bobby, a person I'm nurturing a friendship with, not a parent or professor whose lack of approval will send me down a depressive path.

But dammit, I am aching for his approval. My brain is having a hell of a time categorizing this man. Boss—more intimate possibility, or both? I need a session with Kevin before I make an ass of myself.

My fingers fly over the keyboard to reveal my image of the ancient castle of kings. I drop into my chair as a wave of pride in my work swats feelings of inadequacy aside. It's good. It's moody and broody and intimidating. Just what an iconic castle should be.

"Here's the basic structure of the existing castle set from season two with new and improved layers of magnificence. By that I mean drips." My confidence tank fills. I'm in my element now. Design.

"Drips?"

"The vertical lines I took as shadows are decades of drips adding character to the castle walls. More vegetation springs out of cracks as well. Castles have so much more character than their silhouette. There are more layers. Nature's stamp on the stone. Not to insult Jeff's work, which is amazing, but I wonder if he's been giving castles their full due."

Bobby puzzles through my statements and then his laser focus takes in the screen. He tilts his head one way then the other as I rotate the structure to show him multiple angles.

"I'm also increasing the span here and varying the heights of the turrets."

His hands grip my chair, knuckles barely brushing my back.

"Yes, the distance from the main entrance to the left turret and the height variations adds a new dynamic. No one will guess it's the bones of the same set. Good." He reaches over my shoulder to tap on the screen. "Alan can center a shot there..." His finger slides to the top of my tweaked turret. "And there. It'll read as massive. We'll have to CG everything above that point, but this will give us the money shots." His gaze switches from the monitor to me, eyes bright with no sign of our earlier tension. "With minimal fudging."

"What are we fudging?"

Bobby and I turn in tandem to look at our visitor. The woman is almost as tall as Bobby. Dark chestnut hair wears streaks of magenta, complimenting the color splashes in her tie-dyed peasant blouse. A knee-length denim skirt and cowboy boots add more flair to the ensemble. Her voice commands the room.

"Good morning, Deidre," says Bobby, releasing my chair to give her a peck on the cheek. "We're fudging history."

Deidre! This is Deidre LaRochelle, authoress extraordinaire of *The Chieftain's Son* novels.

"Ah, my favorite pastime, fudging history." She clasps her hands. "I've learned with enough romance and sex; the audience will always allow some straying from reality. Let's be real. Our hero, Donal Cam's lineage is a direct fudge on Irish mythology, and he's a five-star book boyfriend."

I tap a finger to my lip. "Five stars is a little thin for that hunk of Irish dessert."

Bobby gestures to me. "Deidre, the woman objectifying your leading man is Elodie Pettipas, our new production designer."

She sets hands on my shoulders and dips low enough to air kiss my cheeks. It's a bit much for a first how do you do, but I get the sense Deidre is a bit much. "Welcome, Elodie. Gilly sent me over to meet our new visionary." She nods at Bobby. "This one's been counting the days for you to join the party."

"Has he?" I raise my eyebrows and look at Bobby. He's gone a little pink. "Counting the days, huh?"

Bobby covers his sweet little flush by switching back to business mode. "Jeff set the season in motion before he left, but I'm more at ease knowing there's a talented general on the field."

I start to salute but wipe the air instead. "Don't you mean a chieftess on the field?"

Deidre smiles. "You're going to fit right in."

"Yes, she will." He looks at me a beat longer than necessary before his gaze cuts back to Deidre.

"And you two are already flipping castles together," she says with a wink. "How domestic." Deidre crosses her arms over her chest and looks serious. "Mr. Provost, let it be known, I am not backing down on our location shoot on Skellig Michael."

"Wait, backing down?" My mind flips through next season's locations. The island is a focal point of season three. "Isn't that also where Gilly and Jack are supposed to throw their grand wedding shindig?"

"Sure is," says Deidre. "Fantasy at its finest."

Bobby leans both hands on my desk and drops his head. "Dennis crapped the bed on negotiations with the heritage site people."

Deidre pats him on the back. "Bust out your famous Bobby Provost charm and fix it." She smiles at me. "When you've had your fill of his charm, Elodie, come over to the writer's room and meet everyone. We've got the best donuts. Our Maureen is marrying the pastry genius from the Yeats by the Sea Hotel in town. He keeps us in world-class sugar." She turns to leave. "And Bobby, don't you have Maureen work right up to her wedding. Contrary to your idiotic work ethic, people do have lives to live."

This is a woman whose bad side I have no desire to be on. No contest who the real chieftess of this show is.

Bobby points a finger at Deidre. "Says the woman burning the candle at both ends to meet deadlines for the script for our penultimate episode and book eleven of *The Chieftain's Son* series."

Deidre levels a look at him. "Have you not figured out time answers to me and not the other way around?" She waves her arms in a flourish, twirls, and executes a queenly exit.

Bobby shakes his head. "We never should have made her a producer. She's bossy enough already."

"Ms. D. certainly blazes up a room."

He looks after her with adoration. "Yes, she does, and the woman is one of the most creative and insightful people I've ever known. You've read the books."

I shimmy my shoulders. "Sounds like someone has a crush."

Bobby snort laughs. "Talent crush—absolutely. Is she what you expected?"

I mock slap my cheeks. "So—much—more." Replaying Hurricane Deidre, I narrow my eyes. "What's with her winky face and comments about us flipping castles together?"

He waves me off. "Classic Deidre. She'd 'ship the moon with a hole in the ground. It's her currency."

"Am I the moon or the hole in the ground?"

I'm the recipient of yet another Bobby Provost blush that makes it to the tips of his perfectly proportioned ears. "Definitely the moon, since I just dug myself a hole."

"You're fine." I swivel to face my screen. "Shoo. Get to work." I expect to feel the whoosh of *Man-on-a-Mission Bobby* flying from the room. Instead, he lingers then leans one hand on my desk.

"Hey, my suggestion you should cool it with your departmental changes—I'm sorry if I came on too strong."

I turn to face him. "Come on as strong as you want. You're the boss."

It's not the time to tell him I'm going to table his advice and fly my open plan idea to the art department heads anyway. I believe they'll see the merit in free-flowing creativity paths. Maybe they've just been waiting for permission to knock down some walls. Jeff Palmer is mega talented, but old school, which is what makes his designs such a tidy fit for the show. I believe I can lead *The Chieftain's Son* art department to a new vibrant, organic level ala my philosophy of more drips and vegetation as a first step.

His expression is a mix of serious and squish. "I'd rather you didn't pack me into a box with one label."

If he busts out the friend line again, I'm going to scream.

"What did you say about castles? There may be more layers here, Elodie."

I watch his eyes as if a translation of the subtext in that statement will scroll beneath his pupils. I know what I want it to mean. Layers— good. Is it possible I'm not a one-way crush? We share a stare until he breaks it and raps his knuckles on my desk.

"Do come over when you hit a stopping point. Straight down the crossover and through the doors at the end. Follow the arguing." He treats me to a crinkly smile.

"Love to. Save me a donut."

"They go fast."

I leap up, strip off my jacket, and throw it over the back of my chair. "I don't need to be asked twice. Lead the way."

Bobby opens the door. His hand grazes the small of my back as I squeeze past, leaving a delicious heat signature in the shape of a capital B from the contact. Fingers gently close around my upper arm before I can charge down the hall.

"If I haven't said it yet," says Bobby, smiling at me. "I'm very glad you're finally here."

Layers indeed. Now here's a Deidre LaRochelle winkable moment.

CHAPTER 6
MOOSE TERRITORY

The rumble-rumble-bump of the stacked washer-dryer unit in my flat is soothing background noise. I may or may not have decided to obsessively wash all the clothes I brought from home. Doesn't every part of my life deserve a fresh and clean Irish start? What I really need after my mud debut and subsequent debacle with my team is a fresh and clean Irish do-over.

I cringe at the memory of stolid expressions that met me when I bounced through the art department on high energy, proposing cubicle tear downs and free-flowing communal spaces. After the team's initial shock at my sweeping revamp, I nearly froze from the sea of cold shoulders surrounding me. So far, there's no thaw in sight. I've graduated from feeling like an imposter to full-blown idiot.

My laptop signals Kevin has arrived on our video chat. Two of his four cats are nosing their way onscreen, so I know he's at home and not the office. Everyone deserves such a dedicated therapist.

"Hey Kevin." I open my arms wide and chirp out a cheery greeting. "Welcome to Ireland."

His face enlarges as he leans close to the screen. The wolf's line from *Red Riding Hood, The better to see you with my dear,* comes to mind. I settle into my desk chair and pretend to be centered even as I nervously scratch at the knees of my overalls.

"I can hear you scratching, and what's that hum in the background?"

Busted. "Laundry. I'm getting settled."

"Laundry at one o'clock in the morning?"

My face heats, and I hope it doesn't read on screen as hot tamale as it feels.

Kevin executes the half-twist, half-lean of his head, the sign he's getting down to business. "Elodie, talk to me."

I flash my winningest *life is good* smile. "I'm not on the train to Manicland." I lift the bottle of pills on the table and shake it like a maraca. "My little buddies are on the job." Unless I take them too late and end up feeling like I'm sleepwalking through the next day.

"You wanted to chat with me in the middle of your night, while you unnecessarily do laundry, to tell me everything's cherry cola and peanut butter cups?"

I drop my head onto my hands. "I fucked up, Kev."

The computer mic picks up his slow exhale, but he waits for me to speak.

"There are several key fuckups here. First, even though I was advised not to, I dove in with both feet to suggest some major *adjustments* to the art department—"

Kevin flashes me the time-out signal with his hands. "You've been there what—four days?"

"I know, I know. Did you hear the part where I said I fucked up?"

His rubs his lips together.

"In those four days, in the friendliest country on the planet, I've managed to make my team hate me."

"Hyperbole alert."

I twist my hair into a knot and try to jam a pencil through the mass to hold it up. The pencil falls onto the carpet, taking several dark toffee strands with it. My hair settles back on my shoulders. "Delete *hate*. Insert *are irritated with* or *lost respect for*."

"Fixable?"

"Has to be."

"There's your answer. Think of solving this problem as finessing your irritated ducks back in a row. We both know how you need everything lined up and orderly."

"No mocking my penchant for organization at its highest level."

He hefts a cat onto his shoulder to pet. "I wouldn't dream of it." The calico love-bites his knuckle, and he sets it down. "Who advised you against the adjustments?" He air quotes *adjustments*.

"Bobby Provost, the showrunner, my boss."

Kevin's smirk surprises me. "Let me understand. Instead of turning full scale pleaser for your new boss, you went contrary to his advice?"

Huh, I didn't think about my action in that context. "Yup."

"I see progress."

"Don't give me a gold star yet. Allow me to move on to my second fuckup."

For a therapist, Kevin has a very readable face. His *here it comes* look is evident even on video chat.

I blurp out the words at superhuman speed. "I'm afraid I'm doing the authority figure thing and crushing on my boss." I brace myself for the litany of reasons why this tendency hasn't served me well in the past.

"Why?"

His question jolts me into good posture. "What do you mean 'why'?"

"What appeals to you? Is he a father figure? Do you feel you need to win him over for approval or to achieve a goal?"

"Definitely not a father figure, and we share the same goal to achieve what's best for *The Chieftain's Son*."

He clasps his hands and rests his chin on them, waiting patiently for me to elaborate.

"Bobby's kindness appeals to me. His sense of humor has a sharp edge I relate to. Thumbs up in the looks department. We hit it off over the last few months on our transatlantic chats, a definite connection. He's cozy, but not too cozy. There's some heat there."

"Now I'm crushing on him."

I laugh. "Don't tell your cats."

"Elodie, you've just walked into a major life change. Be kind to yourself. Expect what you're calling fuckups. I'm not hearing anything that you can't fix with action or deal with emotionally."

I love this man—in a healthy, appreciative doctor/patient way. My bipolar monsters turn into cute little furry sidekicks under his calming perspective.

"My advice—own what irritated your team and embrace flexibility as you find common ground. You already knew the solution, didn't you?"

I treat him to an exaggerated shrug. "Maybe."

"Ultimately, you are their leader. Guide with grace and you'll be fine even if you're shaking up their reality a bit." He runs a lint roller along his sleeve. "And the crushing on the boss issue—from what you've described, I'm not getting the sense you're falling into an old pattern."

"Kevin, oh favorite authority figure, it sounds like you're giving me permission to crush on my boss."

He lifts a finger and shakes his head. "Don't give me that power. It's your call." He cradles a cat under his chin. "My friend, you're beyond needing validation from anyone but yourself."

I laugh. Such a therapisty answer.

"You know I'm always here if—" Kevin rattles off his litany: manic spikes of non-sleep; compulsive eating, drinking, or shopping; anxiety tsunamis, etc. All the possible weeds that could crop up in my obsessive-compulsive, bipolar garden.

After I pass the quiz, he gives me his kindest Kevin smile. "I do have a suggestion."

"Get out of my own way?"

"Always, but I was going to say, don't slip into the habit of burying yourself behind a computer screen or drawing table without looking at a clock. Schedule in a hike or a long drive. Even better, find a horse."

I clap my hands loudly. A horse. Perfect. Yes, my world always falls into place from horseback.

"Be well, Elodie." With that, my lifeline ends the call.

I didn't put the door back on my office, but wearing the memory of our decent first meeting as confidence-building armor, I've been slapping band-aids on the scrapes I caused with my over-enthusiastic misstep on reinventing the art department layout. A bit of self-deprecation and apologies seem to make inroads at returning to square one. To radiate a less invasive tactic to promote fluid inclusivity, I shared plans and renderings, asking twenty people their advice on the sets we're about to sink our hammers and paint brushes into for season three. I'm not feeling total love or trust from them yet, but they're not erecting gallows for me in the shadows of the scene shop either.

Those don't come into play until season four.

"Matching Jeff Palmer's signature stone and mortar we can do in our sleep," says Lee, one of the CG artists who popped into my office. He chews on his bottom lip, weighing his next words. "I've always thought his style leaned a bit too cold given the heat of the story. We can go so much farther with LED technology for our settings."

My theater scenic designer heart flutters. I'll always love an IRL set better than a virtually created one, but Lee is not wrong. The level of detail and reality that can be achieved with LED-projected backgrounds and locations is beyond heart-skipping. It's heart-stopping. I could add a unicorn riding on the back of a dragon into a scene, and it would look one hundred percent real. If I want to be relevant and forward my career, I must stay in bed with the latest tools and toys today's design world offers.

I want to be flawlessly encouraging even if my fully rendered versions of designs are already embedded in my psyche. "You've got my attention. Play with some looks. Show me what you mean."

Be open, Elodie. Accepting someone else's ideas doesn't signal your failure.

Lee flashes me the friendliest smile of the day. "I'm always up for playing."

Out of habit, my gaze widens to search his ring finger. Bare. Before given a chance to analyze if there was any double meaning, he's out the door.

I'm not disappointed. Why am I not disappointed a cute, ringless man didn't flirt harder with me? Stupid question. He's not the right cute, ringless man I wish was flirting with me.

I haven't seen Bobby today. After Kevin's green light, or his roundabout support that I give myself a green light where Bobby is concerned, I sauntered over to the writer's room, using superior donuts as my excuse. No Bobby, but I did score a dinner invite from Gilly to join her and the hubs for "Dover sole that will change my life" at a restaurant in Waterville famous for it. I'm finally going to meet Jack O'Leary, international heartthrob and secret husband. Oh, the intrigue of it all.

I've got plenty of time before our late dinner, so I take Kevin's advice and head for the horse arena and the stables. I wasn't born in the saddle, rather came into my own there. My mother had a cowboy fixation which killed her marriage to my dad but bought us a life under the never-ending Wyoming sky. Mom got a kitchen gig on a ranch that makes its bread and butter renting out for movie shoots. I had such an affinity for the stable of stunt horses, the head wrangler dubbed me "Master of Horse." In my teens, I helped acquaint some famous folks with their temporary trusty steeds. Best of all, I learned to experience the freedom and special brand of peace only possible from horseback.

The arena is devoid of human and horse. Bales of straw, low jumps, and a plastic wading pool are surrounded by a low, white wooden fence. I trudge across to the stables, appreciating the lack of evidence horses usually leave behind.

Once inside, I inhale deeply, savoring the aromas of horse breath and hay. A perky chestnut-colored friend bobs its head over the stall and nickers at me.

"Is someone lonely?" I stroll over and pet the white streak on its nose. It's gooey lips slurp my hand, looking for a treat. "No cheating on your diet, sweet thing."

Various pairs of large, curious horse eyes take me in as I explore deeper. At the end of the center aisle is an empty office with a glowing computer screen. Next to that is a tack room.

"Hello?"

Stamping and blowing answer me from off to the right. "Wow."

Standing in the last stall, fully saddled and ready to go, is the real star of the show, Streaker, the leading man, Donal Cam's white horse. This is the single being in the universe of *The Chieftain's Son* who traipses through time with the star. Poor Donal Cam must woo his eternal love Nieve in a different incarnation of his chieftain's son role in every book. She never recognizes him at first thanks to a fairy curse the poor guy's parents triggered. Luckily D.C. always wins Nieve over with lots of charm and his prowess between the sheets. Sadly, he's doomed to lose her as he's plopped into the service of a different chieftain. He remembers everything he's gained and lost. Sucks to be him. Donal Cam needs a Kevin.

Streaker nudges her snowy nose against the door to her stall.

"Hey baby, you need exercise?" She's not sweaty or tired looking. The girl is ready to party.

I pop my head into the office to see if there's an inner sanctum where the show's wrangler is hiding. "Hello?"

Grabbing a helmet from the tack room, I secure it on my head and wait for the wrangler to appear. Streaker blows her impatience. Since I've probably clocked more hours on horseback than the wrangler, I consider taking the darling into the arena.

"What's it going to hurt if I walk you out to the playground, Streaker?"

She nickers at me, which I take as assent. Slipping into the stall, I get to know her a little with pats and coos. The beauty bumps her head against me, loving the attention.

"Anyone here?" I call again. When there's still no answer, I lead the obviously ready-for-a-ride horse from the stable into the arena. She's calm and obedient, no horsey shenanigans. We pause next to a mounting block that I'm sure Jack O'Leary doesn't need to jump onto Streaker, but I sure do. It's tempting.

"What do you think, sweetie pie? Should we take a spin while you wait for your daddy? You're all dressed up with nowhere to go." What are they going to do, fire me? I may earn a thank you for saving someone the trouble of exercising their equine leading lady.

I wait another five minutes, and no one comes out of the stables or into the arena. It's not like I'm an amateur who's going to compromise the horse. After adjusting the stirrups to fit me. I nuzzle Streaker's head with my own, climb the block, and slip into the saddle. She's magnificent. I feel her strength and trust as I walk her into the center of the arena. The calm I've always enjoyed on horseback washes over me.

She answers my commands before I finish the question, and soon we're cantering around the track. The ride is smooth and intoxicating. Stress sloughs off me like dust washed away by sweet summer rain. I'm connected to the horse through its rhythmic hoofbeats, but the thread goes deeper. The door at the end of the space is wide open, letting the brisk October breeze send fragrances of grass and earth into the air. This Irish horse moves in harmony with the land outside and beneath us. For the first time I imagine a thread connecting me, through the horse, down into the myth and magic of Ireland. I sense the land of the story I'm meant to tell. It calls to me, inviting me to know it better.

We go faster, and I guide Streaker in line with a jump. Horse wind whips my hair behind me. The two of us are destined to fly. Up we go, clearing the pole with ease. Pounding—turning—freedom.

That's when I hear the shouting.

"What the fuck," bellows a man the size of a young buffalo, with a tangle of brown hair to complete the picture. He and a blond, tall, body builder type race toward me across the arena.

I want to yell at them not to spook the horse, but there's no need. My better half slows to a trot and heads straight for the newcomers, whinnying a greeting. Blinking the blur from my eyes from our last burst of speed, I focus on the pair.

Holy hell.

Mr. blond and muscular is none other than Jack O'Leary. He's as pretty as his horse. Ten times the hunk of gorgeous as he appears on screen.

Jack takes Streaker's muzzle in his hands and plants a kiss on her forehead. "So, lady in the saddle, are you my new horse-riding double?" He laughs. "The shots better be nice and wide to sell it, and you need the hair." He flicks one of his own blond locks and gestures to mine.

"Actually, I'm your dinner guest." I reach a hand toward him. "Elodie Pettipas, the new production designer."

Jack takes my hand in both of his. "And I'm Gilly Bettencourt O'Leary's husband, Jack."

Grumbling buffalo man circles the horse, inspecting her like he's looking for dents or scratches in the paint of a new car. I pull my hand quickly from Jack's to get out of range. I'm afraid Buff may grab my leg to yank me off Streaker's back. He stops next to Jack and points a finger as large as a carrot at my face. "No one touches my horses without my say so. Get your ass off her."

I found the wrangler.

Jack slaps the man on his meaty shoulder. "Moose, I think we can all agree Elodie here knows her way around a horse."

Moose grunts and glares at me. Great, someone else on *The Chieftain's Son* staff I've pissed off. He jerks the reins from my hands and leads the horse to the block so I can dismount.

"Mr. Moose…" Shit, Jack called him just plain Moose. Adding the Mr. makes him sound like a cartoon character. "I promise Streaker was in capable hands. I grew up on a ranch and can handle a horse as well as I do a paint brush."

If my statement softens Moose's ire, there's no evidence.

Take two. "I'm sorry I took liberties." I shrug. "But she was saddled and asked me so nicely." The last thing I want to do is make an enemy of my access to horses.

Jack barks a laugh while Moose stares me down.

Take three. "She's a beautiful horse. Sweet, talented. You must be proud of her."

What, is he her dad? I'm burbling.

I believe there's the barest easing in the creases between Moose's brows before he holds out a hand, jerking his chin at my helmet.

After unclicking the strap, I offer it to him. With a swipe of his giant hand, he snatches the helmet from me and turns his back on us to walk Streaker to the stables. He mumbles something that if my ears don't deceive me, just might be *fine jump*.

I lament the angry set of Moose's shoulders as he disappears into shadow. "He's never going to let me touch a horse again, is he?"

"Did you not hear him compliment your jump. A tick in your win column."

I bounce a knuckle against my chin. "I figured I was hearing things."

Jack flicks a hand at the retreating wrangler. "Moose is really a softy. You can tell by the way horses love the man." He pops his lips. "My advice—show up with a finely rehearsed grovel and a decent bottle of whiskey before you ask for another ride."

I register what Jack is wearing: jeans, flannel shirt over a thermal one, boots, and a helmet strap dangling from his hand. "Shoot, you were coming to train on Streaker for the shoreline battle, weren't you?"

Guilt prickles. The massive war scene, our last shoot for season two, is coming fast and furious. Donal Cam has tricky horseback shots that will work a thousand times better if it's Jack and not his stunt double pulling off the moves.

"Don't think on it. My ass could use a day off from Moose's drills. The man is ruthless." He gestures to the garage door-sized opening leading out of the arena into The Clan complex, and we start toward it. "Gilly told me we're on tonight for Waterville's brilliant Dover sole. Fair warning. It will ruin you for all other fish."

I catch myself staring at Jack. No one could fault me for gawking at this gorgeous human, but it's not his looks I'm after. I want his insight on the pull I felt riding Streaker. Actors thrive on key moments and emotions. "Can I ask you a question?"

"Sure thing."

"Your between season's filler show, *My Two Loves*, what drove you to double your workload considering the brutal shooting schedule of *The Chieftain's Son*?"

Dazzling smile is not just PR with Jack. He does frickin' dazzle. "It's in the name. I love my wife. I love my home. That's worth a bit of being overworked, don't you think?" He grunts. "Exactly why we changed the name from *Secrets of My Ireland,* or *My Ireland."* Even his derisive noises are ridiculously sexy. "And it's throwing the network a bone since I've mucked up their grand publicity plans by daring to marry my soulmate."

Wow, Gilly is a freakin' real-life fairy tale princess to have this near perfect example of manhood calling her his soulmate. I stare a little too long, soaking in the sweetness and beauty that is Jack O'Leary. Crushing on him is a no-go, but I certainly will not miss the opportunity to appreciate him as a colleague and maybe someday a friend.

I pursue my hunch Jack may be key to something I need. As the actor who is the beating heart of our show, he's a resource I'd be a fool to overlook. "Hey Jack, I need a favor."

He raises an eyebrow at the woman he's just met already diving in for an ask.

"I feel I need to gain a deeper understanding of Ireland. I've bathed in the fairy tales and myths, read about battles and kings—architecture and Vikings. But I'm embarrassed to admit my connection still seems surface when it needs to radiate into everything I create for the show. You're doing a whole spin-off featuring that bond. I need help to find it."

Jack starts to speak but I cut him off.

"You may think I'm nuts, but since we're both creatives, hopefully you won't run screaming when I tell you something."

He rests hands on his knees and leans down so we're eye-to-eye, which is no mean feat given our disparity in height. "Let's operate on the notion all creatives are a little bit mad or as my lovely wife would say, bonkers. Go on."

I turn back toward the stables. "On horseback is one of the times I'm not trapped in my own head. I feel instead of think. I felt a vibe when the breeze from outside hit me as I was riding Streaker. There was a—pull, as if a presence was trying to get my attention, give me hints, invite me to grasp something vital about this place I haven't yet embraced."

Damn, his next smile is as warm as lemon ginger tea on a cold morning. How many smiles does this man generate? Jack O'Leary, man of a thousand smiles. "Welcome to Ireland. You're not the first person in our *Chieftain's Son* family who's experienced such a thing. In my opinion, an invitation like that is not to be ignored."

"So not bonkers?"

He straightens. His gaze drifts to the huge doors open to the outside at the far end of the arena. Jack's chest expands as he draws in a breath.

I follow his line of sight to the fields, small hills undulating in the distance, and the deep green trees standing sentinel on The Clan property. He's seeing what I see and more. Depth and appreciation of the country that Jack's called home his entire life shows on his face. It's a mystery I'm dying to explore.

"One of the tragedies of our modern world is that we've disengaged with the ground beneath our feet." One side of Jack's lip curls as he looks down at me. "I've an invitation for you. Can you spare a day to come with Gilly and me on our shoot tomorrow out to the Giant's Causeway?"

Yep, this guy is the key to a treasure chest I'm keen to open and peer inside. My schedule flickers like a neon sign in my brain. Can I spare a day?

"Jack, Elodie, everything okay here?" Bobby blows into the arena, a stronger force than the rising afternoon wind. He waves his cell at us, but his gaze locks on mine alone. "I got a call from an extremely disgruntled Moose."

As he stops a foot shy of ramming me, the loneliness that's lingered around my edges melts away. I've missed him today. Even though I'm probably horse banned, warmth at being with Bobby holds disappointment at bay.

I raise a hand. "Guilty."

Bobby shakes his head. "Nope. Not you." He raises his own hand to grab mine and lower it. Our fingers slide together so easily as if we've clasped hands a dozen times before. "I've been found guilty of not introducing him to the new talented horsewoman on the team." He gives my hand a shake and slowly slides his fingers free. I'm tempted to reclaim them and just stand there in front of Jack, holding hands with Bobby.

"He said I was talented?"

Bobby smirks and leans in for a stage whisper. "He said you were pushy and talented."

I tilt my head to the side and study the design of Bobby's lips. "I own that."

Jack clears his throat, and I realize Bobby and I are floating in our own little flirt bubble. Great, caught in another Deidre LaRochelle winkable moment with Bobby Provost.

"Elodie's granting us the pleasure of her company to the Giant's Causeway tomorrow," says Jack to Bobby. "Didn't you say you've been wanting to see the place as well?"

Bobby's face flares, a ruby caught in a flash of light. He shoots Jack a tight-lipped smile. Jack grins back, the picture of innocence. Am I reading the room, or rather horse arena, completely wrong, or is Jack O'Leary playing matchmaker? Has Bobby said something to him about me? I know they're super close. I tamp down my inner *does he like me* junior high school girl. I'm indulging in some wishful thinking. It's more likely Jack is a textbook example of people in love wanting everyone they know to find happiness as well.

I guess I'm going to the Giant's Causeway tomorrow.

"You're very welcome to join us for dinner, Bobby. Gilly and I are going to educate Elodie on the brilliance of Dover sole."

Bobby claps Jack on the shoulder. "As if I'd ever turn down sole, J." His gaze flicks to me and quickly returns to Jack. "It's a date."

If we're going with his word choice, it's technically a double date. Is this one of the layers Bobby was referring to? A personal layer, one with interesting potential? The two of us are setting off to share a meal with a couple so in love we're bound to received pinprick shocks from the passion sparkles flying off them. Will we get singed or ignited?

I may need to have burn cream standing by.

CHAPTER 7
MY TWO LOVES

The prospect of spending six hours in the car with Bobby on the drive to the Giant's Causeway in Northern Ireland both exhilarated and terrified me as I became a linen burrito flip-flopping in bed last night. Over-analyzing a possible future with Bobby kept me up way past the time I usually give in to the oblivion my meds deliver.

Dinner last night was a blast. Zero awkward. The O'Learys are as passionate about what they do as they are down to earth. Best insta-friends ever. Gilly called dibs again on a sisterly connection between us since her folks took me under their wing. I do love Rich and Amethyst Bettencourt. I wouldn't be here without them, and who in their right mind could pass up the hot and kingly Jack O'Leary as an honorary brother-in-law? Not this girl.

Everything about the evening felt like a double date, from Bobby pulling my chair out to him walking me to Water Villa, which is a short stroll from the Yeats by the Sea Hotel. Well, everything except the absence of a good-night kiss. The end o' the evening embrace surpassed squeeze and release status, but nothing beyond. Am I not sending the right signals? Is it me flashing the friend zone sign over my head? Shoot! Should I have asked him up?

Bobby and I are well past hour five of our road trip, and there hasn't been a single lull in the conversation, even with our pre-dawn start time. Luckily, we're both accustomed to the late night and early morning demands of a production schedule with the assist of highly caffeinated beverages. It's as if we're back on video chat, starting off with show specifics and then veering off into IRL Elodie and Bobby apart from our roles on *The Chieftain's Son*. Comfortable. Fun. Promising?

There is one marked difference from our online get-to-know-you phase. Touching. Lots of touching. Bobby reaches over to squeeze my shoulder to emphasize something he's saying that I've completely lost track of in my fascination with the swoop of a cowlick curving over his left ear. I'm all in with the series of cross-car contacts between us. So far, neither of us has breached the invisible line of casual familiarity. Leg touching is limited to knee patting without straying into thigh territory. No one's lips have snuck into whisper-in-your-ear position. Every approach between us seems to be a test, a question.

Is this okay?

So far, neither of us twitched or leaned away.

Yes—check—okay.

I really should pay attention to what he's saying instead of cataloging every single random brush of his hand. Except, I practically hold my breath, eager for the next touch. I crave his tactile attention to the point where more personal parts of me are getting louder about certain brands of touching they'd prefer.

"Thoughts on the new title of Jack's show?" Bobby's question tugs me back to the conversation.

I swallow and work at acting casual instead of fantasizing over the endless possibilities of Bobby's touches. "Why did they change it?"

Bobby's hand returns to the steering wheel. It still feels like he's on the wrong side of the car. I have intermittent mini jolts I should be grabbing a non-existent wheel on the dash in front of me. I wonder how long it took Bobby to acclimate to off-sided driving.

Bobby straightens his arms, pushing against the wheel. "True Time Network thought keeping the title *Secrets of My Ireland* might be interpreted as Jack being dishonest, keeping his relationship with Gilly a secret or, God forbid, that he was cheating on Niks with Gilly." Bobby squints—his stress tell.

"Are you worried the show is going to suffer when they go public?"

His arms relax. "Maybe social media shit, but I don't see it affecting our numbers. Meg's original timeline was to have Jack and Niks announce their amicable split not long after Cali Con last July, then have them double date with other people at both the Crystal and TVUK Awards the next month. The appearances were designed to kill any toxic *on set feud* rumors." He shares his focus between the road and me. "We know none of that happened. Meg's still waiting for the greenlight from True Time to put her adjusted scenario into action. The delay is eating away at everyone. Ultimately, we're banking the *meant to be* angle of *My Two Loves* will be cause for fan celebration and keep angst to a minimum."

"I know I'm a sucker for a good fated-mates romance."

Bobby's glance darts over to me a few times. He looks nervous. Hell, did he think I was assertively laying out an opening for the subject of us? I pretend to be mesmerized by something outside the passenger window. "Thus the *My Two Loves* rebrand."

"Yup." His voice is strained. "It's going to add ten years to my life when the hush-hush shit and mountain of NDAs are behind us."

This is the closest I've ever heard him come to be pissed about the Jack and Gilly situation. The inkling of what sounds like judgement in his tone bothers me. "People are allowed to fall in love."

He swerves. My stomach lurches as I brace myself against the dash.

"Sorry."

"For the driving hiccup or being angry with Jack and Gilly for shaving years off your life?"

Fingers clamp around my bicep. "Elodie, no. I'm not mad at Jack and Gilly. The opposite. I'm over the moon for them. I'm the head writer of a romance series. Two people finding each other is my spirit animal." He relaxes his grip a bit and lets his hand drift down my arm before he lets go. "The anger you hear is over True Time putting Jack in the position where he had to keep his real relationship under the radar. The strain on both Gilly and him breaks my heart. Fame—publicity playing with people's lives—is fucked up." His knuckles whiten on the steering wheel. "If anything, I'm pissed I didn't stand up stronger to the network on their behalf. Some friend I am. True Time is a medium fish pulling whatever shit they can to become a big fish."

"Like an inhuman production schedule?"

He scoffs. "One of many issues I have with the network."

The lurch in my stomach has nothing to do with Bobby's driving. There's a disturbing degree of *Screw you, True Time* in his delivery. Not a great omen for the showrunner on the brink of season three with seven more seasons to go.

"I don't get the sense Jack and Gilly are grudging against you."

Bobby eases back in his seat. "They wouldn't." A rueful smile twists his lips. "Doesn't mean I don't hold one against myself."

Before there's time to second-guess my move, I've laid a hand on Bobby's leg above the knee. "If they don't, then you need to stop beating yourself up about it."

Just as quickly, Bobby's hand covers mine. "Thanks, Elodie. I needed someone to say that to me."

Shame on me for wanting to slide my hand up higher during this heartfelt moment. I give Bobby's leg a squeeze and let go. He doesn't release my hand right away. I swear the surge of heat from our skin-to-skin contact threatens to fog the car windows.

I'm on the brink of taking control of my emotional narrative, launching caution out the window and initiating a subtle fishing expedition on the topic of Bobby and Elodie when Ireland sends me one of its messages in the form of the coolest castle I've seen yet.

"Wait, Bobby—"

Thank goodness Los Angeles's brand of traffic is non-existent here as Bobby hits the breaks and sends us into a mini fishtail. In California the move would be a guaranteed rear end.

"Oh, crap. Sorry. Nothing's wrong. Drive." I flap my hands toward the road. "I meant wait as in 'Oh my God will you look at that amazing castle.'"

I can tell he's flummoxed by the way he squirms in the seat, trying to readjust after my outburst. "Shit, Elodie. A little warning next time before you explode or do lead with 'Oh my God will you look at that amazing castle.'"

"I want to touch it."

His head cranks back. "Touch it?"

I crane my neck to take in the castle disappearing behind us. "Can we go there after the shoot. I want to absorb the feel of those ruins of…"

"Dunluce Castle."

"That's Dunluce? I thought it looked familiar."

"As I said." Bobby busts out an Irish accent.

"Nice." I swivel in my seat away from the castle back to Bobby.

He nods at the rear-view mirror to reference the castle. "Did you know Dunluce Castle is said to be the inspiration of Cair Paravel for C.S. Lewis in the Chronicles of Narnia?"

I invade his space to stare into the mirror as if it's a looking glass the castle would fill. "Now I totally want to touch it." Too late, I become aware I've clamped my hand on his thigh again to brace myself for the mirror peek. The skin of his neck and face glow with a color I dub *Bobbymelon.*

Ignoring his blush and acting as if the thigh grab was intentional and not a happy accident, I let go and settle into my seat. My, that thigh was delectably firm. I force my thoughts to old stones, moss, and sea fog instead of Bobby's musculature.

He steals a glance at me before paying attention to our winding route. "This castle touching. What do you feel? Grit? Insects fleeing over your fingers?"

Is visualizing bugs the way Bobby attempts to recover from my bold contact? Did Bobbymelon want to recover, or did he share my desire to squeeze harder? "How very superficial of you, Mr. Provost. Engage your writer's soul. What would you feel if you laid hands on an ancient edifice?"

He slides both hands to the top of the wheel and gives the question some thought. "I'd translate textures to emotions and try to imagine the life around the stones when they were in their heyday."

I twist and rest my hand on the top of his headrest when I really want to slide it around to the back of his neck, savor the softness of his skin and the baby-fine hairs surely waiting to be tickled. "Ah, you see the descendants of Viking berserkers sharpening swords and taking selfies with their dragon ships in the background?"

"Get out of my head, Elodie Pettipas."

That's exactly where I want to be, Bobby Provost.

"Do explain what is so alluring about castle groping that forced Patrick into overtime, driving you to Kerry?"

I pull my hand back to homebase and attempt to make myself as small a target of Bobby's discontent as possible. "Sorry. I'll pay for the overage."

Bobby takes his turn at touching and slides a hand down my arm again. "You're fine. I'm messing with you." When his fingers reach my wrist, he lingers over my pulse which is working its own overtime. "Engage your designer's soul and tell me what you feel."

I melt into my seat and close my eyes. "Yes to grit and texture. I also sink into the smells, the temperature, the sensation of the breeze, or if I'm lucky, mist. All the water on Earth has been here for millions of years, cycling from sea to sky and back again. What part of the journey passed through where I stand? Are dinosaur tears dampening the rock? Who hauled the stones and built the castle? Why? How many lives began and ended there?"

I've fallen so deeply into my right brain, it feels as if I'm waking from sleep when I become aware of the dull buzz of wheels against the road. I open my eyes to find Bobby's gaze drifting over me like a lucky mist.

"You are a gift to the show, Elodie, and to me." A rumble warns the car is skirting the rough edge of the highway, and Bobby whips his attention to the road. "From the first time we met online, I sensed you'd understand the story of *The Chieftain's Son* at a cellular level."

That's how I'm a gift to the show, but how am I a gift to Bobby? Here's an opening for me to broach the subject of our *layers*.

As I weigh a few openers, once again the chance is snatched away as Bobby swings the car off the main highway. "Here we are."

Overlooking the Giant's Causeway from the top of the rise, it appears the glacial level of October chill kept all but a handful of hardy souls away from the site. The crew has their pick of choice spots for the shoot. We head toward the sea down stone steps next to a wooden railing. On either side, grasses and plants show off myriad hues of green.

I've seen pictures of the Giant's Causeway, but the real thing surpasses any attempt to capture the phenomenon. Scores of hexagonal basalt columns create this living, geometric art installation. We pass a fortress wall of pillars a good twenty feet high that reach up to the gray clouds on our way to the pathway of hexagons stretching out to sea.

We spot the scant crew prepping a shot near the point where the trail of stones rises to a series of terraces on the way to the water's edge. I see Danna, Bobby's second in command on *The Chieftain's Son* but head honcho for *My Two Loves* deep in conversation with Jack and Gilly. The stars huddle together, bundled in matching show jackets.

Gilly catches sight of us and breaks away, picking her way carefully over the uneven pillars. "You made it."

I gulp air so frigid it burns going down and try to catch my breath from our hike to the causeway. I consider myself in decent shape. Clearly there's LA in-shape vs. Ireland in-shape, and I'm sorely lacking in the latter.

She swipes a pesky lock of strawberry blond hair out of her eyes. "We're on the last setup, but it's the long one—the Fionn mac Cumhaill pages."

Bobby squints at the crew. "You started early."

Gilly shrugs. "Yeah, Jack and I did the drive last night so we were already here. The crew came down yesterday to preview the shots they wanted, and apparently Dermot said today's weather he's tracking isn't cracking," she says, imitating the line producer of their spin-off. "He and Danna wanted to wrap before sloppy rain starts."

For a moment the clouds take five and sun breaks through.

"What do you think?" says Gilly, fanning an arm over the causeway.

I've managed to resume regular breathing. "I'm sure it's magnificent on camera even though it's clearly fake in person." I thoroughly enjoy the way they both gawk at me. "*My Two Loves* has a far superior production designer than the poor slob Bobby hired for *The Chieftain's Son*," I say, thumping my chest. I'm gratified by their duet of laughter.

"Am I right though? This place is so unique it stretches the boundaries of believability."

"Much like the story of the causeway," says Gilly, tapping a toe on the nearest tan hexagon.

Yay, a chance to bust out my research. "Yes, building this dandy road from Ireland to Scotland for Fionn to stage a smackdown with his evil Scottish giant nemesis, Benanadonner?"

"Bobby already told you." Gilly slaps the side of her leg. "There goes the whole mystery of the scene. You might as well leave."

"He didn't tell me. I'm obsessed with Irish legends."

Gilly flashes a satisfied look from me to Bobby. "As is Bobby."

Add Gilly to the Jack, Deidre LaRochelle, winkfest, starring Bobby and me. Gilly reacts with a smirk to the cautionary expression Bobby flashes at her. Are these people giving Bobby a hard time because he's brought me up, or are they just poking at him to poke?

A production assistant hops from stone top to stone top, making her way to us. "They're ready for you, Gilly."

The four of us navigate nature's pavers to the setup. Gilly's facial glow is tamed with a makeup brush, then she joins her hubs in frame. Before we enter the throng, Bobby slides his lips close to my ear. "Let's back up a bit. *My Two Loves* is Danna's gig, and I don't want to hover."

His hot breath slices through cold air, treating the shell of my ear to a slow burn that seeps under my skin and fills my chest with pulsing warmth. Attempting to nod and walk at the same time on the maze of stones goes south, and I stumble. Bobby is there, threading an arm through mine to catch me.

"Thanks."

He changes his grip to my hand and holds tight. "I see some stones just over there that would love to be touched."

His smile is broad and delighted with itself. Hand in hand we scoot off enough to give Danna space but still enjoy the scene. There are a convenient pair of seat-high pillars for us to settle on. To my great disappointment, Bobby breaks our connection. My fingers grip the front edge of my rocky chair. I take in the tumultuous peace of the area. The stones fit together in a tapestry fading from tans to nearly black. The gray sea dips and rolls as a backdrop. Anywhere they can, green shoots and patches of moss make their presence known.

I close my eyes and drink in the essence of this place, the saturation of salty air. The distant hiss of ocean. An old smell, not stagnant but weary. How many thousands of years have these pillars stood as the conduit between Earth's past and present?

A truth that's hovered slightly out of reach finally surges through me. The castles, the causeway, the complicated scents of earth and wind, Ireland isn't only a chronicle of now and then. It's a living storybook, mingling what was and what is, valuing both. It's Donal Cam's never-ending quest to marry his origins to his destiny of loving the same woman through time. This land is a loop of lives and loves, not a straight line. When one tale ends, it's only to make room for the next.

I've interpreted history as static, not fluid. Epochs stacked in a row like these basalt pillars. I create cold castle walls, battle encampments, a bedchamber. Current Elodie, sitting on a slice of eternity finally sees the wavy ethereal film coursing through and between the pieces of Ireland. I recognize the invisible pull I experienced riding Streaker. Honoring that intangible is my duty to the show.

Bobby leans against me and whispers. "What do you feel?"

When I open my eyes to answer him, the first thing I see is Jack, drawing his wife in for a passionate kiss with no acting involved. The kiss goes on past Danna's call of "cut." Afterwards, the couple stays locked in each other's arms, foreheads pressed together, murmuring words in an intimate language no one else is invited to hear.

Danna gives them space without leaking a single drop of her authority. She allows the perfect amount of breathing room before she calls for another shot. The woman exudes confidence and power. I envy her comfort of command.

After today's experience, I will channel Danna and work harder to beat down nagging thoughts I'm an imposter in over my head. That's where the road to confidence lies. I am custodian of the visual myth and must share it with every person watching our show. Deidre understands what I'm just discovering. It's on every page of her books.

I repeat Bobby's question to me, "What do I feel?" and throw my arms around his neck, kissing his cheek. "Everything."

He's so surprised, his body jerks in my embrace. I back off. Yikes. I've found the line where the answer to the *Is this Okay?* question points to no.

I execute a Bobby Provost scamper as I jump up and head over to the shoot, desperate to tell Jack he was so right encouraging me to come out here. I want him to know how much I appreciate his faith in the odd experience I had while riding his horse. The man plays the son of an otherworldly mother on the show, and I'm beginning to believe there may be a touch of the otherworldly about Jack O'Leary himself.

While the camera resets, I make my way to Jack's side. Gilly has pulled away to down a bottle of water. "Hey Chieftain's Son, breaking news, I accepted the invitation."

Jack slings an arm around my shoulders. "Told you the Causeway would do it. Now that you know what to look for, you'll feel it everywhere."

A firm hand presses into the small of my back. "Feel what?" asks Bobby. My entire consciousness slams into the point of contact. Okay, maybe I misread his no to *Is this okay?*

Jack and I share a tacit agreement not to launch into an explanation here in front of the crew. My chest pounds with the urge to share my revelation with Bobby. Surely he's been on a similar journey of seeking connection while writing so many of the key episodes of *The Chieftain's Son.* He'll get me. I want him to get me.

I want him.

I look up into the face I first met on a screen that's become a very desirable part of my daily life.

Gilly rejoins us, hugging her jacket tight to her lithe frame, looking breakable next to her husband. Jack folds around her and nods at the stone steps I'm just now realizing I'll have to climb to get to the car. "I promised Gilly I'd take her across the rope bridge over to Carrick-a-Rede island when we're done here."

She snuggles into him. "It's taken him a few years to pay up, but I'll finally see the place he secretly called me from before his doomsday interview in Belfast."

Bobby winces. "Ugh, that interview."

Jack's face flares as red as a generous pour of cab.

My gaze falls to Jack, Bobby, then Gilly. "Out of the loop here."

The men stay tight-lipped, so Gilly steps up. "Jack and I were dating behind everyone's back and some idiot managed to grab a picture of us." She whirls a hand. "Technically Jack's face but not mine. It started a *mystery woman* rumor when the question about who I was came up in the interview."

"I didn't cover fast enough and nearly gave Meg McGrath a stroke," said Jack.

I cringe. "Ouch. She's intense." The head of PR hit me with a Jack and Gilly NDA before the DocuSign ink was dry on my contract. "Did she order a hit on you?"

Bobby chortles. It's nearly as cute as his scampering. "It was not pretty."

"Did you guys cool it after that?"

Jack tucks his chin into the space between Gilly's neck and shoulder. "Nope. I married my mystery woman."

I nod. "And then Meg ordered a hit on you."

"Thankfully, those type of contracts are above her pay grade," says Bobby.

Danna picks her way over to us. "We've got what we need. Good work."

"To the bridge," Jack bellows, a chieftain calling his clan to battle.

"To the bridge," Bobby answers his liege, and they smack a very loud high five. He takes my hand again as we traverse the uneven ground toward the nightmarishly steep stone steps. I don't care if his purpose is to help me navigate or to keep up our pattern of touchy-touchy, which is something I'm growing very fond of.

CHAPTER 8
CARRICK-A-REDE

I've never been afraid of heights. In fact, I crave them. Super high earthbound vantage points are as close to flying as we mere mortals are allowed. Planes don't count. That's just riding a glorified bus through the clouds.

The Carrick-a-Rede bridge counts.

The rope bridge is one hundred feet above a gap in the Atlantic between the main Antrim Coast and Carrick-a-Rede Island. Our group seems to be the only ones braving the crossing today. I'm first onto the bridge. It takes all my willpower not to skip or see if I can set it swinging. The freedom is intoxicating. The sea beneath is a muted emerald as it flows in and out of the mouth of an enormous cave below in the gap. Black mounds of stone that could be gargantuan pebbles dropped from a giant's hand, maybe Fionn himself, butt up against the island, wearing the frothy lace of incoming surf. Rocks fringed with ten different shades of green grasses cap the mainland's cliffside. Thick fingers of basalt, cousin to the Giant's Causeway pillars, form the craggy face of the small island at the far end of the bridge. Off to the right, nestled on a flat outcropping overlooking the open sea, are the remains of a stark white fishing boat.

My newfound sense of the land and its mysteries sizzle like a live wire. This living world of myth grants me passage to walk upon its surface where giants once tread and fall in love with it. I climb onto the wooden landing as our guide on the island side of the bridge offers me a hand.

"Amazing," I chirp.

The man, who could be cast as an old, wizened sea captain, beams at me, his face breaking into a maze of deep wrinkles.

"I see you're not one to be needing a boat or a helicopter to bring you back across," he chuckles.

"That's a thing?" I ask.

"Oh, t'at's a t'ing," he says with a tilt of his head and a narrowed gaze.

I'm also falling in love with the way some people here trade TH for a T. Ten Pettipas points to Ireland for charm.

I twirl toward the bridge to share my exhilaration with my friends, letting loose a whoop and holler. The forms I find picking their way across the bridge are far from whoopworthy.

Scared shitless-Bobby clings to the ropy railing as he steps forward with one foot and then brings the other to meet it in a cautious shuffle instead of his normal confident strides. His gaze is fixed on the wooden path along the center of the bridge. I want to shout at him to look over the side and not miss the exquisite vista from his bird's eye vantage point. Ten feet behind him, Jack has one hand on the rail and the other clamped around Gilly's waist as he practically carries her across.

I step up the little rise onto the island to give them room to exit the bridge. Bobby gives me a smile almost as shaky as his hands. Jack guides Gilly to join us at the crest of the slope where she promptly turns and vomits behind a convenient rock.

I wonder if puking is a t'ing with people daring to cross the bridge.

With the exception of Jack, I am not in the company of daredevils. I feel a twinge of guilt. Did I actually sway the bridge enough to bring on Gilly's motion sickness and Bobby's shakes? Oops.

Since it looks like he could use support, I hold out a hand to Bobby. It's also an excuse to touch him. He hesitates for a beat and then grabs my hand.

I drag him along a path across the top of the island to give the O'Learys privacy. We veer left and find a cluster of rock to park ourselves on. He reclaims his hand to stuff it inside his sleeve. I fight the urge to dig past his cuff to reclaim it. I convince myself not to take it personally and that hiding his hands is part of his move to regain equilibrium from his cross-bridge shuffle. Maybe I assumed we'd reached hand-holding status when he really was just helping me keep my footing at the Giant's Causeway. Bobby's breathing evens out as we take in the view of two mini islands nestled next to Carrick-a-Rede and the spectacular cliffs of the Antrim coast.

Daggers of frosty breeze slice through our jackets, but the cold doesn't bother me. The air is fresh and unencumbered, with no hints of civilization. I'm not only in a foreign land. It's a new world, an untouched piece of Earth. Seabirds add a layer of wavering grace as they dance near the islands. The sea is not at peace, rather it plays the building crescendo of the violent symphony below us.

This is the Ireland I'm newly acquainted with, a beautiful top layer with hints of wildness churning beneath the surface. Millions of years ago magma roiled, escaping Earth's crust to create the Giant's Causeway. I am becoming convinced the otherworld of Tír na nÓg under our feet, the realm of eternal youth where the characters in *The Chieftain's Son* owe their roots, may control the flow of magic seeping up through the ground to be claimed and cherished by the people who believe it exists. Jack believes it or he wouldn't have encouraged me to find it. I am overwhelmed to be gifted the opportunity to mine the energy of this place and communicate it through my designs.

"You're uncharacteristically quiet," says Bobby, nudging me, his confident tone reinstated.

I close my eyes. "Shh, I'm absorbing."

Bobby's gaze drifts across the landscape. "If given the choice of a personal heaven, this may be mine."

I turn to face him. "Is there room for one more?"

"We usually book a lifetime in advance, but I could make an exception."

Feeling bold, I crook an arm through his. "I'll take it."

He squeezes my arm. "In my heaven, there would be no rope bridge involved."

I love the way his face wears an undercoat of pink beneath his windblown cheeks. "Rope bridges aren't for everyone."

His gaze darts to where the O'Learys found their own private perch. "Clearly."

We sit arm in arm for a few moments. I relish being so close to Bobby, even with the buffer of our jackets between us. He admitted he was a touchy type. I have no barometer to know if this is regular closeness to him, or did I rate an upgrade? Before my overanalyzing ticks to the next level, Bobby pops up. I'm afraid he's going to head back, but he stares intently down at me.

"What were you and Jack talking about at the Causeway?" There's an odd strain in his voice. I'm guessing he's not the type who likes to be out of any loop. A strand of hair whips across his face. "When you told me you felt everything...what did you mean?"

I almost indulge in a teasing smart-ass remark, but a wave of emotion knocks me off course. Patting the rock next to me, I invite him to quit scampering. He looks edgy but complies. "Let us return to your query in regard to my castle touching." Leaning back on my hands I raise my face to the wind. "I've done my research and put heart and soul into my designs for the show, but..." I meet his gaze. "There was an element missing."

Bobby shakes his head. "You're wrong. They're beautiful."

For a moment we stare at one another. The side of my lip twitches as my brain glitches with its usual resistance to accepting compliments. "Maybe nothing was missing visually for you, but for me something was missing intrinsically here." I thump a fist over my heart. "My work hit me as above adequate but incomplete. Up to Jeff Palmer standard but not mine. I expect myself to tell a deeper story, and I wasn't there yet."

He starts to chime in, but I lay an icicle finger on his lips.

"I couldn't nail down what was lacking." I pull my finger away. "I felt it was me. So what did I do? Bulldozed ahead, assuming if I upended the entire layout of the art department, I'd fix the missing link." My ironic chuckle disappears on the breeze. "When I rode Streaker in front of a backdrop of The Clan's countryside, I had a wild, almost out-of-body experience. The tug of an invisible connection knocked at my brain, but I couldn't decode it. Jack was there so I shared what I was feeling. He totally got me and said I should come here today to explore my inkling by experiencing this place.

Bobby slowly nods.

I narrow my eyes. "Is that an *I follow you* nod or an *I'm going to hire a new production designer who has all her marbles* nod?"

His voice is quiet. "It's an *I do get you* nod. I fell for *The Chieftain's Son* because it isn't just a love story, it connects on a primal level to what this country is."

My body superheats, and I'm tempted to throw off the jacket. Instead of leaning into this moment that I desperately want to be a moment as we speak a shared language, I barrel ahead.

"Exactly, it's the vibe of Ireland I was skirting around and not sinking into. The depth of its mystery and deep-seated connection to the story of the show." I mentally kick myself for not defining my deficiency earlier.

Back in my early days as an assistant art director, I relished being the only person shopping the vast studio prop and furniture warehouses where we rented set pieces. I'd sit on fabricated thrones and channel kings and queens. Staring at portraits that had once graced set walls in classic films sucked me back in time to the world of those stories. I've been so caught up in being the big boss and the responsibilities and expectations associated with it, not to mention my constant waltz with imposter syndrome, I shut off my love of whimsy and the poetic emotional time travel objects can evoke. Shame on me. Thank goodness Ireland refused to let me settle for an outline instead of a fully realized rendering of the visual story I'm charged with telling.

I can't tell if Bobby's pulling off a stare or a gaze. Whichever it is, it's relentless and makes me squirmy. The guy is a writer, the head writer of a freakin' time travel romance. He of all people should understand going deeper than the page is not a form of lunacy.

I draw a circle in the air in front of his face. "What is this look?"

His rigidity melts, replaced with a dazzler of a smile. "I've had the moment you found today. I remember it clearly."

I grip his arm. "Tell me."

He chuckles. "I suppose it was my own version of castle touching. Jack has a mate who owns a thirteenth century castle, and he arranged for me to spend time alone there, taking it in. It was just me in an ancient tower house from dawn into the night surrounded by its history of cattle stealing, murder dinners, and generations of lingering souls. You don't come away from that unchanged."

"Does Jack have some magical contract with the otherworld to lead us dumbass Yanks to understand Ireland?"

Bobby barks a laugh. His breath warms my face. "You'd think." He rubs hands over his knees. "It's Jack's generosity, dedication to the show and his country's history that drives him. He doesn't want anyone left out of the richness waiting to be appreciated."

"I see his spinoff is another facet of his passion. I'll bet it wasn't hard to convince him to do it."

Bobby scratches his chin. "Easier when Gilly came into the picture, since he's so eager to share it with the love of his life."

My heartbeats take off running as I stare through the mist at the landscape disappearing around us.

The love of his life

I've been career driven since the art director on the ranch first took me under his wing. I've had my share of crushes and a pair of memorable flings, but to be the love of someone's life…

Bobby stares out over the Atlantic. "I'd let the books get under my skin obviously. I was obsessed with winning Deidre over and getting *The Chieftain's Son* greenlit by True Time Network, but it wasn't until I came here, to Ireland, that the story fully sank into my heart." He breaths deeply. "I understand how special this day is for you."

I'm fully leaning against him now. "Layers," I breathe into the mist.

"Layers," Bobby says, his gaze boring into mine as he repeats what has become a loaded word between us. "You won't just tell the story with your designs now. You'll be the story."

I don't want to be imagining this pull between us. I'll make a complete idiot of myself and pop open a jumbo can of uncomfortable if I'm wrong. An electric charge surges through my body. I have a split second to decide if I'm going to go for it with him or not. Proceeding with caution wins out and sends me to my feet. I pace along the grassy ground in front of Bobby.

"Yes. Jeff Palmer created a luxurious museum piece. I want to give the look of the show a stronger pulse beneath its skin." A gust of wind turns my steps into a skid, but I recover. "I need to move minds, not furniture, and expect from my team what you expect of your writers."

Well didn't I manage to spoil what might have been something tender between us?

Bobby holds up his hands in a *stop right there* gesture. "Moving minds? You are assuming those minds aren't already at the place you've just discovered. People who've lived here all their lives like Jack are miles ahead of we transplants in the connection with the land department."

In an impulse, I lay my palms against his. "Bad choice of words. Not moving minds. I want to sync our purpose to add dimensions. I'll work a day into the schedule for team building, idea sharing, consciousness melding."

Heat rises where our hand touch. Bobby doesn't pull away. "Be careful, Elodie. My philosophy is to gently pull people toward you, don't force them into your mindset. Consider doling out your epiphany in small doses, not a downpour if you don't want a repeat of your department remodeling disappointment."

"How can I keep this to myself, Bobby? I wish for my team to be spectacular not serviceable. Why would they want anything less?" I crimp my fingers between his. "Do you expect me to believe you didn't charge in on a Streaker-level horse to share your passion with your writing staff?"

His fingers remain at attention instead of settling between mine. Is that his subtle hint for me to withdraw my death grip on him?

"Guilty."

I press my fingertips into the back of his hand. "Aha, you agree passion is not to be watered down."

Bobby rises to his feet, finally completing his half of bending our fingers together. The diffuse light through the fog softens his features, and I'm treated to *Youthful-Bobby*. Before I have a chance to step into him, a near-gale force gust drives my body against his, our joined hands the only barrier between our chests.

"Never," he says, a ragged edge to his voice. His gaze lingers on mine and then slides to my lips. I become hyper aware of my breathing, which has deepened, sending tiny bursts of fog between us. Bobby's mouth curves into a gentle smile that dips closer to my upturned face. His hot breath cuts through the Elodie-generated fog, and I return his smile with one I hope is encouraging. Currents of heat from our joined hands run down my arms and straight to my core. My pulse goes nuts in my neck, my chest, and lower regions. Carrick-a-Rede Island is the perfect place for our first kiss.

Bobby's lips brush across the tip of my nose, and he slowly begins to tilt his head when a very loud and unwelcome, "Hello," sails our way from the path. We separate like we've been caught making out under the bleachers at a high school football game.

Jack waves both hands over his head as if we could miss the hulking mass of chieftain's son interrupting our moment. "I'm taking Gilly back across the bridge. We're off for a bite. Care to join?"

I notice the mist has thickened even more around us, much like my disappointment at the distance Bobby put between us. "Right behind you, J," he calls up to his star.

Jack side-eyes us with a smirk. "Meet you at the car park."

In my script, Jack would turn away and Bobby would grab the front of my jacket, pulling me in for a kiss that would render my legs too weak to cross the bridge. We'd huddle under a rocky, bird-free outcropping and make love until the steam from our bodies created their own magical sea mist.

In real life, Bobby gives me a dull smile. I wish my own disappointment was mirrored back to me. Instead, I detect more relief than anything else. Shit. Did Bobby Provost not want to kiss me on Carrick-a-Rede island? I madly rub my thumb over my ring to stuff down humiliation.

Bobby watches Jack retreat. "Maybe I should ask Jack to fireman's carry me across the bridge," he says.

I bend forward and pat my shoulder, offering the service. Humor—the great diffuser.

Bobby guides me upright. "I shall man up. If..." He raises a finger. "You promise not to swing the bridge." With a swoop of his arm, he gestures for me to precede him.

I manage a tight smile as I pass. This is a far cry from my naked island scenario. Inspiration hits and I twirl to face him. "I want to go to the castle where you had your inspiration. Will you take me?"

I hate the conflict running across his face like a strobe light. Damn it. He was about to kiss me. What's the cause of this retreat?

Decision tightens his features. Damn it. He's going to turn me down. Whatever almost happened between us has shifted into a no-go for him, but then his face relaxes except for the intense gaze aimed straight at me. The delicious pressure of his hand against my lower back turns me from a pessimist into an optimist.

"Let me talk to Jack."

CHAPTER 9

PUSHBACK

S

o much for enthusiasm being contagious. I unpacked an entire bookshelf's worth of my research books on Irish and Celtic fairy tales and myths, histories of Irish kings, and even trees and flowers of Ireland. With what I considered a generous offer, I send an email, opening my library to the art department. Egg dripped down my face at the first reply from one of my model makers.

"There are your books and then there's this thing with all the knowledge in the universe. I hear they call it the internet."

Then Rory, one of my most talented CG wizards, perused the spines during a meeting. He shot me the smirkiest of smirks after he pulled out *Wars of the Irish Kings, a Thousand Years of Struggle* and held it up for everyone to see. "And that's Tuesday to us." I laughed with the group, acting like the dig wasn't targeted at the only outsider in the room—me.

His comment is in line with not just my apparently unnecessary resource library, but also the flavor of reactions I got after gushing over my epiphany with connecting to the energy of Ireland and allowing that to be the prime motivator for our visual design. I scored a few polite head nods, but the pervasive reaction was a pastiche of smug looks I interpreted as *the new girl finally caught up*. Great. A second loud *thunk* in my attempt to be an inspirational leader. My brilliant notion of departmental team building activities devolved into pyrotechnics harping over spark vs. flame guns for our upcoming battle scene at the Waterville shoreline, as if I wasn't even there. What the hell must I do to win these people over?

I wish I'd never removed my office door. Settling for showing my back to the room to hide my stupid tears of frustration will have to do for now. Curse Jeff Palmer for allowing his art department to settle into factions. Double curse him for letting them run over him. Or is it only me they're running over?

I'd Facetime Kevin right now if it wasn't the middle of his California night. The familiar chest clench of anxiety tightens until it's hard to breathe. I absolutely refuse to let these people see I'm losing my shit.

What delusional episode led me to believe I could take on this mega show? I've got an entire personal toolbox of design skills, but managing a resistant horde isn't in there.

I do box breathing. In two three...hold two three...out two three... hold two three.

"Miss Boss?" My lead scenic artist, Tim Martin, who could swagger with the best of the cowboys on the movie ranch back home, fills my doorway, blocking light from the main room. I rub my eyes making them even redder and fake a sneeze. I hate the nickname they've saddled me with. It feels both demeaning and insulting. Have I tried correcting anyone? Nope. In my constant *please like me* mindset, sucking it up is de rigueur.

"Hey Tim. What's up?"

He leans against the empty frame, the picture of nonchalance. "Paint shipment isn't coming in until five. Where do you stand on overtime?"

I grab a tissue and mop some of my facial damage.

"You alright there?"

I wave him off. "Allergies." Shit, overtime. My budget is close to busting its seams, especially with all the special effects we need for the Waterville battle. The money mess I've inherited proves Jeff Palmer was no whiz with numbers. The anxiety shackle that's become a permanent fixture around my ribs pinches tighter. "What's left to touch up and get the castle exterior camera ready?"

Tim scratches him arm as his gaze lifts somewhere above my head. "Not much. We're shooting against a section we haven't used before, so matching isn't an issue. The drips you asked for and a bit of spatter are the full menu. The greensman is nipping at my heels to finish so his folks can swoop in with their vines and moss."

"I find it hard to believe you don't have enough paint for drips and spatter."

He grimaces. "Not the right colors. I'll own that one. What with the switch from Ole Jeff to you, I got lax on tracking inventory and might have cleaned house a bit too early before the new stuff came in." He scuffs his shoe.

I bite back my retort of *can't you read a fucking schedule*. I pop a root beer barrel candy in my mouth as I think. "I'll give the greensmen the go ahead to do their thing so they're not busting your chops. Paint will work around them."

He gives me a look of such condescension—I want to fire him on the spot. "I suppose you know what you're about."

A fireball rolls from my gut to my feet. I crunch the rest of my candy and stand. "As a matter of fact, I do."

He flinches a little. I've been full of folksy sweetness, acting like their resistance bounces off me without leaving a mark. My own self-doubt and sense the art department is a runaway train hits critical mass inside me. If they don't want to respect me and play nice, I can match them pissy for pissy.

"And that's a no to the overtime. Light a fire under the supplier and get the paint here before quitting time, even if you have to drive out and pick it up yourself." I target him with a glare. "Since the notion of maintaining a base stock may not have been policy before, apparently, we need to meet and review your material orders for next season. My production assistant will set it up."

I turn to grab my laptop and push past him as if I'm late to a meeting, which I'm not. "And by the way, Tim, my name is Elodie, not Miss Boss." A few heads turn as I stride past the row of cubbies that would be long gone if I'd had my way.

If the art department is not going to let me kill them with kindness and innovation, I'll go another way. Am I a class A idiot for trying to create a team spirit when everyone here seems happy to be a lone wolf, or at least content in their own small specialty packs? Therein lies the fundamental difference I've experienced between theater and film. Theater is a team sport and TV skews more toward clumps and clusters. Not on every show, but *The Chieftain's Son* feels especially factionalized. Hard to believe this dynamic exists anywhere on a show under a main man as generous and enthusiastic as Bobby Provost.

Or am I the problem? Jeff Palmer probably stood the entire art department for ten rounds of drinks at the Waterville pub every night. It's also possible he was so hands off with the day-to-day, the art department never had a shot at the cohesion I'm striving for. Whatever shape my department is in, instead of improving it, I'm fucking it up.

I crash into the corridor and head for the shadowy end away from my colleagues. Have I become the imposter I fear? Was Rich and Amethyst Bettencourt's faith in me misplaced? I rest my head against the cool metal of the double doors leading to other arteries of The Clan. My next burst of self-doubt sets my hands shaking. Did Bobby make the wrong choice trusting me with his epic baby?

The urge to walk out the front doors of The Clan and go back to Wyoming and a much smaller life nearly chokes me. Why did I ever buy into anyone who claimed I should pursue my talent? They not only praised, they pushed me, and I let myself be pushed. Words like gifted and wunderkind went to my approval-starved head and set me on a path I clearly don't deserve. I should have stayed on the movie ranch and married a freaking stunt cowboy. Then I wouldn't be drowning in this pressure.

I need sugar.

The best place for that is the writer's room before all the daily yummies from Maureen's fiancé, Grady, have disappeared. I'll be happy to snag the last half of a donut or pastry someone cut in two attempting to save calories.

My charge to Mount Sugar stalls when I think of who might be in the writer's room. Bobby and I haven't spoken for days after Carrick-a-Rede Island. The man is insanely busy, being pulled in a dozen directions with his show responsibilities, but he did almost kiss me. Doesn't that deserve a text at least? Is he planning on following through with our castle tour, or did he only offer it to deflect the awkwardness of Jack catching us in the ramp-up to a kiss?

The meal and long drive to Waterville didn't feel awkward, but I was so lit up by my revelation of *Elodie Gets Ireland* I chattered most of the way about my plans and visions. It's not as if Bobby didn't contribute, but he also didn't try and kiss me again. I wish I knew if he was *Team Regret* or *Team Lost his Nerve*.

I use the sleeve of my plaid flannel to pat my face dry. If my eyeballs are still a furious red, I'll stick to the allergy story. Best case scenario is an empty writer's room and at least a quarter-full donut box. A gal needs sugar choices.

Worst case scenario rides again. The writer's room is teeming with humanity. At the center of the melee Beth, one of the production assistants, is handing out white boxes.

"We're goin' green," she announces as the writers step up one by one to get their new tablets. "Bobby says our old-school holdouts will still get a paper script if they want one."

Cam Stephens, Jack and Gilly's shared PA, grabs two boxes and raises them. "Anyone who needs tips for using these new beauties can hail me."

I skirt the crowd for the snack table. No donuts. All that's left is a plastic bag with bagels. Crushing disappointment. I scan the room for Bobby. Nothing but a big Bobby void. Crushing disappointment number two.

Wrangling a bagel out of the bag, I stick it in the microwave for ten seconds.

"There's a perfectly good toaster just there," says Collin, one of the senior writers. He trains a thick strand of black hair off his face. "Don't let Maureen catch you microwaving a bagel. She'll school you on proper snack etiquette."

I'm even incapable of prepping my own damn snack the right way. If I didn't feel like an utter failure before, I do now. When the microwave beeps, I turn tail and escape the scene of my bagel crime. Fleeing down the hall I pass a room with a huge electronic white board at one end, filled with Jack and a handful of other burly men. I catch a fleeting glimpse at a tall, thin, gray-headed man who must be Doolin, the Irish language teacher, poking at a phrase written on the board. I'll be at his mercy soon enough. Cast learns first, then novice me.

To my left is a businessy-looking office behind a glass wall where a brown-haired woman with a tight bun in a burgundy suit paces behind a power desk with a phone glued to her ear. I recognize Meg McGrath, head of publicity, from her NDA-waving cyber attack on my person. My heart skitters when I see who's sitting in her leather guest chair, Bobby.

The moment his attention flashes to me, I race along the carpet. I'm too unglued to talk to him. I need alone time. I need escape.

Navigating The Clan complex has become easier since I poured over the hand-drawn map of the place Bobby made for me. I cling to the edges of the sound stage to avoid any of my crew and head toward wardrobe. Their workroom is buzzing.

I greet the costume designer, who is one colleague who doesn't think I'm a loser. "Hey Marie."

"Ah, Elodie. You're very welcome to my shop. What can I do for you?"

Help me hide. "Can you direct me to the drapery room?"

"Go through that door, pass the last row of wardrobe racks, and you'll find the accordion door to the drape cupboard." She cocks her head. "Do you want help?"

"I'm fine, but thanks."

"Go on then." She returns to her table of pins and rich, wine-colored brocade.

Thankfully costume storage is empty and blissfully dim from a single fluorescent ceiling light over the exit sign that bathes the room in a blue-tinged glow. Appetite gone, I toss my incorrectly heated bagel into a trash can and walk slowly down the center row of racks, letting my fingers trail over silks, furs, and leather. The contact slows my hammering heart, and I breathe in the scent of fresh laundered clothing with a tiny hint of dust. At the far end of the room, in an open space, I find a trio of velvet covered benches in front of two tri-fold, full-length mirrors. A cart with pins, chalk, and cloth measuring tapes sits next to an empty rack. I've found Marie's fitting room.

Dropping onto one of the cushy benches, I rest my head on my hands and let the world spin around me. I expected this job to be monstrous, but I didn't expect it to be a monster. How would Kevin, therapist extraordinaire, address my mini breakdown?

"Trust yourself, Elodie. Stop trying to please everyone, Elodie. Take it one step at a time, Elodie. Do your fucking job, Elodie."

Okay, maybe he wouldn't say the last one, that's all me. I signed on for this. I must see it through. If I bail or fail, it's career suicide. I check my watch. At least six hours until I can take the pill to master my faulty serotonin and allow me to enter the void of sleep. I won't let anxiety overtake me and tick into depression. I haven't had a depressive episode in years now. There's a sign in the scene shop with the numbers of days it's been since an injury. I should wear one celebrating the days I've managed to stay out of depression dungeon.

Then again, I've never been under this level of pressure. What made me think I could handle it? Oh, yeah, the temptation of a supportive art department, a team.

"Dammit!" I launch off the bench. I'm not a damsel in distress who needs a therapist on a white horse to save me. The work I've done on myself these past few years has to count for something.

My gaze lands on a gorgeous yellow damask dress. Even in the low light, it glows like a neon buttercup. I'm not a fan of dressing nicely and uncomfortably. If I can't get paint on it, the piece doesn't fit into my wardrobe. This yellow dress calls to me. I run a finger over the smooth fabric. What would it be like to wear such a fancy gown, to twirl in it, to playact medieval royalty? To feel beautiful?

I'm alone in here. No one is going to know if I dally with the costumes. I pull the dress off the rack and hold it against me. Probably a bit too long, which is my constant refrain when trying on clothing. What the hell, I'm going to play dress up. It's not as if I plan to parade around the halls in the costume. I just want to be someone else for a red-hot minute before I walk back into my world and do my job.

Shucking off my overalls and flannel isn't enough. My modern bra doesn't play nice with the built-in corset and the plunging neckline of buttercup. Once I'm bare save for my panties, I manage to slip the dress over my curves. Thanks to the magic of magnets and Velcro, it's not hard to secure it in place. I giggle as I realize if there be magnets, this costume is destined to be ripped off quickly on camera. I carefully pick my way to the mirrors and snap on the pole light next to them. Mama pajama, my cleavage is transformed into something spectacular. My entire silhouette achieves a rating of *fine*. I twirl. It's as distracting and satisfying as I hoped.

"Chieftess Elodie demands your presence. Bring me a slice of boar." I point at an imaginary suitor. "You will bathe before you touch the royal personage."

"Elodie?"

Shit. I snap off the pole lamp. Caught yellow-dress handed by the last person I want to witness my attempt to pull myself together.

Bobby.

"Everything okay?"

"Peachy. Give me a minute, I'll meet you, uh…outside."

His voice is closer. "Why do we have to meet outside? Can't we talk in here?"

I slip a few racks over. "Sure, go ahead."

He's close to the fitting area. "Is there a reason you're hiding from me?"

My heart can't decide whether to clang like a church bell or fall into tachycardia. "Why would I hide from you?" I scooch between two fur and leather tunics to put another aisle between us.

The light in the fitting area snaps on. Bobby's low chuckle floats to me over gowns and breeches. "This might explain it."

I peer around the end of the rack to see Bobby holding my bra aloft.

"Elodie, is running naked through wardrobe more of you getting in touch with the pulse of the show?"

"I'm not naked nor running, and I'll thank you to unhand my delicates."

The rumble of his laugh starts a rumble between my thighs. "If you're decent, come out, come out wherever you are."

His playful tone adds heat to the rumble. Lifting the too long skirt of my borrowed gown, I round the end of the rack and as gracefully as possible princess-step toward the light.

As soon as Bobby sees me, his laughter dies. No scampering now. He's full-on gawking. My bra falls from his hand.

I decide to go all in with my dress up fantasy and curtsy. "Lord Provost." Yep, his gaze rockets to my near-to-busting from the neckline boobs.

"Why are you...what...you're..." he stammers.

I'm a little put out he's so shocked. Either I look ridiculous, or Bobby's uptight about messing with the costumes.

My face heats as my girlie parts cool. "Like I said, give me a minute, and we'll meet outside."

He continues to stare.

I release my hold on the skirt, and it pools around me. "Hello?"

"I...you're...I've never seen you in a dress before." I don't know who wins for most saturated blush.

"Don't get used to it." I decide *what the hell* and go for a full twirl. "I've never seen me in a dress like this before."

As soon as I finish my revolution, Bobby is right in front of me. His hands grab my hips. "You're stunning." The heat between us swirls, and I ache to sink into it, into him.

I rest my hands on his shoulders. I will not miss my chance to take advantage of the lust haze in his eyes. "How stunning?"

"Shit, Elodie."

When he starts to slide his hands away, I snatch them, replacing his grip on me. I'm so damn thirsty for him, I refuse to let him slip away. "Shit what, Bobby?" This time I reach up until my hands rest of either side of his face.

"I shouldn't."

"Oh, you should." I pull him toward me. That's all the encouragement he needs before his needy mouth crashes into mine. There's not much preamble before I open my lips and grant his eager tongue an all-access pass. Bobby's hands slip around to my ass, and he lifts me flush against him as our mouths compete for most energetic taster. Even through the layers of buttercup's fabric, I'm aware of Bobby Provost's admiration.

He carries me over to one of the velvet stools and sets me on top so I'm looking down at him. "Is this okay? Are you okay?"

"Shut up, Bobby, and kiss me again."

With a growl he pulls my mouth back to his. Teeth graze my tongue before he sucks as if I'm made of candy.

"You taste like a root beer float." His lips blaze a slick trail down my neck to the top swell of my breasts. My nipples strain against the fabric, waiting to be sampled by his eager tongue.

Suddenly, he pulls away, panting. I jump to the floor, skirts billowing around me to reach for him. He captures my hands. "Shit, Elodie. This isn't fair to you. I'm not being fair to you."

"Oh my God, Bobby. Will you stop." I raise a hand. "And I don't mean stop. I mean keep going."

He takes a step away, and I want to scream.

"I don't want to just plunge and run with you."

My gaze takes in the swell at the front of his khaki's. "I beg to differ."

It's adorable the way he tugs at his pants as if to hide his enthusiasm and sputters. "I haven't used that attractive term since college." He flashes a lopsided smile. "You make me feel twenty, Elodie."

I step closer and rub a hand down his arm to twine my fingers through his. "Don't stop, Bobby. I want this too."

He rubs his temple with his free hand. "I believe enough blood has found its way back to my brain to elaborate."

"That's a shame," I say, squeezing his hand. I love *Off-kilter-Bobby* more than
Showrunner-Take-Charge-Bobby. "I do enjoy a good plunge. Not so much the running away after."

His gaze is a seductive mix of gentle and intense as it meets mine. "Oh, I suspect there will be plunging, but not here. I'm not the kind of guy who'd slam you against a wall in wardrobe."

"There are benefits to a good wall slamming." I'm so ready for him. The thought of Bobby rucking up my medieval skirts and taking me hard and fast is sexy as hell. With my free hand, I start to lift my skirts to guide our joined hands to the place that will prove just how primed I am for a plunge or slam.

He steps away before I get the chance and lays a hand on his chest as if it will slow his heavy breaths. "Elodie, I'm the showrunner. I respect this show and you too much to mess around in here where we might get caught. It borders on sleazy. I'd like to believe I'm better than that."

He moves close and slides his hands along the sides of my face, tilting it up to meet his gaze. "I want to be better than that for you." His fingers quiver with the energy he's trying to contain. "You're...you're special, no exciting..." He raises his face to the ceiling and shouts. "Ach." His gaze returns to mine. "What I'm trying ineloquently to say is that you're something big to me."

I turn my head to kiss his palm. "You're something big to me too."

His lips press against my forehead, and he speaks against my superheated skin. "I'm sorry if I'm coming on too strong. I'm falling for you, Elodie. First online, and then once you were here it got worse. I just can't hold back any longer."

My arms wrap around him. "What finally flipped your switch? Oh, God. Don't tell me it's the dress. You would be so cliché." I pitch my voice low, imitating his. "Elodie, I finally see you as a woman."

He snorts. "I've wanted to kiss you since I saw your ass covered in mud. I don't care if you're wrapped in my towel, which was extremely hot by the way." He waggles his eyebrows. "I'll take you in paint clothes, a dress, or buried in a puffer jacket. I want you."

"Why did you hold back?"

"I do have some class. I wasn't going to jump you the minute you got here and assume my feelings were mutual. Then when the transition with your department has been—" He hesitates.

"I believe the term you're looking for is a disaster."

His hand strokes my hair. "Not a disaster, maybe more challenging than you anticipated."

I lean into his touch. It's everything I want it to be, sweet, comforting, exciting.

"El, I didn't want to add a complication to your adjustment process."

Oooo, I like him calling me El. I lay my head against his chest. "You are not a complication."

"Okay, to prove I am a classy guy, will you join me for a late dinner?"

"How late?" I've got to be up pre-dawn to triple check the castle set is camera ready. I mentally calculate how late I can take my meds and not be a zombie in the morning.

"Danna and I will be in editing until at least ten or half-ten. Fucking True Time sent absurd notes on episode 209 we've got to finagle. Those idiots don't know a good plot point when it bites them in the ass."

I don't know what's more jarring, Bobby's dig at True Time or the image of Danna and him locked in a dark edit bay. Is she married? Boyfriend? Does she harbor a cache of unrequited love for Bobby?

"Yes," I blurt.

"It's a date."

I narrow my eyes. "A real date?"

His soft damp lips tap mine and linger in a brief kiss that's sexier than our tongue battle. "Yes, Elodie, a real date."

When he backs away, I notice one breast with a very *happy to see him* nipple has worked its way free from its bodice boundary. His gaze falls to my neckline, but to my disappointment, Bobby deftly tucks temptation back into the costume but not before his thumb brushes over my peak a time or two. Such a gentleman.

I wiggle the corset into place and try to tame the quaking between my legs his touch sets off. "I wish you were a little less classy."

He grabs the top of my skirt and slams me against his body, driving his hips into mine so I can confirm how classless I make him. He takes my earlobe in his teeth and then growls into my ear. "Not as much as I do." With a groan he drops his head onto my shoulder. "I—am—walking —away," he says, taking one step backward with every word.

"You know everyone in wardrobe is going to check you for swollen lips and a hard-on when you walk through that door."

Bobby laughs. "I won't give them the chance. Watch this." He pulls his cell from his pocket, bends slightly forward, and holds the phone to his ear as he flies down the center aisle between two racks and then back to me, deep in mock intense conversation. He flashes a smile, tempting me to raise my skirts despite his protests. "People know not to mess with me when I'm in *Bobby-Mode*."

"They call it *Bobby-Mode*?"

"So Jack tells me. As you can see, it comes in handy when used properly. I can be very sneaky."

"I like sneaky," I say, dipping into a curtsy and treating him to one last peek at my cleavage. He'd better zip through the land of needles and pins fast for the well-trained eyes of costumers to miss the party in his pants.

His mock bow is quite accomplished. "Tonight, Chieftess Pettipas."

"Tonight, Lord Provost." I admire his rear attributes as he darts out of costume storage in *Bobby-Mode*. I'm so freaking giddy at this about-face in my terrible, horrible, no-good, very bad day, I nearly rip buttercup as I tear off the dress and rehang it.

Giddy is fleeting in a brain as programmed for self-doubt as mine. Instead of giving myself more than a damn moment to celebrate what just happened, what I've been hoping for, I start stressing. Wait, what did Bobby mean by complicating things for me? Is he concerned how my prickly crew will react to an Elodie-Bobby pairing? Will they use it as more evidence to disrespect me? Damn it, they may take me even less seriously once they suspect there's plunging going on between Bobby and me.

I tuck in the tail of my flannel and fumble with the straps of my overalls. What felt like heaven moments before begins to curdle into the possibility of a bad idea. My chest constricts. It hurts. I know it's anxiety, the bud of a panic attack, but knowledge doesn't ease the pain. My breathing is shallow as nausea gurgles in my stomach. Unable to focus on a breathing exercise, I resort to gulping air.

I've wanted things to go forward with Bobby, and now that they are, I should be dancing a jig. Instead, I'm panicking. If he's worried about complicating things, then I need to pay attention to his warning. Oh God, what if the man I'm crushing hard with may be a career misstep?

My tendency to bolt and leave it all behind rises for the second time today. I squeeze my eyes shut. "What should I do? What should I do?"

Grabbing buttercup, I bury my face in her skirt and scream.

CHAPTER 10
CHEMICAL READ

A lone on the deserted sound stage, at least I can think straight. I wish I had a mother who I could call because she gave a crap about my mental/emotional reality. I wish I had a therapist in the same time zone. I wish I had a brain that could stand on its own without meds. I wish I had a text from Bobby on my phone telling me he was on the way to meet me instead of an apology cancelling our date. Zero on all the above, but at the moment, I've got a paintbrush and a purpose. Those will have to do for now.

I want to be relieved tonight fell through and take it as my sign maybe despite my longing for Bobby, we shouldn't move forward. The problem is, he doesn't fall into the category of a transient show hookup for me. If he did, my mind wouldn't be cycloning. The answer would be an easy call. Get in—have fun—get out. My crew would never know. I keep trying to create a Bobby/Elodie pro and con list in my brain, but my mind skitters off the cerebral page. First, I doubt my desire to get closer to him is a smart choice. Then I doubt backing off is the best call.

I growl and pound the set next to me with my fist. Why can't I make a damn decision and be confident it's the right one?

Breaking what I'm sure are a handful of union rules, I straddle the top of a rolling ladder to reach the high point of the castle set. This is my therapy. Since I issued the *no overtime* edict, the finishing touches to the castle scenery fall to my paintbrush. The aged stone walls with their newly applied encroaching moss and vines would do for Jeff Palmer, but not me.

I dip the brush into the watery mix of brownish-black paint and smush it against the set wall to unleash a cascade of thin rivulets. Even without the still-delayed shipment, I was able to cobble together what I needed from the dregs of paint from several cans. Obviously more effort than Tim was willing to put in. We are so going to have a serious chat.

The drips meander down fabricated stone faces and seep into mortar. They may not like me much, but I take a moment to admire the talent of my plasterers and Tim's scenic artist crew. I could be working on the surface of an honest to goodness castle.

There is something grounding about paint under the fingernails. It's reassurance I've given over my entire being to the artistic task at hand. For the dozenth time, I climb down the ladder, flip off the wheel locks, and roll the a-frame over to the last turret to be baptized in drips.

My legs complain as I make my way back to the top. A long hot shower and ibuprofen will be my companions this evening since Bobby had to stand me up. I press the bristles harder against the base of one of the turret's arrow loops. And now I'm in a snit? God, I'm a case. I do respect Bobby's first loyalty must be toward showrunner responsibilities.

"Shut up, snit." Having the gift of a night to mull over our potential change in status and the repercussions is a good thing.

I lean a hand on the set. Yep, sturdy as hell. Unlike my mental state.

"Here's a worker's comp claim ready to happen."

Bobby's voice startles me enough to lose the grip on my paint brush. It slaps hard on the stage floor, sending splatters across the base of the set. They look good.

"Only if someone scares the piss out of me while I'd straddling a ladder."

Bobby grips the bottom of the ladder and checks the wheel locks. "What are you still doing here? It's half-one in the morning."

"My job."

Bobby picks up the fallen paintbrush. "Seriously, Elodie, please come down."

"Why don't you bring me my brush so I can finish?"

His eyes widen as he takes in the height of the ladder. I remember his lack of love for the Carrick-a-Rede bridge and regret the ask.

"Never mind." I do my own version of scampering down the ladder while he holds it in a death grip.

"Are you part squirrel," he asks as I hop to the floor.

"On my father's side." I feel oddly shy around him. I'm being an emo adolescent over his cancellation and my doubts as to the prudence of going forward with him.

He releases the ladder and studies me. "I'm still confused why you're here in the middle of the night alone on top of a ladder, painting a finished set."

I scrunch my lips together. "Therapy."

"Are you open to alternatives, like say…" He shrugs. "Talking to me about what's bugging you?"

I want to tell him part of what's bugging me is the subject of us, but I hold back. "As my boss or my Bobby friend?"

He takes a step closer. "Either. Both."

Isn't this what I'm missing? Someone to open myself up to besides Kevin. His eyes are darker green in work lights than they are in sunlight. What's my issue? I kissed Bobby and told him he mattered to me only hours ago. If that's not opening a door, I don't know what is. Whatever we are or may become, he's here now and he cares.

I walk over to the curving faux-stone steps of the castle set and sit, patting the step next to me. Bobby follows. Hugging my knees, I turn my head to face him. "Dump warning. I'm a woman with issues."

He nods solemnly. "Dealing with issues is one of my skill sets."

I manage a half-smile. "One would hope." I fuel up with oxygen and unload. "You were right about my department takeover not going as planned. My crew thinks I'm a joke. First, I piss them off with my suggestions of reorganizing our space, and then they think I'm an idiot when I share my passionate insights and goals for going forward with designs." I hide my face on my kneecaps. "My feeble attempt at teambuilding was laughable, and then I got bitchy. Now I'll never gain their respect." I pop my head up. "Do you know they call me *Miss Boss*? Does it get more condescending?"

Bobby swivels to face me, one knee resting against mine. "Where do you stand on tough love?"

I sit straight, bracing myself. "Go." It comes out more forceful than I intend. Surprise causes him to jerk back. I grab his arm. Muscles tense beneath my fingers. "Not go, leave. Go ahead and be honest with me."

"You're too nice." He leans back against the curving wall. "You want them to like you. Fuck that."

Not the answer I expected. "This coming from the friendliest showrunner I've ever worked for, and the man who told me not to barrel in and mold the department to my expectations."

He leans so we're almost nose to nose. "I can be a real bastard if the situation calls for it. And using your words, I did suggest you not barrel, but never told you not to make it your own."

Sugary breath swirls across my face. Someone found donuts.

Bobby is thoughtful for a moment, his gaze trailing up the stone wall. "Jeff definitely had a different leadership style than you do."

"And I'm not who they pictured as a replacement."

His gaze rockets to me. "You're no one's replacement, Elodie."

Because I'm tempted to kiss him for that, I stand and pace over the fake flagstone floor. "You're telling me to grow a pair."

He leans back on his elbows. "Please don't. That could be awkward."

His crooked Bobby Provost smile increases the urge to jump into his lap and do naughty things with my tongue.

"I'm telling you to do what you do best. Keep producing magnificent designs and trust in your leadership. It's not the first art department you've run."

I twirl my ring. "It's the most complex with the highest stakes. I guess I fell into the trap of seeing that as an obstacle rather than a challenge." Wow, it's easy to lay this on Bobby.

He leans forward, forearms on his knees. "I've said it before, but I wouldn't have hired you if I didn't think you'd be amazing. I didn't want another Jeff Palmer. I need an Elodie Pettipas."

Our gazes lock and we move toward one another, gravity turned sideways. When the moment comes where we either fall into an embrace or call it off, I lay a hand on his chest. Oooo, there are very tempting muscles there. It throws me off for a half second.

"Thank you. Best boss talk ever, but…"

Weariness takes over his expression. Clearly, he's not a fan of the "but." Bobby backs away and reclaims his seat on the step. "Go, and not go as in leave?" he asks.

"About tonight—"

He's up again, striding around the set in a blur, a hummingbird searching for nectar. "I feel like crap cancelling on you tonight." Hands rake through his hair. "The True Time cuts weren't working, and then Danna and I got into it over cross-boarding and block shooting for season overlap to maximum time and talent." He groans. "Sometimes this show is building a jigsaw puzzle with all the edge pieces missing. And oh, my fucking hell, our crowning scene for the season finale is going down like two-week stale bread. I'm going to have to disrupt Niks's life and fly her here to fix the damn thing. After tomorrow, our final shooting days of the season were supposed to be the damn shoreline battle. And the new tool True Time hired is nitpicking at the budget."

This is new. *On-the-Verge-of-a-freak-out-Bobby*. The man is an anxiety tumbleweed being blown back and forth across the expanse of the castle interior. He reminds me of…me. An incurable workaholic with a thousand strands of stress twisting inside.

I counter his moves with some flitting of my own to meet up. Here we are a pair of hummingbirds stressing out together. What could happen if our wicked beaks collide?

He skids to a halt, and I catch up to him. "Sorry, Elodie. I'm a great help. Here you are trusting me with your problems, and I unload on you."

I don't mind Bobby sharing his crap with me. In fact, I like it. It takes a bit of a stretch for me to lay hands on either side of Bobby's head to tilt it toward me and kiss the top. "Anytime."

Our gazes settle on one another, appreciating, questioning. His hands find my waist. This can only end in a kiss unless I step back. Which I do. Confusion compounds the questions in his eyes.

I study the pipes above that hold massive stage lights to steal a moment to think. My focus slowly finds its way back to him. "There's something else."

His lips press into a tight light as if he's already decided to be unhappy about whatever is going to come out of my mouth.

I summon what I hope comes off as a caring expression and flick a finger between the two of us. "I'm considering what you said about creating complications for me if we're together." *Considering* sounds so civilized when in truth I'm freaking out.

His *huff* is a basecoat of frustration topped with a layer of anguish. "I'm so sorry. I should have held back. This is exactly what I didn't want to do, add to your stress level with the kiss and acting on the spark between us." He stares at the rolling podium and line of directors chairs set up for tomorrow's shoot.

I growl and it gets his attention. "Bobby friend, not Bobby boss, please shut up." I feel the callous growing on the tip of my thumb as I furiously twirl my ring. "Did you notice the way I kissed you back? That's not a spark, my friend. It's a freakin' bonfire."

"Then—"

I point a finger at him. "You're supposed to be in shut up mode, not what does Jack call it—*Bobby-Mode?*"

He sets his fists against his mouth.

I stroll over to the massive oak table in the center of the castle interior and lean back against it. "I'm kinda screwed up. I want to move forward with you, but my problems with the crew... I am worried they'll get worse if we take this any further."

Bobby comes to lean next to me. "If we're discreet—"

I rest my shoulder against him. "If by that you mean clandestine, I won't be involved with someone and hide it. Look at Jack and Gilly. It must be hell for them to pretend to the world."

He sighs. "It is. I hate what True Times's PR fantasy of Jack O'Leary's image has put my friends through. Put all of us through. It's a miracle the truth about their marriage hasn't slipped thanks to Meg, and Jack and Gilly of course."

"I hate games, Bobby. Give me a blunt truth to face, even if it makes me want to climb into a hole to recover from the backlash." I lay my hand over his. "Full disclosure—I'm a waffler. It felt good at first to go bitch today on my lead scenic artist when he tested me, but then I felt horrible and wanted to bring him baked goods and ask for forgiveness." I take a fortifying breath. "And now I'm waffling about the advisability of us."

Bobby tries to speak, but I press two fingers against his lips. "Before you repeat your advice to 'fuck them' because you're trying to build me up, let me finish." I slide my touch to his chin. "I truly believe there will be a balance with my team I haven't figured out yet. I'll probably earn some scars trying to find it, but I will find it. I'm committed." In voicing my dilemma, the promise to myself feels solid and doable. Is it saying it aloud or sharing my purpose with Bobby that's allowing little beads of strength to start flowing through my bloodstream.

He nods. "Maybe if I call an official reorganization meeting—"

My fingers whip back to his mouth, mostly because I love the touch of his soft, damp lips against my skin. "Don't you dare try to rescue me, Bobby. This is my challenge."

He gently grasps my wrist so he can speak. "Where does that leave us, Elodie?"

"In a mess."

Bobby slides his cheek against mine to whisper in my ear. His late-night stubble scratches a trail of longing everywhere it brushes my skin. He kisses the shell of my ear, then nuzzles his nose in my hair. I'm dying to allow my mouth to wander to his. I stifle a giggle at an image of him sweeping the carefully placed props off the tabletop and laying me across it for some serious plunging. Never. The prop department is one group that seems to like me. I must protect their interests.

"Am I tickling you?" he murmurs, stirring the fine hairs next to my forehead as he nuzzles his way inward.

I wrap my arms around him and find a perfect spot to snuggle my head to his chest. "I'm not saying no to us. It's only fair to you that I should get my head on straight about how to deal with my crew if there's backlash about us being together before we take another step." I sigh. "My tendency is to panic and run. I don't want to run from you."

In answer, Bobby wraps me in an embrace I never want to leave. We enjoy the stillness of the empty sound stage together for a few moments before I pull away. "You may stay while I finish my last drip run, and I'm not just letting you because I need a ride home." I blow him a kiss and head to the ladder.

"How did you plan on getting to your place? Did you sweet-talk Patrick into being on call twenty-four seven?"

I stop halfway up and look down on him. "I thought I'd ride Streaker, share a nice bowl of oats with her before bed, and then settle the ole girl on my couch for the night."

He raises a concerned face to me. "Seriously."

I shrug. "I was going to crash in an empty dressing room. They do have showers."

Bobby shakes his head. "We've got to get you a car."

At the top of the ladder, I sling my leg over and reach toward the paint bucket hanging off the side for a non-existent paintbrush. Peering down, I spot it on the floor where I dropped it. I groan. "Damn it. Will you toss the paintbrush to me."

Bobby grabs the paintbrush and gives me a dubious look. "I won't be the cause of you leaning out too far and falling off."

I point to myself. "Squirrel, remember?"

He eyes the ladder like it will attack. "I'll bring it to you."

His foot is on the first rung before I can protest. I'm going to be ancient or asleep when he finally makes it to the top, but the gesture is so sweet, I let him climb. Easing my body down the other side of the ladder to counterbalance, I wait for him. Bobby is flushed and sweaty when he reaches me to hand over the paintbrush. Our bodies echo the angles of the ladder, bringing our faces close.

"About that mess..." he says, fingers turning white as he grips the wood. Gingerly, he leans the last few inches, open mouth heading straight for mine. His fevered breath reaches me first and my own lust makes me clamp my fingers around the top rung. Careful not to shake the ladder, he delivers a slow, scorching kiss. It's crazy sexy to only be able to move our lips and tongues or risk upsetting our precarious perch. Gently he disengages. "Is it too pushy to ask if you have an estimate on how long I should back off?"

The words *back off* clang in my ear like a sour note. "Are you afraid you can't squeeze me into your schedule?" I tease.

"No, it's just something to look forward to." The low tone of his voice sets off a rumbling south of my belly button. "Something to wish for."

Our gazes lock. What do I honestly hope to gain by keeping a man who affects me like this waiting? There's cautious, and there's *what the fuck are you thinking*? It's fear bullying my heart. Bobby immediately respected my need for time instead of pushing me into what he clearly wants. Why do I need time? It's not as if my feelings for him are going to disappear. We're not only hot for each other, there's a great friendship going. Who else in my life has ever sat with me in the middle of the night on an empty set and validated my problems? To use a popular term around the shop, for feck's sake, the man just blew off his crushing fear and climbed a ladder to kiss me. How is my life truly any better not going forward with him? Ugh, I never would have had any doubts if he hadn't brought up concerns about complicating my life with my crew.

Fixate on your problems much, Elodie? For once in your life, don't be a waffler. Take what you want. What you've been wanting since before you met him IRL.

Well look at that. There is something to be said for the combination of paintbrush therapy and a worthwhile man. My head feels on straighter already. The mess of my life recedes when Bobby is in on it. He's right. Fuck the crew and whatever resentment they may drum up because Bobby and I are together. We're smart people. We will keep our professional life and our personal life in their own lanes. The plasterers will just have to deal with it.

"Wish no longer, Lord Provost."

He peels his hand off the ladder to lay it on top of mine. "Dammit. I pressured you again, didn't I? Please be honest with me, El."

He El'd me again. That's worth several Pettipas points. "I know how busy your schedule is. I wanted to get first dibs on an opening."

"Seriously, if you need to take a step back—"

"You may notice I have a smidge of self-doubt issues. I'm sorry I almost let them get in the way. I do want to give us a shot, Bobby." I dot a kiss on his knuckles. "Hey, no acrophobe has ever scaled a ladder to kiss me before. It's a convincing argument."

"I'd do it again."

"Oh God, please don't. It's making me nervous watching you shake. I'll meet you at the bottom."

Bobby plants a quick kiss on my lips and with painful slowness eases down the ladder. He drops into one of the director's chairs and lowers his head between his knees. By the time I finish my dripping and join him, he's mostly recovered. I walk straight between his knees and throw my arms around his neck. "You're one of a kind, Bobby Provost."

His kiss is much more confident on solid ground. I wait for doubt to scream in my ear that I've blown it by saying damn the consequences and following my heart. Instead, I breathe in Bobby's scent of sweet, nervous ladder-climbing sweat, and if I'm not mistaken, a hint of pencil lead, second cousin to the smell I adore of fresh cut wood in a scene shop. I smile against his mouth before breaking away for a yawn.

He slowly curls a strand of my hair behind my ear. "Do you want to bunk at my place tonight? I can have you there in a few minutes."

I collapse against his chest. The thump of his heartbeat is perfect to fall asleep to. "Must—sleep—now. I think we both know that won't happen if we have a slumber party." I emphasize the point with a blue-ribbon award-winning yawn. "Let me go grab my stuff, and I'll meet you at the car." After a peck on his high cheekbone, I head toward my doorless office, trying not to fixate on the room-filling bed in his little house. Being a responsible adult can be no fun at all.

The sound of Bobby's voice follows me. "Since tonight didn't work out for dinner or..."

I turn back and his hooded gaze seriously makes me question if sleep is all it's cracked up to be.

"What do you say to a rain check next weekend...in a castle?"

CHAPTER 11
DEEP DIVE

The way Jack O'Leary's Irish warrior frame fills the gothic arched doorway of an actual castle is damn impressive.

"Billy Boy," he chimes when a dead ringer for Santa Claus throws wide one of the double doors of Coolderry Castle and opens his arms to Jack. Friendly growls of greeting emanate from the pair embracing on a raised stone expanse in front of the entrance. The term *bear hug* certainly fits these two ursine fellows.

I study the rows and columns of squares on the metal castle. Huh, not wood. I suppose metal is more practical. A gargoyle door knocker is on point for the left side, but the intercom embedded in the center of the right panel screams *wrong wrong wrong* to my designer brain. I remind myself this is someone's home, not a museum or a set. Authentic doesn't necessarily translate to livable.

My gaze continues to soak in the castle. A formidable rectangle of dark gray stone looms above us. In some places raw granite or possibly limestone peek through cracked layers of plaster. Ten-foot-high Gothic windows echo the silhouette over the main door and stand guard on either side. I feel a great sense of satisfaction seeing the weathered drips embedded in the face of the tower house. Two stony wings attach to the main house and stretch on either side. Golden yellow lichen climbing the tower catches the fading afternoon light. I make a mental note to extend the color palette of my castle set vegetation.

It's the crenelations that captivate me. Their detail and design have been preserved for eight hundred years, waiting for me to worship at their feet.

Santa pushes wire-framed glasses up his nose and inventories Jack. "Jackie Boy, it's fine to see you."

Jack reaches a hand to Gilly, who joins him on the castle's threshold. "Meet my beautiful bride, Gilly Bettencourt-O'Leary."

Next to me, Bobby executes a full-body shudder. I find his hand and give it a squeeze. While the O'Learys exchange pleasantries, and Billy Boy engulfs Gilly, I side-whisper to Bobby. "If Jack trusts him with classified intel, Santa must be able to keep his lips zipped." When the creases across Bobby's forehead don't ease, I add, "He's kept a lid on the whole elf-labor thing for centuries."

Bobby's explosive laugh draws the trios attention. Jack extends an arm in our direction. "Billy Kelly, you remember our big boss, Bobby Provost, and here's Elodie Pettipas, production designer extraordinaire."

The intro touches me and adds buckets of water to my confidence well that's reached critically low levels of late. Would it be wrong to kiss Jack? Since there's no step stool handy, I'd be hard pressed to pull it off anyway. No wonder the world has twinkle eyes for the man.

Bobby and I take our cue and step up to the castle doors.

After Billy shakes Bobby's hand, the Lord of Coolderry Castle's gaze falls to me. "Aren't you a darlin' wee thing?" He swallows one of my hands in both of his. "You're very welcome to Coolderry Castle."

I bite back glib comments about the North Pole and reindeer. I'll save them for Bobby when we're alone. "Mr. Kelly, I'm thrilled for the opportunity to hang out in living history."

"Bah with the Mr. Kelly nonsense. I'm Billy." He gives my hand a shake. "Jackie tells me you want to get a taste of castle living." Billy inhales a great gust of air and then cocks his head. "Be good to my ghosts, will you?" With a wink, he steps aside, gesturing for us to enter his tower house. We step into a medieval open-plan first floor. The huge metal, wood-burning stove stuffed into what was once a fireplace large enough to fit five of me is incongruous with the rough, natural stone walls. Yep, it's a castle all right.

To call Billy's aesthetic taste eclectic is to downplay the mish-mosh of African tribal statues, ornate teak side tables, Tiffany lamps, and collection of overstuffed knock-off antique armchairs from various time periods. He's a garage saler. There's even a Gothic style bookcase with a collection of Nora Roberts paperbacks. Ah, Billy likes a good romance, or maybe the ghosts enjoy a saucy scene. My design eye goes on the hunt for anything middle-agey but comes up empty.

Billy claps Jack on the back, aiming him toward the side of the room opposite the front door. "Jackie, let me show you and the missus how to take care of my babies."

A splash of green and fuchsia catches my eye, and I follow them. There's the oddest annex off the main room consisting mainly of more Gothic windows with thin strips of stone between each that wear a mix of carvings from basketweave to very Catholic-looking images, including a detailed crucifix. In what I assume is the brightest room in the castle, Billy has created a beautiful atrium, filled with exotic blossoms, bonsai masterpieces, and skinny fruit trees.

As he instructs Jack and Gilly on the care and feeding of his flora, I join Bobby in front of the ancient, yet modernly retrofitted fireplace. When Bobby invited me for a night in a castle, I didn't picture Jack and Gilly joining us. My fantasy consisted of me looking over the edge of a parapet to where Bobby recites love poetry or maybe a merry lustful chase up a curving stone stairway to a regally appointed bedchamber.

Bobby slides his hand around to the small of my back. "What do you think so far?"

"I think Santa needs a decorator."

He pulls me against his side. "Too bad for the jolly old elf, this one is taken."

"Join us, will you," Billy calls from his greenhouse.

We walk into the sunlit paradise. I catch Jack's self-satisfied glance at our joined hands.

"Now the payment from you two for the stay is to keep an eye on my cattle." Billy gestures to the rolling green pastures and clusters of trees below. A smattering of brown and white cows dapples the verdant landscape.

It's only then I realize the castle is on the very edge of a cliff overlooking the expansive land holdings of Lord Billy of Coolderry. I push closer to the window, reveling in the sensation of floating above the ground. Bobby backs up, going as green as the foliage.

Billy stares me in the eye. "If you see any O'Briens coming over that ridge for my cattle..." He reaches behind a tree to retrieve a nasty looking axe. "Get down there and give them what for." Billy places the axe handle in my hands and shows me how to swing.

I hold it aloft, ready to attack. The weapon feels amazing in my grip. I wish I could have spent more prep time here in Ireland, bopping from castle to castle, slurping up authenticity. My last job didn't wrap in time for that to happen. "Does it work on ghosts?"

Billy retrieves his treasure with a chuckle. "You're on your own there."

Gilly squints out the window. "Wow, you own all this land. Impressive."

"God, no. Give me an African violet over a cow any day." He heads back into the main room. "Taxes are bad enough on what I've got, and the fixing up is a lifelong job." Billy nods to us. "Remember to close any doors you go through. I'll be wanting the heat to stay put in here for my orchids."

There's one bed in the room, not far from the fireplace, that barely reads as a bed. The structure is a massive beast with tall dark wood panels carved with what seems to be scenes of the crusades rising on three sides. It could be a daybed for a giant.

"You and your Gilly will be warm enough down here by the fire," says Billy, gesturing at the bed. "I hope the other pair of you brought your long johns for sleeping in." Walking over to a wooden door mid-wall, he takes a pair of handheld fluorescent lights off hooks and hands them to Bobby and me. "The stairs are through here. If you want to get exploring, take these along. We're only wired on this floor."

November light fades fast, so I'm raring to start picking around.

Billy lifts his chin. "Any questions for me before I'm off?"

I scan the room, looking for an archway or another door leading to a bedroom, or I suppose to be more accurate, a bedchamber. "Where will Bobby and I bunk?"

He looks puzzled. "I thought the two of you were staying the night as well."

Bobby interjects. "Elodie means where will we sleep?"

Shoot, *bunk* or rather *bunk off* means to get outa town. I do need to watch more Irish TV.

Billy treats us to a look I'm sure translates to *idiot American.* "Through the door and to the next floor. You can take your pick of the beds. They're made up for guests."

I copy his earlier gesture and take one of his bear paws in my two hands. "Thank you for letting us barge into your home."

His smile is broad, revealing a missing top tooth near the back. "It's a pleasure." Billy turns to Jack and Gilly. "I'm off and away. Jackie, you know how to lock up when you leave." He grabs a suitcase I hadn't noticed before by the front doors. With a wave, Santa heads for his sleigh in the form of the rusty mint green truck parked out front.

I pull my phone from the pocket of my jeans, ready to start snapping research pics, and turn on the fluorescent. "Let's get this party started." Grabbing the black metal ring on the door, I tug. Damn thing is super heavy. Bobby catches the edge and helps me wrestle it open.

I wave a light toward Jack and Gilly, who gaze out the window over the never-ending swath of green, whispering. Her hand is tucked into Jack's back pocket. Hmm, how long will it be before I'm allowed to pull off that move with Bobby? "Coming?"

Gilly twirls so her back rests against the ample real estate of Jack's chest. He wraps arms around her. I'm envious at their ease with being snuggly adorable.

She sighs. "We're heading over to Maureen's parents place for a wedding summit with Grady and her. Maureen was my maid of honor. She's returning the favor."

Heat flutters in my stomach. I do get to be alone in an honest to goodness castle with Bobby.

"How will Grady and Maureen's wedding hope to compete with your…" I flash air quotes. "*Official* wedding on Skellig Michael."

Gilly drops her head back against Jack. "At least for their big day, Meg doesn't have to work on restricting air space from newsy helicopters." Jack kisses her temple.

I shake my head. "I didn't picture helicopter invasion being an issue over here."

Gilly playfully prods Jack with her elbow. "Have you met my insanely famous husband?"

He pretends to take a blow instead of a nudge.

She extricates herself, retrieves her tartan bag from where she left it on the floor. Before she can sling it over her shoulder, Jack takes it from her. The look of adoration she wears for him makes me squishy inside. "We won't be long. I've got work to do, right Bobby?" Gilly's look flashes daggers at him before she sighs. "We should do a writer's retreat with the staff here."

"Maureen would definitely freak out the ghosts," says Bobby, shaking spooky fingers at Gilly. "And we'd have to deal with Benj and Benny nearly fainting every time they heard a creak."

Jack shifts Gilly to his side, freeing one hand. "Toss me your keys, Bob, I'll haul in your bags with ours before we go so you two can get on with enjoying the castle."

I'm going to start calling him Jack O'Smirky if he flashes one more suggestive hint at us.

Jack catches the keys. "We'll grab takeaway on our way back."

Bobby and I slip into the stairwell. If my light wasn't on, we'd be in total darkness. Complaints about the lack of windows in the castle must have given medieval relators fits at open houses. Before I share my wit, I'm backed against the door with a hungry wet mouth finding mine for a delicious ravish. Who needs a burly Irish clansman castle fantasy with a lithe and ready body pressing against the entire length of mine?

Lips trail a path down my neck. Each kiss a delicious bead of warmth. If the heat of Bobby's breath is any indication, sleeping, or not sleeping away from the fire will not be an issue. How cold can a castle really get? When I dip my tongue in his ear, he moans. Quivers between my legs rev their pace to a pleasant *thump thump thump*. Bobby's hand slides around to enjoy a handful of my ass. He starts a slow grind against me.

My voice is not much more than a breath. "You're good at this. How many against the castle door trysts have you enjoyed here on the Emerald Isle?"

Bobby tongue tastes the shell of my ear before he answers. "None." His raspy voice encourages me to wrap a leg around his. "Which accounts for the blue glow coming from my balls." His fingers slide under my jacket to find the waist of my jeans, then slip inside heading south.

"There's something to be said for a date where you're guaranteed to get lucky." I'm embarrassed at how ready his fingers will find me. "I would have been all for you pulling over on the way down here to remedy your blue situation."

"I did consider it every time we passed a little side road. If we didn't have to get here on time to meet Jack and Gilly…" His voice trails off as his lips finish the sentence.

We savor one another for a long moment before I run my fingers along the side of his face. "Probably best for the show to avoid being hauled in by the Gardaí for lewd car conduct." My hands find their way to his wonderfully firm bottom and yank to bring those aching balls flush to my *thump thump thump*. "Now lewd castle conduct is an entirely different matter." The shift in position drives something sharp and painful into my back. "Ouch!" Reflexively, I push away from the door and clutch the base of my spine.

"Are you okay," says Bobby between heavy breaths.

I reach under my jacket to check my back while he lifts his light to examine the door. The round head of a rivet pokes out of the metal band spanning the wood. Turning away from him, I lift my jacket and shirt. "Am I bleeding?"

He bends close and runs a fingertip over my spine. "No, just a red spot." Bobby kisses my exposed skin.

I don't want to stop him from kissing every inch of my skin, but we will be losing the lingering sunlight all too soon. "As much as I want to be plunged against a castle wall..." I press a quick kiss to his puffy lips. "I'd like to see the place while we still can."

Bobby tugs my jacket into place. "I'm sure there are softer options in here to plunge." Together we lift our lights to the curved stones stairs and begin to climb. "Did you know these clockwise spiral stairways favored right-handed swordsmen?"

I snort. "Did you know that's bologna?"

"It's not."

"It is. Perhaps you should deepen your research dives." I give his ass a little smack. "What I mean is, general wisdom points to the fact this stair design allows one to brace their right hand against the wall before the dawn of handrails when picking your way down these narrow tricky fuckers was no picnic."

Bobby reaches back to take my hand. "I have a lot to learn from you, Miss Boss."

I slap his hand away even though I deserve the dig for being a know-it-all. "Don't even go there."

We reach the next level. It's freezing and just as sidewalk-sale chic as the first floor. I stroll around the room. There are no less than three Henry the Eighth worthy, four-poster beds set against the walls at intervals. In the center of the room is a kidney shaped glass tabletop, supported by a thick gnarled branch. Off in the corner is a full-sized Irish harp, the only nod to authentic Ireland in the room.

"Oh goody." I shiver. "A middle ages sleepaway camp." I grab a magazine from a stack on the table. It's an old copy of the Irish Sun tabloid featuring a famous non-couple who made the mistake to embrace at a public event. "Nora Roberts downstairs and tell-all mags up here. Billy Kelly is into the classics." An involuntary *Whoo* escapes as the next shudder ambushes me.

Bobby moves alongside, draping an arm around my waist. Is he always this warm, or is residual lust heat wafting off him?

"Jack and I agree the real beaut is the next floor." He gestures to another door. "Shall we?"

I'm about to agree when a splash of color on the white plastered wall near a small niche leading to a tiny window catches my eye. "What's...

Wow!" Painted on the wall is a spectacular fresco of a magnificent Irish chieftain. "Look, it's Donal Cam's daddy." I run a finger over the image, imagining the long-ago artist who bled this beauty into wet plaster. Grabbing my cell, I snap pictures.

"Which daddy do you suppose?" asks Bobby, joining me.

"This is the find of the trip."

He takes my shoulders and twists me. "Here's another."

Behind me is a second fresco of a woman clad in fine clothes with long snaky braids intertwined with gold fabric, staring out over the room. My chills aren't from the cold. "It's like Nieve is waiting here for Donal Cam to find her."

Bobby touches the fresco. "Our fan hoopla centers on Donal Cam's quest to keep finding Nieve across time." His finger pauses over her heart. "I've always felt for Nieve. It wasn't her parents who defied fairy rules and prompted the piseog that separated her from her great love."

"Piseog? Does it mean pissed off?"

Bobby laughs. "In a manner of speaking. It means curse." He takes my hand and leads me over to another wooden door. "Are you ready to enter the scene of the Black Blood Ball?"

"Creepy."

"Extremely," he says opening the door for me.

Up another curving flight we arrive in an empty room as long and wide as the tower house. The floor is strewn with rock rubble and dust. Here stones of the structure itself protrude from untreated walls. Four recessed alcoves each hold a pair of skinny Gothic windows so dirty the light shining through them has a greenish tinge. The view of gray clouds over a picture-perfect landscape seems to mock the heaviness surrounding me. Icy drafts crisscross through the room, giving off low moaning whines.

"No gossip rags here," I say, using my phone to capture every detail in closeup as well as full panoramas of the deserted space. My fingers learn every texture, every temperature of stone and mortar. There's undeniable energy around us. It skitters through me like a confused static charge.

Bobby walks up behind me and sets hands on my shoulders, leaning his cheek close to mine. He shifts into storyteller mode. "In the sixteenth century the first daughter of Coolderry Castle wed the son of the clans greatest enemy, the murderous O'Bannions. The blessed union was to allay threats from these vicious rival warriors. On the night of the wedding, a ball was held in this very chamber to celebrate the nuptials. All was candlelight and dancing until from the floor below, the head of clan Coolderry heard the blood-chilling scream of the bride, his only child."

I snuggle back into him, preparing for the story to go dark.

"He rushed upstairs to where we now stand to find his heir bloody and lifeless, the new husband dangling her body over the oubliette." Bobby's hand slowly lifts to point at a low square of stones near the corner of the room. "As the devastated father watched, the groom let go and dropped his bride down the shaft to her eternal rest."

He walks me over to the oubliette. I peer over the edge into the dark channel where the new Mrs. O'Bannion got screwed and not in a good way on her wedding night.

"Before a wail of grief escaped from Coolderry's lips, an O'Bannion sword found its way between his shoulder blades and through his heart."

"He must have offered one cheap-ass dowry." My voice plummets into the tunnel of the oubliette.

Bobby grips the stones to stare into the death hole. "Coolderry joined his daughter to rot in in the bowels of his castle. His wife, the lady of the castle, was given as a prize to O'Bannion soldiers. When they finished with the poor woman, her corpse was tossed into the nearby Rapemills River."

"Well, that name's a bit on the nose."

He nods at the oubliette. "It's said the bones of the Coolderry sire and heir still dwell here today. Centuries later, the pair continue to protect the castle and lands they lost to the O'Bannions that fateful eve by haunting any usurpers who attempt to lay claim to their ancestral home."

"Billy Kelly must have his hands full."

Bobby hip-checks me. "Jack says Billy is a distant cousin to the Coolderrys. Free ghost pass."

I thread my arm through Bobby's. "And I thought bad lighting was the biggest downside to this place."

He pivots to take me in his arms. "Any ghost that tries to toss you into the oubliette will have to go through me first."

I twist to call down into the Coolderry's tomb. "We're only here for the research." As I turn back, Bobby's long, slow kiss dares any avenging spirits to mess with me.

CHAPTER 12
FIRESIDE CHAT

All those historical novels I love so much were right. Whiskey does warm you up. I hold up my glass for a refill as Jack, Bobby, and I lounge in front of Coolderry Castle's woodburning stove on pillows scavenged from armchairs. We lean back against the bed behind us that Gilly claimed to stretch out on. The men and I are doing a respectable number on the bottle of whiskey Jack received as a gift from a Tipperary distillery and brought to tonight's party.

Jack holds his glass to the firelight. "It's a bit on the fruity side for my liking."

"Easy on the tongue though," says Bobby, taking another drink.

Gilly guides Jack's glass under her nose. "Let me smell." She's begged off the whiskey in favor of hot tea, claiming morning, especially an early morning with a hangover, is not her happy place. Since they carpooled with Maureen and Grady, our companions have to leave at daybreak to get to Waterville in time for Grady's brunch shift at the hotel. "Citrus?" she asks.

I've got a long way to go with being able to ID the nose, taste, and finish of the whiskey Jack and Bobby analyzed. My only experiences with non-Irish whisky variations are Fireball and peanut butter. Those none-too-subtle differences I can taste.

Jack relaxes back against the front of the clunky bed. "What did your Wyoming cowboys drink?"

"With pizza?" I gesture at the two empty boxes of takeaway pizza we polished off. "Beer and Jack Daniels."

Bobby perks up. "Have you ever had steak in Jack Daniel's sauce?"

Jack and Gilly groan in unison. She digs a chin into Jack's shoulder. "At Cali Con in San Diego, Bobby dragged us to a steak house three nights in a row to indulge his new culinary obsession."

Bobby acts affronted. "Do you disagree it was delicious?"

Jack drains his whiskey glass. "I'll give you it was worth one return visit, but two was pushing it."

I was so worried I'd be a solo act in Ireland, and here I am a month in, enjoying the company of people rapidly become great friends. If the night lives up to its promises, one of those friends will be my lover come morning. The level of contentment I feel luxuriating before a fire in the castle is unexpected and wholly welcome. Ach, and to think I nearly let Lady Panic take this away from me by not going all-in with Bobby because of a cranky crew balking at the transition in leadership.

Gilly drapes her arms over Jack's shoulders. "Do you miss Wyoming, Elodie?"

I stretch out my legs next to Bobby. "I miss the horses."

He squeezes my knee. "Not the cowboys?"

"Are you fishing for my cowboy past?" If he only knew I lost my virginity to a theater nerd behind a set in my senior year of high school. It could be fun to tease him about cowboys, but it doesn't sit right to be anything but honest with Bobby. Well, mostly honest. I don't share my mental illness with anyone. Giving out that intel opens me up for people to dismiss any legit emotion I have with a flippant 'she's so bipolar.' I hate the ignorance of people who fling the label around, callously oblivious to what it really means to be saddled with the disorder.

"Hot cowboys are my mom's weakness, not mine." I wave a hand. "Don't get me wrong, I was always in awe of the stuntmen's way with the horses. Those guys were sweet to me when I was younger, giving me riding tips, but it was the behind-the-scenes action that I fell in love with." I take a deep breath. "One day I was hanging back, sketching my version of shots they were filming on *Through the Western Dust*." I turn to my companions. "Do you know the show?"

Gilly gives Jack's chest a gentle slap. "It's one of Jack's guilty pleasures."

"The production designer, Will Tremblay, caught me drawing." I shrug. "He said he saw talent and took me under his wing whenever they'd come to Wyoming to shoot the series for the next couple of years." After another sip of whiskey, I go on, alcohol making me chatty. "I secretly pretended Will was my dad. He was French Canadian like my real father." My surrogate pop and I shared olive skin, dark toffee-brown hair, and cola-colored eyes so different from my mom's blond-haired, blue-eyed beach girl look. "I couldn't get enough of Will's stories about growing up in Toronto and adopted them as ones I might have learned from my bio dad if mom hadn't left him in the dust and dragged me to a movie ranch in the middle of Wyoming to chase her cowboy dreams.

Bobby sits straighter. "Will Tremblay! He's big stuff. I initially tried to get him for *The Chieftain's Son*."

"Fate brought you his protégée instead," says Gilly, smiling at me.

"Will not only gave me an on-the-spot education in art direction, he also mentored me to build a portfolio that eventually got me into top-notch theatrical design program." I wrap my arms around my middle to squelch a sudden burst of homesickness for my erstwhile dad.

Jack squints at me. "You're French Canadian? I had mates in a play back in Dublin from Toronto—French Canadian fellows. They were much swarthier than you."

I give him mock stink eye. "Are you profiling French Canadians as pirates?"

Jack laughs and tips his head back to allow Gilly better access to play with the long waves of his dyed blond hair. "Pirates and cowboys," she coos. "I'll bet we could find a steamy paperback with both on Billy's shelf."

Jack grabs his wife to slide her over his shoulder onto his lap. "If it's steamy you want…" Tilting her sideways, he kisses her in a pose worthy of any romance paperback cover.

"Hey, we're on a first official date here," says Bobby. "Don't make Elodie uncomfortable with your third date level kissing."

Jack flashes us a wicked look. "You know what else happens on a third date?"

I *pfft* my lips. "Do you expect me to believe the way you two are all over each other that you waited for a third date?"

"Technically," Gilly says, meeting Jack's gaze. "Was it our third date before...?" A red flush apart from firelight deepens the color of Gilly's face. "Are we embarrassing you, Elodie?"

I sip my apparently fruity tasting whiskey, but the only thing I can identify are numb lips. I raise my glass. "Remember...mother-cowboys, I don't embarrass easy."

"He did kiss me in a pub within hours of our first meeting at a golf tournament."

"Couldn't help myself," says Jack, tapping a kiss to her lips.

Gilly counts on her fingers. "I didn't count that as our first date."

"I did." Jack grins.

They rub noses. "Jack also counted driving me home and giving me a protein bar as a dinner date."

Bobby is quiet. Can we count any of our numerous late-night video chats as dates? We certainly got to know one another substantially over those months. Maybe he tallies the trip to his house after my mud bath as our first date? If so, was our costume storage smooch date two? Uh-oh, that would make our ladder kiss date three. Damn, we missed our shot to live up to third date expectations. Bad omen or admirable restraint? Judging from his kiss attack at the bottom of the stairs, restraint won't be an issue on this date no matter what number it is.

I snuggle closer to Bobby. "Please continue, I do so enjoy prying into the love life of people I've only recently met."

The four of us share a laugh.

"You're easy to fall in with, Elodie," says Jack.

I reach out to pat his leg. Damn, it's like a marble pillar stolen from a colonnade on Mount Olympus.

Jack pours one more trickle of whiskey into his glass and raises it. "To the first of many double dates."

Bobby and I join him in the toast.

I reach forward and set my empty glass on the stone hearth. "So back to Gilly and Jack, date three."

Gilly's smile sets the bar high for the look of a *woman in love*. "A beautiful trip around the ring of Kerry. Jack introduced me to Ireland." Jack and Gilly gaze into each other's eyes as if they're alone in Coolderry Castle. "I fell in love twice that day."

"Come on, Bobby," I say, slapping his thigh and then standing, albeit a bit wobbly. Whew, I didn't think I had enough whiskey for my level of buzz. "I hear our exit cue. This..." I gesture at the happy couple. "Might be contagious." I offer him my hand, which he accepts as he finds his feet.

He pulls me close, intending to whisper, but the ole castle bounces sound quite well. "One can only hope."

Mr. and Mrs. Smirky O'Leary don't even attempt to hide the fact they heard him. The toasty combo of flames and whiskey fades as we leave the range of Billy Kelly's fine fireplace. I have the answer to my previous question of how cold a castle can get——freaking freezing. I retrieve our jackets from a chair. We throw them on to trap any last remnant of heat from our fireside cocoon.

I grab the two fluorescent handhelds off their pegs while Bobby retrieves our bags and heaves open the door to the stairs. We conquer the uneven stone steps to the second floor. With a cry of, "Cooooold," I cross the room at a gallop to the four-poster bed furthest from the window. After kicking off my sneakers, I waste no time scrambling underneath the covers fully clothed and pull several layers of blankets and bedspread over my head. It's like sliding between sheets of ice. Where's an old fashioned bedwarmer stuffed with hot coals when you need one? My remedy is to make snow angels—sheet angels, hoping friction heats the frigid fabric.

The edge of the bedding lifts and Bobby's face appears. "Are you battling a ghost?"

"Get in here," I command through chattering teeth.

Bobby slides in beside me. He's shucked his jacket and shoes. The man must have superhuman internal body temperature not to worry about death by exposure, or maybe it's copious amounts of whiskey warming his blood.

I grab his arm and turn onto my side. "Spoon me."

When he obliges, I tuck back into a body not a whole hell of a lot warmer than mine. So much for superhuman.

"Not enough. Lay on top of me."

I roll onto my back, and Bobby eases on top of me. "If the whole night is going to be this bossy, I approve." His lips graze my neck, and he breathes deliciously hot breath over my pulse point.

I moan more with relief than pleasure as his heat cranks higher and begins to seep into my frozen skin. He takes it as encouragement and slowly begins to glide up and down my body. The heat-inducing friction is much more effective than my sheet angels. "Don't stop."

He kisses his way from my neck to the corner of my mouth. His hot tongue travels across my lower lip and then my upper, treating me to more of his warm breath. I'm almost recovered enough to kiss him back when he pulls away. "Your thin California blood needs to adjust."

I give his bottom lip a gentle bite. "It's November in an unheated castle. Anyone's blood would need to adjust. Why aren't you colder, LA boy?"

Bobby finds my hand in the tangle of blankets and guides it between us. His arousal is an impressive heat source.

I tease him with a few gentle over-the-jeans caresses which he answers with a long slow hum. The sound kindles a spark in my frosty lady parts. Moving as best I can with Bobby nearly squashing me, I enjoy a more thorough exploration of his length clearly begging to be free of denim. "If you think I'm getting naked with you in this ice cube, think again."

Bobby is a bold kisser. He plunges his mouth down on mine, using his tongue to force my lips open. It's his own special brand of bed warming. My hands thread through his hair to pull his mouth harder against mine. I use my tongue as a paint brush, kissing with techniques I use in watercolor. Quick dots and languorous slides with the tip of my tongue across his and then juicier strokes with the flat side, wet into wet.

A pocket of heat surrounds us under the covers as Bobby purrs into my ear between kisses. "Don't knock it 'til you've tried it." His fingers sneak under the bottom of my jacket, popping the snaps open one at a time as the back of his hand glides over my stomach and then between my breasts. "Still cold?" Those same fingers find their way to my nipple, transforming it into a plump raisin at his touch. "Hello there. We've met before."

His slight pinch and the memory of Bobby tucking my boob back inside a yellow bodice sends a jolt straight between my legs. I hook a leg around him so his hard cock strains against my softer parts.

He frees his hand to work the buttons of my flannel until it lays open along with my jacket. The silky ice blue layer of my thermal shirt is the last defense before bra and bare skin. Lifting our sexy tent covering with one hand, Bobby uses the other to peel up my shirt. He skims two fingers beneath my bra to roll each nipple until raisins shift into newly budded grapes. The whole time he's rocking his hips in a slow rhythm against mine.

Suddenly I don't give a flying fuck about the cold. I need naked Elodie under naked Bobby. I flop in a frenzy to free myself of every top layer. Bobby lifts above me, laughing as I manage to wad my jacket, shirts, and bra together and shuck them out of the blankets. I pull his head to my breast. "Get to work."

He does. Oh, mama pajama, he does. His tongue dances, then his lips close over me, sucking me deep into a hot mouth that makes me forget I'm in an ice palace. My fingers dig into his back under his sweater as I writhe and moan. If this is how my body reacts to his teeth teasing my nipples, I may not survive the full plunge.

Pulling the tail of his flannel and thermal toward his shoulders, I growl. "I need more skin."

Bobby is so fast, his shirts seem to fly off his body. When he lifts the edge of the blankets to toss them aside, a blast of frosty air forces its way into our haven of heat. Instead of a shock, it's cool relief from the fire rising between our skin.

"How's this?" he croons into my ear before he slips his tongue inside, bringing me closer to sexual Armageddon.

I return the favor, which sends a delightful shudder through him. "I'm amending my decision on naked."

That's all the encouragement he needs to kneel over me and undo the front of my jeans. He slowly slides the fabric down my legs. The pace of his movement ignites me. I writhe and groan with anticipation. Losing control, I finish the job by kicking my pants into a bunch and sending them beneath the covers toward the end of the massive bed.

Bobby laughs at my impatience. "I was getting to that."

The stall gives me a moment to realize our sexy party has an audience downstairs.

I grab his shoulders and pull him close so I can whisper. "Will Jack and Gilly hear us? Should I bite a pillow?"

Bobby gives me a wicked smile. "I'm a big fan of pillow biting activities."

I nip the side of his jaw. "Biting in general could be fun." I stick my tongue back in his ear, my new favorite thing to do, just to make him shudder again. "You didn't answer the question."

"Hard to tell. We are under a mountain of blankets, behind two closed doors with a stone floor and twenty feet between us. Maybe they'll think it's ghosts."

"A sexy Coolderry ghost-romp is something I can wrap my head around."

"I think I'll wrap mine around..." His hand sneaks inside the front of my panties, a finger dipping slowly into my pool of damp heat. "Umm... who needs a fireplace when I have this?"

Each twirl of his fingertip primes me higher for a mind-blowing explosion. I stop giving a damn how loud I am. He hits one perfect spot and knows it from the way I buck into his touch.

"Here, babe?"

The way he circles and presses, it's like I've never been touched there before. I squeeze a handful of blanket and groan.

"Come for me, beautiful Elodie."

His movement speeds up, faster and faster until my mind is nothing but static as pleasure explodes through my core. I'm barely aware of

Bobby slipping my panties the rest of the way off while I treat him to my post-release shudders.

"I'm not sure they heard that," he whispers against my ear. "Let's try again."

The upper halves of our bodies are freed from heavy covers. The contrast of frigid air and hot skin are maddeningly seductive. Bobby's lips kiss their way down my stomach, then lower until he finds new ways to coax pleasure with his tongue. He grins at me as I become a quivering mass begging for a second release.

"Oh, my fine glass of whiskey, your scent is toasty marshmallow." His tongue slides over every sensitive nerve before he looks up again. "Your taste, creamy caramel. And the finish..." He sucks just the right place to launch me a second time. I try to grab for a pillow to bite, but I'm not in time.

I clutch his shoulders as my psyche peels itself off the roof and returns to the bed. Bobby slips his fingers through my hair. "You're the perfect blend of smokey and sweet." He stretches out on his side, pulling my leg over his hip.

I kiss the underside of his jaw. "They're deaf if they missed that one." He chuckles until my hand slips over the bulge in his crotch, still trapped in his jeans, and begins to stroke him. "I believe I was promised a plunge."

He starts to kiss me tenderly and slowly, but when I increase the pace, he does the same, shifting into lip-bruising passion. Panting, he draws away. "I don't want to rush you." His hands grab my ass, and he fits me to his arousal. "I'm afraid I won't be very graceful. It's been a helluva long time. I want to be sure you're ready for me."

If there is one benefit to my tendencies of mania, it's my ability to go from sexually satisfied to *take me again* in record time. I guide Bobby's hand between my legs.

"Oh—fantastic," he says and treats me to a few flutters with his fingers that leave me panting.

I work the buttons on his fly open and yank his jeans down over his hips, taking his boxers along with them. "Your turn to kick 'em off."

"I'm more of a wiggle man." Bobby shimmies out of his jeans.

I wish there was some light besides the sanitized glow of the fluorescent discarded on a table near the bed so I could appreciate more than a shadow of the eager cock pressed against his flat stomach. Luckily, I've always been a more tactile person. "Wanna see what really revs me up?"

I feel the low chuckle in his chest. "Is that a trick question?"

Sex with Bobby isn't only setting me off like a string of firecrackers, I'm having fun. I pull the covers to our necks, then disappear underneath. My fingertips learn every delectable contour of his silky shaft and linger on his smooth tip. He pushes against my touch and my gentle travels grow fierce. I wrap my palm around him, stroking faster until I drive him to make sounds that echo off the castle walls.

My core tightens and pulses in time with the blood pounding in my new favorite part of Bobby. It's then I dip low enough to circle his tip with my tongue. His body begins to shake harder and harder. He yanks me up for a quick savage kiss before he practically leaps out of bed to rifle through his duffel. He's got the condom on before he's back under the covers.

I smack his chest. "Hey, maybe I wanted to help."

"Next time. Get on your back, woman, so I can plunge." He playfully pushes me down and rises on his knees before spreading my thighs apart. Hands lift my bottom, and he slowly sinks partway into me. His thumbs slide to either side of my opening, coaxing it wider as he goes in farther. His touch is everywhere, finding the best places to unravel me. He continues to peel me apart, maddeningly gaining new ground with each approach. I'm so wet, it's a miracle he doesn't slip all the way up to his hilt.

He's being a gentleman when I know how badly he wants to go for the full plunge because I share his need. Bracing my arms against the headboard, I thrust my hips to take him deeper. His cry of surprise treats Jack and Gilly to another blast of our saucy symphony.

"Fuck, Elodie."

"Yes, please." So much for slow. He rocks into me again and again, increasing speed in time with his ragged breaths. I arch to meet every thrust and clench tightly around him with my own rapid-fire rhythm.

Our sexy skin-smacking dance will surely paint a blush on every Coolderry ghost.

I can tell he's trying to make it last, but we've blown past fourth gear. With red velvet covers draped around his waist, he plunges with a force that's utterly mind-boggling. Sheer appreciation of his unrestrained power rips a bubbling orgasm from me as we share a Coolderry Castle climax.

After we both manage to stop breathing fire against each other's necks, gasps downgrade to a more regular rhythm. I squeal from the frost surely forming on my bare ass. We sprint to the bathroom to ditch the old condom and in my case, freshen up. Bobby grabs more foil packets from his duffel and spills them onto the bedside table. We've barely dived between the covers when Bobby lounges on the pillows then lifts me to straddle him.

With fingers clamped on my hips, he slowly guides me back and forth over him to reawaken his beginning-to-party cock. "Okay, bossy. I'm at your command."

"Turn the light off."

He reaches over and kills the fluorescent. The night is moonless. I can only feel, not see him beneath me. Inhaling, I savor the fragrance of our previous joining and his pencil shavings scent. Savoring my top position, I'm able to better appreciate his sizeable asset as it grows harder beneath me. If there'd been more than the scant glow from the handheld light before our first romp, I might have freaked pre-plunge that we wouldn't be a comfortable fit. Lucky for me, our initial success tossed that concern out the window. I realize why he tried to be on the careful side the first time. As Billy Kelly said, I'm a wee thing, and Bobby is far from wee.

"Sit up." He obeys. I kneel between his legs, using touch alone to take my turn at slowly rolling a fresh condom over his pulsing length. He moans at my unhurried progress as I enjoy every inch of him. I'm blind in the moonless night as I slide my fingers all over his chest, enjoying the slight texture change from the planes of his smooth skin to the barely there layer of hair between his pecs. Next, I trace the thin, corded muscles of his arms. He squirms when my travels skim across his ribs.

"Someone is ticklish."

"Maybe." His voice is husky. "Don't let that stop you."

"Shush. I'm giving the orders." Continuing down his stomach, I smile when he tenses beneath my touch.

"Are you mapping me for future torture?"

I lean close to drop a kiss on the middle of his chest. "Maybe." Swirling one fingertip through the soft downy trail below his belly button and another along the side of his arousal, I shiver. I never guessed pitch-dark sex could be such a turn on. My inner thighs begin to quiver and the shocks slowly wind my core into tighter spirals. I skim fingers around the base of his cock to learn the shape of all his other bulges and enjoy their feel within my grasp. This is oh so much better than laying hands on old castles.

"I need to touch you," he gasps.

I find his hands in the dark and lift them to my breasts. He cups and squeezes, stroking my nipples over and over with his thumbs. I lean in to fit his hot length against the front of my slit. A finger delves between us, curving down and around until he thrusts it inside me. A second finger joins and begins to pump, in and out. I rock slowly against him, languishing in the steady build of lust.

I groan when his mouth clamps over my breast, matching the rhythm of his dancing fingers as he sucks, increasing his intensity from hungry to ravenous.

Hugging the covers around me like a cape with one hand, I climb him, hovering above his cock long enough to grasp it with my other so I can guide him to my entrance. It's his turn to run his hands over my arms and down my sides, learning me the way I did him. When he grasps my ass, I tilt forward and hiss in his ear.

"Face to face."

I sink onto his shaft, testing the limits of how far our connection will go. My knees squeeze his hips as I circle and grind, attempting to take him deeper.

"Ride 'em, cowgirl," he murmurs, fingers digging into my hips. After tonight, I probably will be walking bow-legged.

I'm about to answer with witty snark when he shifts slightly, and I swear the new angle makes me levitate. With a throaty laugh, he relentlessly teases the same place he hit inside me, coaxing sounds I've never made before. My hands find the sides of his face in the dark, and I thrust my tongue deep into his mouth until he's the one gasping for air. His arms wind around me, crushing me to his chest as the intensity of the ride unleashes a long wail from my lips.

We pant into each other's mouths as we press together harder, reaching for the moment until he is finally destroyed. I refuse to end the gallop until I follow him not long after. If we haven't disturbed the snoozing O'Learys below, they need to get their hearing checked. Serves the pair right for all the winking and insinuating glances they threw our way, even if their encouragement turned out to be dead on.

We hold tight to one another, not breaking our ultimate point of contact. Bobby is first to regain the power of speech. His chin digs into my shoulder. "We will definitely be doing that again when I can see your face."

We collapse together onto our sides in a heaving tangle. I pull the covers over us to trap in the fresh blast of heat we generated. Bobby's barely out of me before he starts snoring. It's not wheezy grizzly or even bear cub. He softly rattles and hums. I imagine it's degassing of the tons of ideas his subconscious produces while he sleeps. I wish I could see his face. I raise my palm to his cheek and find a fist pressed against his lips as we lie curled into balls facing each other.

I'm suddenly aware the humming has stopped. "Did you suck your thumb as a kid?"

His voice is crumbly with sleep. "Until I was six. It was hell on orthodontist bills."

I wrap my fingers around his fist. "I hope there are pictures."

"Plenty," he says, pulling me flush against him. "Are you sure you're okay with this, El?"

I tiptoe my fingers across his hip. "The nickname?"

"No."

"The sex?"

His laugh is soft. "Hopefully." A nose nuzzles my cheek. "Us, being together."

I rub my toes through the soft hair on his leg. "The you and me part, absolutely…" I trail off.

"But?"

I reach around to pinch his solid ass.

"Not that butt, El."

Trailing my finger around the curves of his behind for the pure pleasure of touching his skin, I breath in. "I'm still stressed about winning over my staff on my own merit, not because I'm with the showrunner."

"So we keep it pro at work and very very naughty after hours." He grabs a handful of my ass. His rising hard-on works its way up my stomach. Apparently, the short snooze was enough to refuel him.

"Very very naughty, huh?" I snuggle closer. "When my mom had the sex talk with me, besides the mechanics, she said sex ranges anywhere from one bottle of hot sauce to five. For years I thought sex actually involved hot sauce, although for the life of me, I couldn't figure how it fit into the equation without burning something delicate."

Bobby's chest vibrates with laughter. "How many bottles did we manage?"

I kiss him long and slow, tasting lips then cheekbones and the space between his eyebrows. "Oh honey, we cleared off the whole shelf."

The moment I relax, my buddy, self-doubt, crawls across my shoulder like a spider. I order myself not to think of work or the repercussions of Bobby and me being together right now. He must feel me tense because he shifts his hand from my ass to rub circles on my back. "What?"

I duck my head against his collarbone. "Ignore me, I'm a head case."

He strokes my hair. "Then be a head case. We're in this together. We won't lie, but we don't have to throw our private business in anyone's face either. Between the insanity of both our schedules, apart from meetings, how often are we going to see each other at the studio anyway?"

I play with the sparse hair smattered across his chest. "That could work."

"It will work."

I kiss his Adam's apple. "I want it to work."

"Me too."

I've always felt like a vagabond, dragged to Wyoming by my mother and then leaving it all behind for college in LA, only to dart from location to location on the shows and movies I worked on. Bobby grounds me. Is this what it's like to call a place home: a dream job and a man who's as into you as you are into him? Gilly admitted to falling in love with Ireland when Jack took her around the ring of Kerry. Castle touching, the Giant's Causeway, Carrick-a-Rede island, riding Streaker, designing history, Bobby—all those things could be the tiny tendrils of Elodie roots testing the Irish soil. We potentially have years. If we can move forward together, this just might be more than a show fling. I hold my breath. I've never imagined longevity with anyone. The feeling is foreign but comforting at the same time. Maybe I've never found someone where longevity mattered. *The Chieftain's Son* has a ten season pick up, ample time for those tendrils to dig deep if I choose to water them and turn my TH's into T's.

After a slow burn round of O'Leary-disturbing activity, we scoot deeper under the covers, twining together for warmth, and fall asleep .

CHAPTER 13

CHEESE AND ONION PIE

J ack has his two loves, and for the past few weeks, I feel as if I have two lives. Unfortunately, time-wise my work life is out of proportion with my personal life. For a pair of perfectionists, Bobby and I bumble through figuring out our relationship and boundaries. When I dared to suggest he might be spreading himself too thin, I swear he started working even harder. He's frustrated I'm not home-basing it at his Hobbit hole to give us longer stretches of night together, but I don't want to move too fast. I'm savoring the excitement of our newness. I won't shove aside fresh and thrilling for routine just yet, even if those thrills must fight their way through our schedules.

Gilly shared how fast she and Jack went from lovers to partners. Great for them, but I need gradual to avoid overthinking that could lead to a freak-out. My favorite part of the design process is the discovery phase. Finding a catalog of possibilities and then glomming onto the best of the best is the ultimate reward. I feel the same way about my relationship with Bobby. I want the rendering of us to be multi-layered with subtle shadings and surprises.

"Is there a kissing boundary for your office?"

My lips curve into a smile as I review the series of photos taken of the castle set we plan to cannibalize for parts and transform into the Rock of Cashel, the new fortress for next season's chieftain, Duagh, before he abandons it to bail to Skellig Michael.

"Do Gilly and Jack kiss in front of the crew?" I swivel my desk chair to face him. "What about Meg and her guy...?"

"Cian," says Bobby with a grin. "Who kisses Meg when he visits at work to annoy her."

"Are you trying to annoy me?"

He walks right up to my chair until we're knee to knee. "Would you like me to annoy you?"

I notice the bustle in the art department behind us has stilled. Pitching my voice low, I raise my eyebrows. "They're pretending not to watch what we do."

He matches my tone. "It's been weeks. Don't you think they're aware of what we do?"

When I swivel around to face my monitor, Bobby is forced to back up. "Let's keep them guessing."

He leans over my shoulder as if studying the screen. "Now I'm annoyed, and by annoyed, I mean aching to drag you into costume storage and lock the door."

"As romantic as that sounds, they're doing final fittings for the shoreline battle today."

He huffs. "I'll tell wardrobe to throw a leather tunic over their heads and call it a day."

I turn my face so our lips are inches apart. "Says the king of authentic detail." Counting on his body to shield us from view, I give him a quick smack on the lips and then pull away. "Now go away, I have to take a run at the armory for a final check to make sure there's enough period correct steel for mayhem and murder."

Bobby runs the tip of his tongue over his lips, tasting my kiss. "I'll see you at the meeting."

I spin around as he leaves. "Don't forget we're going to dinner at Jack and Gilly's place in Sneem."

"Where you'll finally meet the illusive Cian."

I tap my lips with a finger. "Will there be annoying kissing?"

His smile is of the naughty variety. "Oh yes."

"Go be professional, will you?"

Bobby's gaze lazily takes in my chest. "If I must." His cell buzzes. "*Work-Bobby* on duty." With the phone to his ear, he scampers out of my office.

It takes me a moment to refocus on what I was doing instead of Bobby's naughty smile. Tonight, I will definitely agree to bunk at the Hobbit hole.

"Are you free then, Elodie?" Tim hovers at my door.

I wave him in.

"Can you come to the shop? I've got the Cashel wall treatment samples to show you."

"Sure." Tim's been ten shades friendlier since what I coin as the skirmish of the castle drips. He was very contrite and complimentary after viewing my drippage and spatter on the old castle set, as were several members of his crew. *Don't ask anyone to do what you are unwilling to do yourself* worked its charm once again. No complaints from the union. I must have passed some unwritten test, or maybe the prop department's approval is catching. I'm not beloved by any means, but the tacit resentment I walked into seems to be breaking down ever so slightly.

The work of Tim's scenic artists is exemplary. I bust out genuine heartfelt praise and suggest the group picks the wall treatment they think is best. Any of the samples work well. I'm happy to hand-off some decision-making power and hopefully earn Pettipas points.

"When the panels are finished, we'll let you touch 'em to see if they speak to you," says one of the painters. It's a friendly jibe, lacking the condescension that first met my revelations of sensing the influence of Ireland through stone.

After a meeting of the minds with my head armorer, Garrett, about a few details to tweak on a pair of battle swords, I make my way to the conference room. This is it, my biggest moment yet. I hug the binder and my laptop. The director of photography, Dougie, and I are going to lay out our finalized sequences for the Battle of Waterville shoot to Bobby, Danna, the director of the series, Alan Rafier, True Time infiltrators, and other key players. I've spent hours with Dougie, the special effects departments, and the fight coordinator to nail everything down. We've designed the zonal type shot progression I suggested, maximizing our drones, dollies, and cranes. It's efficient and will insure we get all the necessary shots during our sure-to-be grueling multi-day shoot. The follow-up on the LED stage for close-ups and angles should be fairly painless to match.

In theater speak, I nailed the callbacks, and now it's opening night.

Dougie turns the meeting over to me to go over some visual details after he has his say. I cast my laptop screen onto the huge flat-panel monitor and go over my contributions to the plan. Producers and department heads nod along at what we've orchestrated.

Alan Rafier turns to me at the end, chin in his hand. "Where have you been all my life?"

My look of surprise raises chuckles around the table.

"This is the most comprehensive taming of moving parts I've seen in a while." He nods at the True Time rep near the corner of the table. "Got yourself a good one in Ms. Pettipas. More pizazz than Jeff Palmer to be sure." Smacking the table with both hands, he rises. "See you on the beach." With his own laptop tucked under his arm, he leads his cadre of assistants out of the room.

Dougie slings an arm around my shoulders. "Well done, Shorty. Brilliant job. You've won crabby ole Alan over to your side. Not an easy feat." He takes a deep breath. "He'll still give us hell on the day, but it's part of his process."

The room drains of more and more teams until just Bobby, Meg, and me are left. She fusses with a strand of hair that's escaped from her bun, and then leans on her elbows. "We'll get a load of publicity shots, and the after-the-episode team will shoot interview bites throughout the day. Are you ready for your on-camera debut, Elodie?"

"My what now?" My control freak side doesn't like the wave of cluelessness washing over me.

Meg shoots a look at Bobby. "You didn't think to mention it?"

I shoot my own dagger stare his way. "No, he didn't."

She stands and collects her laptop and leather-bound notebook. "Och. Nothing to dwell on. You'll share insights on the bits and pieces of the battle. Folks are keen to hear what happens off camera." After adjusting her pencil skirt, Meg strides toward the door. "Ask Bobby to show you the extras on the season one Blu-ray. You'll get the gist." She's got the *Work-Bobby* pace down cold. Maybe he got it from her. Meg tosses us a final over-the-shoulder glance. "See you at dinner."

I wait until she's out of earshot. "Interview?"

He shrugs. "I didn't think it would be a big deal." He gestures at the big flat-panel. "You just nailed the meeting. An interview will be a piece of cake."

I drop into a chair. "Have you met my anxiety?" I've held back on being completely honest with Bobby about my mental health issues. I need to give him a memory bank of me handling my job and staying in control of my emotions before I bring up the hot button word bipolar. If I ever do. I can't deal with Bobby thinking of me as flawed. It's the way my brain is wired, a hereditary gift from dear ole dad, not criteria on which people are allowed to judge me. I function in the world plenty successfully. Granted, it may be a bit tougher for me. As if therapy and meds aren't routine these days for tons of people.

Bobby comes around to massage my shoulders. "You don't need to explain to me about needing to be in control. It's a song I know all the lyrics to. I'm sorry I didn't clue you in to the interview. It's such a regular part of production nowadays, it slipped my mind." He kisses the top of my head. "You don't have to do it if you don't want to." He sits next to me and takes my hands in his. "Think of it this way. You're a woman in a key position on the production team of a hit show that's been traditionally male dominated in the past. Dare I use the words 'role model'? I believe there are people out there who'd be interested and inspired by your perspective."

With my gaze downcast on the table, I mull his words. The spotlight has never appealed to me. If it did, I'd have gone into acting. I clocked time as an extra on the ranch and never was bitten by the performance bug. Working hard and creating tangible things are my passions. I'm not going to act faux humble and deny my talent as a designer. It helped me climb the ladder of my profession faster than most, but I don't choose to flaunt it in interviews either.

"Elodie?"

I drop my lips to our joined hands and kiss his knuckles. "I'll get over myself and go full chatty, but next time, a little heads-up please."

Bobby scans the room and the hallway on the other side of the glass walls. "Can I give you an annoying kiss now?"

In a move intended to shock him, I slip into his lap, throw my arms around his neck, and kiss every upcoming meeting, writing session, and editing deadline out of his head.

Jack and Gilly's adorable little red cottage type house in the equally adorable village of Sneem is not what I imagined for an A-lister TV star, and his Crystal Award-winning wife. It's set back on a side road off the main drag through town at the top of an incline past an even smaller little yellow house behind a restaurant called the River View Bistro.

I play with the soft hairs on the nape of Bobby's neck as he pulls off to the side of the unpaved road behind a few other cars. "Bring me to this cute little village when it's light enough to explore."

He kills the engine and leans across the console to kiss me. I pull away before I have to do lipstick damage control. His thumb rubs the skin at the side of my lip. "Only if it ends up as successfully as our night of castle exploring."

After checking my face in the visor mirror for dinner-guest acceptability, we walk hand in hand to the front door. When Bobby knocks, I pull free, but he slides his fingers back through mine. "Relax. There's no one here who isn't on board with us being together."

A buttery glow pours into the fading dusk when Jack throws the door open. I'm nearly tripped by a pair of cats trying to dart inside. He deftly retrieves his pets from storming the castle gates. "Oh no you don't, my wee pair of devils." The tabbies attempt to lounge inside the crook of Jack's muscled arm before he unceremoniously dumps both, paws down, into the empty flower bed next to the open door.

The bolder of the pair rubs against my legs, seeking an ally to get them past the gatekeeper. I bend to scratch a gray-striped head. "Thank goodness we didn't try to sneak in."

Jack lets loose a sharp whistle and flaps an arm toward the cats. With indignant trills, they disappear around the corner of the house.

"Tomasina and Maxine are the true ladies of the manor. Gilly and I live here at their pleasure." He steps aside and gestures us through.

"And our quartet of power couples is complete." Deidre LaRochelle raises her wine glass. "Happy Thanksgiving."

I get my first good look at Doolin as he rises from his perch on the arm of the couch next to where Deidre sits. The language master is quite the handsome silver fox, in slacks and a dark magenta V-neck sweater that compliments the streaks in Deidre's hair. He meets us with an outstretched hand. "Elodie is it? I'm Doolin Byrne. It's grand to put a face to the woman Bobby's been on about for months."

Finally, confirmation Bobby did mention me to his friends. It explains the constant winks and knowing looks we've been subjected to.

His grip is strong and decisive. I always planned to greet him with a well-practiced Irish phrase I'd learned from my app, but the entire language flies right out of my head. "Hi."

Doolin points a finger at me. "You're long overdue in my classroom." He claps Bobby on the shoulder. "I don't see a golf club in her hand yet."

"It's on my list," calls Gilly from the archway to the kitchen. "Jack, will you put the leaves in the table? The pies are almost ready."

"Cian'll help," says Meg from an armchair in the corner of the room near the fireplace. She vacates the lap of yet another hot guy. Ah, this is the infamous Cian, Meg's fiancé, an excellent souvenir she brought back from the show's debut at San Diego Cali Con last July. His khakis and blue dress shirt could have come from Bobby's closet. Cian's cropped hair and facial scruff read more LA than Kerry.

The main room is so small, he has to squeeze around us to join Jack in the dining nook. "Hi, Elodie. Heard you're shakin' things up over at The Clan." Instead of a handshake, Cian leans down to dot a kiss on my cheek. A charmer for sure.

The look Bobby shoots him is a thinly veiled *hands off*. I already got an earful about the network shenanigans True Time pulled by trying to replace Meg with Cian as head of PR for the show. Bobby's grudge is targeted more at True Time than Cian, but I get the sense my man isn't a big fan of Cian's. Judging from the smitten way Meg watches her man cross the room, Bobby's going to have to mellow out.

"You can stick your coats in the bedroom and then come get something to drink," calls Gilly from the kitchen.

"Two men walk into a dining room and turn into a pair of fools," says Doolin, crossing the room to help Jack and Cian, who don't seem to be able to unravel the mystery of which way the table leaves fit in the space they've created after yanking the ends of the table apart.

Bobby's hand on my elbow guides me toward the door into the bedroom. Once inside, he helps me out of my heavy cardigan. It's cold enough to wear my puffer jacket, but I wanted to look a little classy for the evening.

"Power couples, huh?" I say, straightening my recently acquired Aran knit pullover and giggling.

He tosses his leather jacket onto the bed. "Deidre is into defining character dynamics. Have you read her books?"

"Do you see us as a power couple?"

He gives me an enigmatic grin. "Do you?"

"I…" I whisper as I step past him, "am not into defining character dynamics this early in a relationship."

"So noted," he says with a sneaky pinch to my ass before we rejoin the others.

When we near the kitchen arch, a dishtowel comes flying through the air and almost smacks Bobby in the face.

Jack catches it with one hand as Bobby ducks. "I already wiped it, love."

Gilly fills the kitchen arch with hands on hips. "Not with the leaves in. It's so fecking dusty around here with the construction. I'll throw a real party when the add-on is finished."

"Did Gilly just say 'fecking'?" Cian grins.

Deidre's robust laugh fills the room. "Our girl is going native."

Gilly leans on the jamb. "I think fecking is much cooler than its

American alternative. Cursing-adjacent is all the rage with we transplants."

Doolin rolls his eyes and reclaims his seat next to Deidre. "Yanks. Are there any of you left in America or have every one of you come here to torment us?"

"Bobby, Elodie, Guinness, cider, or wine? Deidre brought something very pink," says Gilly as Deidre raises her glass.

"I'll grab a Guinness," says Bobby, turning to me. "El?"

"I'm feeling half a glass of pink since I've got a predawn call to start prepping the beach."

Bobby disappears with Gilly into the kitchen. I tense in expectation of an awkward moment, since Deidre and I are the only ones left in the living room.

Before I formulate opening remarks, she pats the couch next to her. "Sit yourself down, Elodie, and tell which of my books is your favorite." My ass is barely on the cushion when she offers her glass to me. "You should taste this before you dive. It's a twelve on the sweet scale."

When I devoured *The Chieftain's Son* series of books, sipping out of the author's wine glass was nowhere on my radar. To be polite and buy a few moments before answering her question, I taste the bubbly pink liquid. "Wow, dessert before dinner. I'm in."

"Ah, a kindred spirit."

I rub my nose to alleviate the bubble tickle from the sparkling wine. "No contest—book three, *Skies of Mist and Wind*. I'm thrilled to help bring that story to life."

"Why?"

And here I was afraid of a behind-the-scenes interview on set. Deidre's pointed look is hotter than any spotlight.

"I love a good chicken shit chieftain whose escape plan is to flee to an island a stone's throw from the mainland. When I read it, I went straight to the Monty Python place and imagined ole Duagh standing on the highest point of Skellig Michael, blowing *come and get* me raspberries at his enemies."

Deidre's explosive laugh draws everyone's attention. Thank

goodness I timed my comment to avoid a bubbly pink spit take. She snaps her fingers. "Opportunity missed."

I rest my arm on the back of the couch. "Is book eleven finished? If not, the Pythons could swing by and give Duagh the chance to mock them from his island."

She pats my hand. "Alas, wrong era, my dear."

Jack's voice booms through the little house. "Chow time." Gilly's Americanisms are rubbing off on him. I hope they don't go too far. Jack is freaking iconic as the quintessential Irish warrior. It would be a crime for him to lose a single shade of his enchanting accent or witty native phrases.

Gilly sets a bowl overflowing with roasted veggies on the table followed by a gorgeous cream-colored, stoneware platter with tiny shamrocks around the edges piled high with medallions of beef. She and Jack together carry in the grand finale, three steaming glass pie plates. "My cheese and onion pie opening night," she says with a curtsy.

"I've been at all her rehearsals," says Jack, slinging an arm around his wife's waist. "Your lives will never be the same." He kisses his wife with passion usually reserved for private.

I seem to be the only one who gives typical O'Leary PDA a second glance. There's a stitch of longing in my chest for a similar demonstration from Bobby.

"What, no turkey?" says Bobby.

"No Thanksgiving here, no turkey," says Doolin, spearing the beef.

"Maybe I'll do turkey next year," says Gilly. "I'm not up to the challenge with the insane work schedule my boss insists on." She purses her lips at Bobby.

Bobby raises both hands. "Don't turkey shame me. Aim that sneer at True Time."

Jack wasn't kidding. The savory pie is the stuff of poetry and song. The table erupts in the chatter of cross-conversations. I field so many inquiries about myself it feels like a rehearsal for my on-camera interview. The swirling anxiety over being a focal point begins to dissipate.

Meg wipes her mouth with one of the fancy linen napkins from the table. "I wouldn't make a habit of these, Gilly, if you want to maintain your fighting weight for the wife-carrying competition."

"Let my woman eat," roars Jack. He pounds his breastbone with a fist, then flexes his arm muscles. "Nothing's too big for these fellows."

I swallow down another delectable bite of cheesy heaven. "Wife carrying?"

Cian, who sits on one side of me, answers my question while the others jab at Jack for his muscular hubris. "It's a worldwide competition. Husbands literally carry their wives over an obstacle course to vie for the win. Championships are in Finland."

I swallow a mouthful of wine. "What do they win, a divorce?"

"The wife's weight in beer." Cian grins and eyes his fiancé with affection. "Having Jack and Gilly compete in the Irish prelims is part of Meg's plan for the big reveal of their relationship. My future wife is master of the big-ticket PR splash."

"The more eyes on your people, the better," says Meg, who leans into Cian for her own kiss.

"Meg, I'm still holding out for you and Cian to join Jack and me," says Gilly with a twinkle in her eye. She nods at Cian.

Cian snaps his fingers. "Darn. We won't be married by then. Maybe next year."

Gilly shakes her head. "Nope. Useless excuse. You don't have to be married to enter."

Deidre leans one arm on the table and targets Bobby. "Maybe Bobby and Elodie should give it a go."

My face heats. I'm sure I'm as pink as the center of the beef medallions at the suggestion. Sure, I'm econosize, which makes sense for wife carrying. I wonder if her suggestion means she's caught a glimpse of the golf muscles Bobby's hiding under his sweater. I prejudged his physique as being gawky high school basketball player, and boy was I off. The man has gorgeously defined chest muscles, tapering to a thin waist. There are some serious sleek guns lurking in those sleeves. Picturing *Bare-chested Bobby* spikes my temp even more. I guzzle the rest of my wine, which only increases my flush.

"Aren't you going to be in the states then, Bob?" asks Jack.

I don't think much about the comment, since I know Bobby flies to LA intermittently to bow down to the True Time overlords until Deidre pipes up. "You're the prettiest fellow at the Hollywood party lately, aren't you Bobby?"

Bobby takes a turn at red face. He waves a dismissive arm around the table. "It's a game. Your show does well, your stock goes up."

"And the offers get shinier," says Meg.

Offers? What offers? I want to ask but I seem to be the only one at the table who isn't savvy as to what they're talking about. It'll embarrass both Bobby and me if I open my mouth. My happy cheese and onion pie-filled tummy suddenly feels bloated and miserable.

Cian chimes in. "And True Times's luster gets duller." He attacks the last chunk of roasted carrot with his fork, aiming it at Bobby. "I don't miss those sorry sons of bitches one bit."

When I realize it's shaking, I drop my hand to my lap. Under the table Bobby crooks his ankle around mine. The chatter resumes, except for Gilly, who reads the tension in my scrunched forehead.

Bobby leans toward me as she intercedes. "Elodie, will you help me carry some of these plates to the kitchen, then I'd love to get a designer's opinion on the window placement in the add-on." Gilly sets her napkin on the table and stands.

I detangle my leg from Bobby's. When I move away, his fingers brush my wrist and linger as if he's afraid to let me go.

After we dump a few plates in the sink, I follow Gilly through the kitchen door into the dark construction zone. I'm greeted with the smell of freshly cut wood and the brisk air sneaking in through gaps in the heavy plastic sheeting around what appears to be the frames of a trio of rooms. The mingled scents work wonders to de-escalate my anxiety.

She glances back at the kitchen door. "I could tell by your face Bobby didn't let on he's got the Hollywood hounds sniffing around him."

"Not a peep."

"Do you want my advice, or should I walk around and gesture, pretending we haven't already figured out where the windows go?"

I suck in as much air as my lungs allow. "You're the writer. What subtext did I miss in the scene back there?"

"Let me lead with this... I swear Bobby's been giving off light since you arrived." She laughs. "Don't get me wrong, he always buzzes with energy, but there's something softer about him lately, happier. It's you, Elodie."

"I make him happy, but I'm not entitled to the big picture?" My quiet gut rumble threatens to flare.

She wipes the air between us with flat palms. "Absolutely not. Secrets are their own special brand of poison where I'm concerned. I'm sure what's going on with Bobby is the same thing going on with Jack. They've hit a homer with *The Chieftain's Son* and proved themselves. Hollywood feeds off lightning striking twice. Of course studios and networks start dangling offers."

I draw a squiggly line with the toe of my black ballet flat through the thin layer of sawdust on the floor. "Is Jack considering any?"

The sweetest smile blooms across Gilly's face. "We're both content here. The two shows fill our lives fine for now. Jack and I are homebodies at heart." She sighs. "We know we're in a bubble. There will come a time when he'll jump at movie offers. We'll adapt."

Homebodies. The Irish roots Gilly has put down with Jack are fat and sturdy whereas mine are thin and tentative. Where do Bobby's roots land on the spectrum? I know he loves the show. It's his dream come true. Would any offer be big enough to supplant that dream?

I run a finger along an upright post. "You adapted to this life quickly enough."

"I so didn't." She shakes her head. "I was a failed novelist who ran away from a bad relationship to join *The Chieftain's Son* circus." Her gaze drifts through the maze of wood. "Bobby saw something in me and my work. When I thought I was a fraud, he convinced me I wasn't." Gilly meets my gaze. "He's a special person. Ask Meg or almost everyone on the staff or crew, and they'll have a similar Bobby story."

For once, I have no comeback. Gillian Bettencourt, who won a freaking Crystal Award for a script she wrote before she was officially on the writing staff, is in the imposter syndrome club. I shore up my nerve with a deep breath. "I've been questioning my right to be on this show since day one."

"I heard you've had challenges with your team."

"Okay, now I'm embarrassed."

She lays a hand on my arm. "Don't be. I should have kept that to myself. Bobby tends to confide in Jack. He's been frustrated he couldn't help you more."

I nod at the kitchen door. "Off-camera lives are every bit as messy as Donal Cam and Nieve's onscreen, aren't they?"

"Messier." Gilly leans against what appears to be a future built-in bookshelf. "You and Bobby are brand new. I'm sure he's still figuring out how it all works. He's one of the best people I know, but that doesn't mean he can't fuck up."

"Do you mean feck up?"

"Nope, this ranks a fuck."

"Thanks for the rescue, Gilly." I go in for a full hug. She admitted Bettencourts are huggers when we first met, and heck, aren't we sisters by proxy?

The kitchen door opens, and the rest of the dinner party joins our tour.

Bobby's scamper is subdued as he scoots in close, grabbing my hand. "Sorry for the Hollywood blindside," he whispers. "Apology to be continued?"

I squeeze his hand. "I love a good sequel." Even though he's just opened the topic for future discussion, I can't fight the feeling being kept in the dark about what's brewing for him is a step backwards not forward. If we're forging the foundations of a relationship, shouldn't discussing something as behemoth as career trajectory be high on the agenda? Even if he's not entertaining offers, why isn't he sharing that with me? Shit, what if he is considering one of them?

The itch to call Kevin chafes red and raw, but running to him seems like backsliding. I believe I've graduated from hot mess to warm mess since I've been with Bobby. He's the one I need to talk to and share my doubts with, but not tonight. My gut tells me these next few days of pulling off the Battle of Waterville is the make-or-break-it moment for me with my crew. I can't let a personal pothole in the road knock me off course.

Bobby pulls me away from the others. "Are we okay, El?"

I hate the need to bust out my plastic smile. "Sometimes sequels are better than the originals."

His laugh is as dry and as unconvincing as the upward curve of my lips.

CHAPTER 14
THE BATTLE OF WATERVILLE

I fan a gust of prop smoke out of my face to read Bobby's latest text. He's earned plenty of Pettipas points for effort in the days since the O'Leary Thanksgiving by sharing elevator pitches from the offers that came his way.

I squint at my cell screen with the latest project blurb.

A sitcom pilot about a single city gal, hiding a magic fairy mushroom circle in her walk-in closet...as if.

I text back.

I'm picturing a sitcom pilot about a single city gal, growing magic mushrooms in her walk-in closet thinking fairies are real.

Three dots popcorn back.

Fairies are real. Did you forget where you are?

Bobby and I haven't found enough together minutes in the past few days, between the battle shoot, an inhuman editing schedule, and his head-writer hat. He's buried nailing down season three scripts.

Even though I could tell he was upset over my change of decision to stay at my Waterville flat after our power couple Thanksgiving, he was generous as usual about accepting it. Our goodnight kiss hadn't even cooled before my regret set in. I gave myself a mental ass-kicking and had to admit derailing our sleepover plans dipped a toe in overreaction territory. Somewhere in LA a therapist developed a sudden headache.

The burn of being left out of the Hollywood offer loop wasn't even first degree. I should have gone home with Bobby that night and talked it out. Instead, I matched his relationship faux pas with one of my own. What did I gain except an empty bed?

If I want to keep our relationship on healthy ground, Bobby and I need to set ground rules for communication. Visions of making up for lost time in Bobby's bed dance in my head like sugar plums on Christmas Eve.

The battle sequence wraps season two except for an LED stage, special effects session. Because True Time insists on rapid release between seasons, we're already in hyperdrive to prep for the first setups of season three right after Christmas. When I get to The Clan, there will be no trace of Chieftain Brian Boru's world. Castle repurposing is well underway. Luckily, the production schedule for season three calls for banging out as many location shoots as they can at the beginning since we often get screwed with weather and the best laid plans fall apart.

Now there's a topic Bobby doesn't hold back on. He's a raging ball of anger over True Time's ball-busting demands that force him to do so much holiday season/winter shooting. Our second unit team would agree. They'd probably hold down the True Time execs while Bobby kicks them.

Exhaustion pokes holes in my avoidance filter and allows an ugly thought to break through: Could Bobby's growing anti-True Time sentiments grow intense enough to jeopardize his position on the show?

Pull your head out of worst-case scenario land, Elodie.

I only have time for a closed-eye, tongue-out emoji to answer Bobby's last text before I'm hailed across the rocky shore. Making my way under the wires that look like a vacay zip line for a camera, past two parked drones, fog machines, and through bloody, limbless extras, I enter the fray. Dougie, pyrotechnics, a gaggle of producers and their PA's are locked in a renewed debate whether fire sparkle guns or a flash gun fireball works best in the composition of the final set up. On-the-day changes are always a party-in-a-box.

I scan the gray cloud-filled sky and pluck at the wristband granting me access to the location. Gardaí line the street keeping onlookers out of range, and so far, none of the curious have spoiled any shots.

Speed of light swiping through my tablet confirms this is indeed our last shot, not just a manifestation of my wishful thinking. "If we hustle, can you sneak in both versions to give Bobby and the director choices?" A particularly loud wave smacks the rocks. "And by hustle, I mean haul ass." I bring up my tide and sunlight charts. "We're on our last hour of decent light and the tide is ignoring its schedule and coming in early for a look-see."

The moving pieces start buzzing as everyone takes their places, including a very bulky man in a blue Lycra suit who will become a ghost after special effects gets ahold of the footage. I back away.

A lovely peace settles over me. My carefully laid plans were set in motion and went well. Departments found the sought-after brand of magic synergy that you strive for on a monster shoot like this. By all rights we should have had a week to ten days to tame the beast, but thanks to True Time, we had to conquer what we could in three days. I think we've pulled a miracle out of our asses. Hopefully, editing will agree.

"Elodie." I turn to find Garrett, the armorer, approaching with a load of weaponry. "Just wanted to say crackin' job." He rattles his swords and dips his head in a bow.

My first instinct is to rush into his arms, weep, and thank him for validating my existence. "Back at you, Garrett. I think it went well. Take the night off."

We share a laugh, knowing this breather between the shoot and our meeting tomorrow morning is technically our only scheduled time off.

Hours later, the Waterville beach is returned to its rocky solitude. High tide has staked its claim. The last fire pipe has been extracted from the ground and equipment trucks are en route to The Clan. Any lingering actors or crew are across the street at the pub for some well-deserved celebrating. Jack and Streaker were only here for the first day. I wish he were here now so I had a pub pal. I'm alone on the small stone wall by a statue of Charlie Chaplin, enjoying the shush of the Atlantic.

It's the same quiet satisfaction of being alone in an empty theater after cast and crew left for the night.

One of my favorite gigs early in my career was as an assistant scenic designer on Broadway. The show had been a jukebox musical full of joy and fun. I remember pulling the ghost light across the stage after opening night. It was the final day of my responsibility before I was on to the next project. I sat on the edge of the stage, swinging my legs over the orchestra pit to soak in every last drop of theater energy lingering in the air. It was one of the rare occasions I enjoyed wearing a dress. I'd already been hired on a Tudor era limited series which I eventually took over for the final two episodes when the production designer had a family emergency. In my bones, I knew that night was my moment to bid farewell to theater and hello to my dreams of reproducing naturalism for the camera.

I swirl the toe of my waterproof hiking shoe through a pile of rocks. Even though we raked the beach and used a bazillion pictures to return it to its pre-Battle of Waterville state, I'm still on the lookout to rectify any square inch of disruption.

"Waiting for moonrise?"

Bobby's voice startles me. "Damn, Bobby."

He climbs over the knee-high wall and sits next to me. "I looked for you in the pub."

I love that he came looking for me. That's ten Pettipas points. "I thought you were in editing hell."

"We put the penultimate episode to bed with no more interference from True Time." He slides an arm around me. Who knew mashing together our matching show logo puffer jackets could be so sexy? Or did Bobby using the word *bed* flip on my electronic ignition? "Is it crazy to say I've missed you?"

I snuggle closer. "If it is, we're both nuts."

He lifts my chin to angle my lips to his. The kiss is the perfect slow burn for a frosty night. My mind flies to Coolderry Castle and the imaginative ways we warmed each other. Bobby's teeth gently graze my bottom lip as he ends the kiss. He swings one leg over the wall so I can relax back against his chest as he wraps his arms around me. His chin rests on my shoulder. The sound of the waves, the top curve of the moon deciding if it's going to join us, and the solid softness of Bobby's body combine to create a delicious peace.

His hot breath meets the cold air in a gray puff. "I get caught up in things, El."

I squeeze his leg above the knee. "I've noticed."

"It's not an excuse, but that's what was going on with not sharing the job offers. They were just one more thing on my endless to-do list to deal with as they came up." He pulls me closer. "I'm used to problem solving and moving on. It's how I stay afloat."

"*Plate-Spinning-Bobby* gets the job done," I say.

He releases a gentle snort. "I got sloppy and allowed our game plan of separating work and personal life become too black and white. There's crossover I'm not used to figuring out. I promise to work harder at including you in everything."

I lean my head into the crook of his shoulder to look up at him. "Your texts bringing me up to speed with what's going on with you mean a lot." Stretching, I kiss the stubble on his jaw. "My reaction to feeling excluded may have bordered on drama queen. I'm sorry about that. We're not exactly in a long-term committed relationship."

He brings his cheek next to mine. "I am."

"Bobby, we can count our weeks together on our fingers."

"Months."

I execute my own leg swing over the wall to face him. "You still count our online chats?"

"Why wouldn't I? I'm not a professional dater, but I clearly recall the getting-to-know each other phase. You can't deny that wasn't happening during our screen-time conversations." I rub my thumb over my ring, contemplating as he continues. "It's a viable way to start out in our modern world. You can't claim to be tech savvy in your day-to-day and hold on to luddite status when it comes to online dating."

He has a point. Even though we never defined it as such, technically it's what we were doing. "Okay, I'll give you Pettipas points for that." His look of utter confusion is delightful. "I'll explain later when my ass isn't growing icicles."

"Need a rub? I'm happy to warm it up for you."

I stand and aim my fanny at him. He takes it in both hands for a squeeze, warming much more than the real estate under his fingers, and then maneuvers me onto his lap. "Does this mean I'm forgiven, El?"

"Let's take that word off the table. It's too loaded. We both mis-stepped. You inadvertently withheld information and I...well..." If there's ever a time for blunt, it's now while we're engaging in what Kevin would term *transparency*. "Backpedaled from intimacy."

He tightens his arms around me. "Thank you for being gracious."

"And while we're chatting..."

"Should I duck or..." He does duck, but it's to plant a lick and kiss on my neck.

"Stop please. This is the talk."

I feel him draw a deep breath through our jackets. I grimace in anticipation of the truth-telling I'm set to verbally vomit. "I'm crap at dating overall, which I hate—the dating. Even worse at relationships, okay the one real relationship I attempted after grad school. I've got no natural instincts or decent examples among the disastrous catalogue of my mother's dumpster-fire hook ups. I'm romantically inept." I lean my chin on the heel of one hand.

"I find you very ept."

"I'm not, which explains why I have to ask this clarifying question." I stare at Bobby's nose instead of his eyes. "You say you're committed, but truthfully, is what's between us beyond a very nice but transient, offstage friends-with-benefits hookup?"

His eyes wobble in a look I've come to know signals rapid-fire brain activity. Icy fingers cup the sides of my face. "Elodie, please tell me you seriously don't believe that's all we are." Bobby drops his head back to blow a long breath to the stars. "This is on me." He snorts. "You should ask that question after I kept you outside the loop on my fucking offers." His lips rest against my forehead. "My relationship track record ranks somewhere below abysmal. Writing, and then my path to becoming a showrunner, has always been my priority."

"We're a matched set of romantic sink holes."

He laughs against my skin, then dots a kiss before he breaks away. "There's an image."

I treat him to a wicked grin. "I'm a very visual person." I take his chin in my fingers. "So, to clarify...Elodie Pettipas's status: in a relationship with Bobby Provost."

"Same."

I shake my head. "Nope. Sounds like you're in a relationship with yourself. Didn't you just admit that's been your problem?"

He clears his throat. "Robert Benjamin Provost's status: in a gloriously fulfilling and planet-rocking relationship with the exquisite Elodie Pettipas."

"I call writer showing off, but oooo, I rate Robert and Benjamin." I kiss the corner of his lips.

"That makes it legal in several countries."

"Nice touch." I run the tip of my tongue across his bottom lip. He quickly captures it with his own, and we seal our relationship declarations with a kiss.

"Now that you've got my heart rate up..." The cad sneaks a hand under my jacket to fondle my breast before he groans. "Too many layers."

As an apology for my barriers, I wiggle on his lap in a way that makes his breathing speed up. "Since we're talking legalities, I'm willing to grant you relationship longevity credit for all previous online interactions in exchange for being included in Bobby World privileged information from now on."

"Sounds fair." His hands position my warmest parts against his growing appreciation. "I agree to your terms. Now kiss me like you mean it."

"Did you agree just to get lucky?"

He pulls back. "This isn't a quid pro quo, Elodie. It's a promise." His gaze sweeps the beach. "I suspect our relationship is going to have as many challenges as the Battle of Waterville, but I'm invested."

An arctic-level blast ripples our jackets. I slide off his lap and tug on his hand. "Let's find a warmer place to continue."

He tucks my hand into the crook of his elbow. "My place or yours?"

"Lots of eyes at my place." My flat in *The Chieftain's Son* company housing in Waterville isn't exactly private. Even though there aren't a ton of others bunking there at the moment and most of them are leaving tomorrow now that the battle shoot is over, Bobby being spotted leaving my flat could fall into the *flaunting our relationship* category. "And I believe I owe you a sleepover rain check."

"Happy to cash in."

I squeal as he lifts me onto the wall so he doesn't have to bend to kiss me. "You do love putting me on a pedestal, don't you, lover?" I crush my mouth to his, darting my tongue past his lips and then retreating to make him chase me. He does an excellent job. "Catch." I jump into his arms and wrap my legs around his waist, popping the bottom three snaps on my jackets.

When we part, our heavy breathing raises an impressive fog bank between our lips. "Keep calling me lover and we won't get farther than my car." He moans when I slide down his body to the ground. "Is this part of my penance?"

"Nope, just a perk." I reclaim his hand. "I should pop into the pub to be sociable first. Solidarity. I made real strides with my peeps on the shoot. I want to keep the love vibes flowing."

"If I buy a round, can we leave right after?"

I reach around to pat his cute rear end. "Works for me, lover." I pour plenty of over-the-top seduction into his title.

We laugh and head across the street. Bobby stops on the sidewalk in front of the pub. "I hope you've been privy to all the compliments I've been hearing how well the shoot went. Your stock is off the charts."

My insides fill with a toasty buzz at his news coupled with the sense of comradery I felt over the last few days. "Everyone has been very sweet. It's nice." I crook my pinkie around his and take a step onto the stone walk leading to the pub.

He holds me back. "El, here's the thing." His previous lusty tone settles into full-scale caution. The Bobby tension that melted away after our talk starts to ratchet up again. I did ask for full inclusion in his life. It looks like I'm about to get my first taste.

He gazes at the newborn moonglow bobbing on the surface of the restless Atlantic. "There was one offer I haven't shared yet."

A rush of anxiety encircles my renewed tension forming a lump in my chest. "And you left it out why?"

Oooo, the expression on his face wears too many shadings of guilt. "Because I wanted to go over it in person."

My shoulder muscles tense. Did we just get back on course so he could knock us off?

He blows out a breath. "I didn't bring it up because it's probably nothing."

Probably. Shit, I knew it. I give his chest a firm but gentle shove. "Damn it, Bobby. Quit talking around your point. Why didn't you text me about that offer like the others?"

He stares into my eyes. "Because maybe, and it's a super thin maybe, there might be something to it."

CHAPTER 15
STORM WARNING

There's always satisfaction, hitting *send* on work you're proud of. I sit alone at Bobby's teeny kitchen table for two. The times when we both work here, we constantly bump laptops until one of us retreats to the couch. My final revisions on what will become the virtually created top of the Rock of Cashel to be added in post are now in the talented hands of special effects. I tap a text on the chatty CG department thread that now includes me.

Incoming

Three different folks send me goofy gifs, atta girls, and one super sweet message about how kick-ass the castle turned out. The Battle of Waterville was a turning point for more than just Donal Cam and Nieve's story. Something finally shifted in the art department's acceptance of me. Skeptical sourpuss faces morphed into pats on the back. Condescension melted into, dare I say, admiration. This new lovefest has made the last few weeks a blast at work.

Bobby and I had a quiet Christmas, my first one officially in a relationship. He spilled about the one offer he entertained for a minute and a half about a development deal with the Stream Up network, a new power player on the scene. It received a label of tempting, but in the end, not juicy enough to snag him.

Our Christmas present to each other was a weekend in Dublin where we were not allowed to bring up work for two whole days. Like tourists, we did selfies on the Ha'penny Bridge and in front of the Molly Malone statue. We checked off visits to several of the famous pubs and had the best damn Guinness Stew at the Brazen Head, the oldest pub in Dublin. I got a small taste of the museums. I'm itching to go back.

It was our only respite from work apart from Christmas Day which we spent with Jack's extended family. The insanity of a large holiday gathering was novel to me. I loved it. I finally got my holiday turkey. His mom teaches little kids, and I promised to find time to pop in and do an art lesson for her class. The day felt, well, settled. Everything is starting to feel settled with Bobby. I'm allowing myself a tiny sliver of hope we might be the real deal.

A different thread pops up on my cell from the carpenters and greensmen.

Pub call U in?

They give me shit when I say I'm already tucked away for the night. That sense of family I always experienced working in theater started sprouting a few buds with my *Chieftain's Son* crew. I bust out the goofiest smile in Ireland.

The alarm on my phone intrudes on my happy dance. I play the keys on my laptop until I get to the *Entertaining For You* website and click on the live stream of their morning show. Bobby should be home by now. We planned to watch this together. I dart off a text.

Are you almost home? It's starting.

I quickly delete the second sentence. He's fully aware of what's about to start because it's a hot-button issue for him. Thanks to True Time's hemming and hawing, this monumental announcement is months behind Meg's meticulously planned timetable.

The almost too gorgeous, blond poster girl for Hollywood adorbs and woman-most-likely-to-aggravate-Jack O'Leary with her fawning, Cici Storm, stands in front of a huge screen. Splashed across it is a collage of photos featuring Jack and Niks Tellefson, the leading lady of *The Chieftain's Son*. Wearing an obviously over-dramatic sad face, Cici Storm plays directly to camera.

"And now some big news from the set of The Chieftain's Son *in not-so-Merry Old Ireland."*

"It's Merry Old England, honey."

I understand Bobby's choice words in private to me regarding Ms. Storm's IQ or lack thereof. He forces himself to keep a civil tongue in his head publicly since she's uber popular with fans of our show. There's also the wrinkle that *Entertaining For You* and True Time Network are on open-mouthed kissing terms.

"The IRL romance that had all our hearts pounding between Jack O'Leary and Niks Tellefson will not live out the same happy ending as their onscreen counterparts Donal Cam and Nieve."

A steamy season one shot of Jack and Niks kissing fills the screen, followed quickly with a huge black diagonal slash filled with red broken heart emojis.

"It feels like only a moment ago when the couple's secret love affair and engagement was leaked last summer at Cali Con in San Diego."

Cici Storm pouts.

"Even though our hearts go out to the pair…"

Ugh. This is gag inducing.

Cici winks conspiratorially at her audience.

"There's a super shiny silver lining."

Her hand covers her heart.

"Ladies, Jack O'Leary is back on the market."

Behind her the screen shifts to a close-up of Jack with bedroom eyes. Cici sprinkles way too much sugar over the story for my taste. I'm sure Mom is swooning right along with the *Entertaining for You* spokeswoman and legions of other Donal Cam fiancée wannabees. Even though my mother has made inappropriate lusty comments about Jack on our few and far between phone calls, he isn't cowboy enough for her. Thank goodness. If he was, she'd catch the first flight over here.

When the show switches to its next salacious story, I click off the site. Jack and Gilly can finally stop holding their breath. The plan is to wait a few months before Gilly enters the zeitgeist as Jack's new love, and when we shoot on Skellig Michael in June, their PR wedding will take place.

I text Jack and Gilly a congrats with confetti. Gilly texts me the barfing emoji and then a meme of a sloppy drunk Cici Storm hanging all over Jack at a red-carpet event with the caption: *She wishes*. I wouldn't be surprised if Gilly created the meme in the first place. I can't imagine the hell those two go through keeping their marriage a secret. Meg has Jack and Gilly slated for their first public debut together on Valentine's Day.

I bust out goofy smile number two of the evening. I'm going to have a Valentine's Day with a boyfriend. Another first. I've been doing my damnedest to live up to our shoreline proclamations of relationship status and be an award-winning girlfriend. Sometime overachieving is called for.

Bobby's done the same on his end. I even scored flowers. And the firsts keep coming. Definite Pettipas points for that one. Our sneaky stolen kisses with the occasional inappropriate grope at work are a definite turn on. If Robert Benjamin Provost had his way, I would move into his place. It does make sense, since I spend most nights here anyway. I'm considering it. The biggest downside would be having to use the machines in wardrobe to wash my clothes the way he does. Free laundromat—whoo hoo. I can't wrap my head around literally displaying my dirty laundry in public yet, so we hang at my flat while I take advantage of the washer/dryer and he works on his laptop. We can be adorably domestic.

Speaking of which...I check my phone. No return text from Bobby. I resist the urge to nudge. He's probably got some poor editor in a headlock over whatever episode they're working on. The aroma of the cottage pie that Pat dropped off warming in the oven makes my stomach growl. Mrs. Pat has taken it upon herself to send over a couple of homecooked meals to Bobby's place each week. It's sweet. This *Chieftain's Son* bunch is a family, and I'm so grateful to feel like a part of it after my less than spectacular beginning.

As much as the casserole calls to me, I'll wait for Bobby. He does the same for me when I'm the one with a crazy late schedule. I've also got a surprise for him tonight. I've been on the pill for a couple of months now, and we both passed our insurance physicals with high marks. It's goodbye condoms. We should have a ceremonial fire to burn our remaining supply. Sadly, his electric fireplace would just melt them over the ceramic logs. It could be fun to watch *Mortified-Bobby* explain the damage when the unit had to be replaced.

I cross to the bathroom and flip the wall heater on. A shower to transition from the workday to a yummy meal and sexy evening with my handsome man beckons. As I strip, I think about the first time I took advantage of Bobby's tankless water heater. I wonder how long it took him to chase my residual mud down the drain. It hits me how much I wanted him that night. He's right. The time we clocked online before I came over was truly our beginning. We were courting. My mind was so cluttered with anxiety over proving my worth and the upcoming move to Ireland, I missed out on enjoying what we were building.

Stepping under the decadent toasty water, I smooth my hair back and make a vow to myself. I will not miss another moment of being with Bobby. Despite my hesitant way of entering into this relationship, I'm here now, heart and soul. He is my person. A niggling voice in my head interrupts with the thought *for how long*.

I swallow a little water and cough. Curse my mother for her string of relationships with expiration dates. Curse my obsessive need to calendar start and end dates to everything as if I'm mapping a production schedule. Curse the part of my brain hellbent on preventing me from embracing contentment without worrying something will go wrong.

The click of the shower door and a blast of cool air scares the crap out of me. Instead of the slasher I fear, a very naked and very aroused Bobby slips in with me.

"You're very welcome to my shower," I say, borrowing the standard Irish greeting, surprised how husky my voice sounds.

He's already breathing hard, pupils tantalizingly large. When I try to step into him, he grabs my hips and spins me. Fingers circle my wrists, and he guides my hands to flatten both palms against the molded plastic shower wall. His arms circle my waist, and he squeezes us together, fitting his hard length to my ass.

I turn my head, aching to kiss the drenched naked man pressing his body to mine. "I'm loving this hello."

"Shh," he says, biting my shoulder. The light sting of his teeth against my wet flesh makes my legs wobbly. Hands slide up to my breasts, kneading and pinching. He's rougher than usual as he tugs my nipples in a way that does crazy things to my body. My core clenches with almost painful spasms of longing. I'm going to finish in record time.

I push my ass back harder to rub against his cock. Since we're not face-to-face, my mind supplies the view I'm missing. Bobby's so frenetic and always on the move, he doesn't maintain an ounce of body fat. He's tall and skinny, but unwrap the package and nicely corded muscles sculpt a body that inspires what's happening to me right now. Before I had the privilege of enjoying his body, I assumed his cock would match his thin lanky physique. Such a delicious surprise to discover one of my favorite parts of him was not to scale with the rest of his proportions.

My raspy plea bounces off the wall. "Bobby, I need you."

He rocks his thick shaft against me, bending low to find new places to tease but not enter. I try to free my hand from the shower wall to encourage his grasp to switch from my breast to the scorching flow between my legs. He takes charge and with his hand guiding mine, orchestrates long, slow strokes along my seam. Up and down, he works me in a tantalizing rhythm, changing speed with every pass. I buck to increase the pressure until a jolt of release nearly makes me crumble. He holds tight to keep me from dropping onto the drain as the orgasm takes its time fading.

I want more.

I try to turn in his arms, but he stays locked behind me.

"I want you bent over while I take you screaming under the spray. Stay here." He jerks his hips against me once and then starts to open the shower door to retrieve the condoms in the bathroom drawer.

I stop him by reaching down to close my hand around the base of his cock, effectively keeping him in the stall. My grasp is a little slippery, but I hold firm and relish the pulsing against my palm. Sliding up his length, my thumb brushes over his tip to feel the hot bead of liquid, thicker than a water drop, signaling his readiness. "We don't need it. You've got clearance for takeoff."

"You're sure?" He can barely get the words out. *Lose-Control-Bobby* has me hotter than the water pouring over our bodies.

Of course he'd double check. I slide my grasp none-to-gently along his length. "Make me scream, lover."

With a growl, he slams the shower door and returns my palms to the drippy wall. Yanking my hips toward him, he invades me in the most delicious way. Now this is a plunging. He's completely inside me fast and rougher than I ever imagined he'd dare. It's heaven. The scream he requested rips from me as I teeter on the edge, encouraging him to thrust harder.

"Bring me with you, babe," he growls.

I clench and pump my own rhythm around his hard length until his own guttural cries answer mine. My first release was nothing compared to what threatens to burst out of me now.

Bobby's body covers my back as he sinks in deep with a powerful thrust like a lightning strike, and I'm the tree. A stream hotter than the blissful shower spray pours into me, and I get my first treat of what I've been missing. One hand snakes around my thigh, yanking me tighter to him while the other darts to grind the side of his palm against my pulsing sex. I howl as my vision becomes a splash of red filled with pinpoints of silver light.

We both groan and slump against the shower wall, my head resting on my arms, his hands flat on the surface above me, waiting to recover enough to move. When I do try to stand, he gently presses against my back to keep me bent forward, still filling me with his half-mast cock. I expect him to slide free, but he begins to sway against me in a slow and steady pace, returning us to plunging formation.

"I need you again, Elodie." Each approach is punctuated with a word. "Will—you—wait—for—me?" His hand sneaks around, and fingertips press between my folds. I cry out and jerk at his touch, surprised at how sensitive and already on the rise my body is again. I can't seem to get enough of *Lose-Control-Bobby*. My sudden shift sends us both off balance. He breaks contact to catch us before we become a sexual shower casualty.

He slaps off the water, kicks the door open, and scoops me into his arms. There are romantic benefits to being my size. His wet, hungry mouth collides with mine as we drip our way into the bedroom. I'm lost in the wildness of the kiss and the savage need in his actions. I barely register when we fall onto the bed. Bobby crawls on top of me, hunting like a ravenous predator. I yearn to be caught. We're both sopping wet and drowning in lust.

I dig my nails into his back and arch up against him. He slides down my body so fast, it's a shock when his head drops between my legs. He laps at me in a ferocious pace. It's fantastic and excruciating. My fingers thread through his hair as I push him harder against my aching need. He groans. The heat and vibrations from his voice flare across my skin, and I'm freaking dying.

His fingers swirl in and out of me. I grab his wrist to keep him there as he coos. "Are you ready, lover?"

I've lost words as he braces himself over me, eyes dark and savage. I feel a surge of anger, but not at him. My body is crazed to have him back inside me. I stroke him with one hand followed immediately by the other to pull him as close to the brink as I am. It's so fucking sexy how he swells against my palms. Covering my hands with his, he tightens my grip as together we nearly set him off.

His knees press my thighs apart, and he enters me unyielding and fast, echoing my angry need. He hums *Elodie* in my ear over and over as his hips pound against mine. Our mouths devour, tongues roll together. We bite and kiss and moan. How will we survive this primal attack?

I wrap my legs around him and reach between us to caress the sexy parts of him not sunk into my depths. Bobby returns the favor, going straight for the swollen nub he's learned will launch me into fucking space. I'm fully primed and burst against his fingers. Moments later, he arches back and does the same inside me.

I'm breathing so hard, my chest aches. I rest my palm over his heart and find equal intensity. Bobby ducks his head against my collarbone, and I hold him tight. This sense of trust and passion is beyond anything I've ever wished for. We stay joined as if parting will take something away we're not willing to give up. It takes quite a while to clear away the haze of pure emotion and become cognizant of the present.

I rub my nose over his cheek as I regain a little sanity. "Why does it feel like we just had make-up sex? Were we fighting and I missed it?"

Bobby flops onto his side and slings a leg over my hip, unwilling to disconnect too far. "Was it too much?"

"It was incredible." I give his face a gentle slap. "There's no such thing as too much with you."

He pinches my ass. "I can't wait to test that statement. Maybe we should reenact some of the scenes from *The Chieftain's Son's* books."

"I vote for the hot sex in book four, right before Nieve thinks she's going to be burned as a witch."

Laughter rumbles in his chest. "I'll have to join Jack in his workouts before I'm up for that one."

We kiss for a long time until I start to shiver.

"You're still wet," he says, grabbing the edge of the comforter to fling it over me.

I rub my satisfied lady parts against his thigh for emphasis. "That's the understatement of the century." My hand strokes his slick cock. "You're not so dry yourself."

He pulls me closer and sighs into my hair. "I got carried away. I was agitated driving home, and all I could think about was getting lost in you."

I play with the curvy strand of hair in the shape of an S on the back of his head. "Horny agitated?"

"As soon as I heard the shower I was," he says and gives me a thorough kiss. I'm surprised when he buries his face in his hand. "I was pissed about the fucking *Entertaining For You* piece. I watched it in my office before I left."

"Pissed? Really? It was sappy, but it did the job."

Bobby sits, pulling up his knees and wrapping arms around his shins. "It didn't. True Time was supposed to cut this bullshit of Jack being free months ago. What did those assholes do? Delay releasing the news his ridiculously staged relationship with Niks is finished and then sic Cici Storm and her hormones on the poor guy. That disgusting announcement made it sound like it's open season on Jack."

"I texted with Gilly. She didn't seem upset." I throw my arm over his shoulder. "It's one step closer for them to stop hiding."

He kisses my hand and then pops out of bed to pace in the narrow space between the bed and closet. "Yes, but it continues to fuck with the show."

As much as I enjoy the scenery of *Naked-Dangling-Bobby*, I don't like where his train of thought is going. "How are they fucking with the show?"

He runs a hand through his hair. "They want to push the starting air date of season three. That's why I was late coming home. I had to lay out how accelerating their *rapid release...*" He puts air quotes around the phrase. "Will hurt the show."

I pull the blanket closer around me. "Did you convince them?"

"They'd already decided. That rat bastard, Dashell Everett, insists since the show doesn't have reoccurring cast except for Jack and Niks, we can rev up the schedule. Banging out second unit location shit for season three first is what they call a break for our stars."

A burn starts in my chest. "But Jack and Gilly are still shooting *My Two Loves*, how does True Time's plan give him a break?" And how the fuck am I going to get my end of things ready on time?

"It doesn't," roars Bobby.

Our production schedule is already completely unrealistic. If they're cutting our time even more, quality is guaranteed to suffer. My department's quality. I'm going to be ripped apart in reviews and social media for the watered-down the look of the show.

He smacks the bed. "True Time's heads are so far up their asses they can't see the misery they're creating." Bobby drops down next to me. "I can't keep doing this, El, watching while they drive my show into the ground." He digs his fingernails into the bedding.

I can't draw a decent breath. I'm dying to ask him what exactly that means, but I'm too afraid. He hasn't mentioned pursuing any of his offers, and I can't imagine him bailing on *The Chieftain's Son*. It's the nature of show biz, the push and pull of profit vs. product. I shouldn't overstress, but that's my default.

I pull his fingers free to twine with mine. "What about Deidre? Doesn't she have clout with the network?"

Bobby clenches his fist, squashing my fingers. "She's going to war for us." He drops forward to bury his face in my lap and not in a sexy way. "I'm terrified everything I built will go to shit if we can't reach a compromise." His arms come around me. "You are my sanity, Elodie Pettipas. My reset. My light."

I stroke his hair as a top layer of the internal house of cards representing my sanity begins to topple under the weight of his expectation. The pleaser in me rises to the surface. Yes, I want to live up to Bobby's vision of who I am to him, be loyal and supportive, but his constant feuding with True Time is a low frequency hum of anxiety that seems to permanently reside in my chest.

Soft snores send a trickle of warm breath against my belly. Asleep, Bobby loses ten years as his stress lines smooth under the magic spell of unconsciousness. I continue to lightly run my fingers through his hair. I love this carefree version of him, *Soft-and-Still-Bobby*.

I love him.

I love how easy it was to fall for him. Ours is the quiet and steady progression of a relationship I've always craved, friend becoming lover. The drip of the shower echoes from the bathroom. Flashes of our recent underwater antics bring heat to my face and slightly overworked lower areas. Okay, so not always quiet and certainly not without addicting passion.

My heart doesn't need him to say the words. I know Bobby loves me too. I chuckle, imagining the look of bafflement I'd get if I asked him straight out if he loved me. Those jade eyes would wobble as his mind searched for confirmation he'd never said it. Bobby is not a guy to state the obvious if it is obvious. I've seen that tendency in the way he deals with storytelling and his style of guiding the show. My payoff would be a proclamation of love from him to make Donal Cam and Nieve's steamy scenes look like a bad junior high crush.

Bobby grumbles in his sleep and the stress lines ruin the soft landscape of his face. I hate True Time for invading his well-earned peace. The delicate love bubble I float in pops. I'm aware of every cold damp spot on the blanket and uncovered body part dotted with goose bumps. This animosity between the network and my darling showrunner feels not only like a creeping shadow closing in over *The Chieftain's Son*, but a threat to a future I've barely begun to believe in.

My ribcage clenches with the onset of the first anxiety attack I've had in months. To allay it, I bury my nose in Bobby's hair to breathe him in.

Stop it.

I should tell Bobby I'm scared. Hell, doesn't he deserve to be let into my mental health issues? I'm applying a double standard to our relationship. He's expected to share everything with me when I'm keeping my lip zipped about myself. That can't be healthy.

I just can't seem to convert *should tell* into *will tell*. Not yet.

CHAPTER 16
SOUL-TO-SOLE

The smell of the training room at The Clan is high school gym meets whatever pine-scented cleaner they use to wash the mats.

"Or flip her like this..." says Jimmy, the stunt coordinator, as he dangles his wife, Mary, upside-down along his back with her legs draped over his shoulders, her face looking directly at his ass. "For Estonian style."

Gilly and I share a skeptical look from our piggyback perches on the backs of our men. Jack roped Bobby and I into joining Gilly and him for the wife-carrying competition. Turns out Jimmy and Mary are old pros at the event so we're treated to after-work training.

"That's not pretty," I say, sliding off Bobby's back. "Hard pass."

Gilly shimmies down Jack and backs away. He pursues until his chest meets her outstretched arms. "Don't even think about it. As much as I enjoy looking at your ass, I'm not going to do it at a run with blood rushing to my head."

"Then we'll stick to this," says Jack, effortlessly tossing Gilly over his shoulder in a fireman's carry.

She giggles and slaps his back. "Unhand me, you historically accurate brute."

Jimmy, now Mary-free, downs his water bottle. "The wife carrying is good fun, but you do want to practice." He pulls his cell from the pocket of his sweatpants. "I'm texting you some YouTube links. Watch 'em to get a sense of potential obstacle courses."

The door to the training room flies opens hard enough to hit the wall. T.J., one of Bobby's assistants, barrels through. I smile, imagining that Bobby's PA interview process includes how fast the candidates can walk and text at the same time.

"Bobby, you're on live chat in five," says T.J., bracing the door open and sweeping his arm for Bobby to scamper through.

"Be right there." Bobby gives me a quick kiss. "I'll come to your office when I'm done."

I don't shy away or flinch from kissing Bobby in front of the group. Despite my fears, our being together proved to be a non-issue for *The Chieftain's Son* team. Our separate schedules are so bonkers, we barely cross paths at work. In fact, one of my prop ladies asked me if we'd broken up, and was I doing okay? I don't think she believed all was well and offered a friendly ear if I ever needed girl talk.

"I'll meet you at the restaurant. Patrick's delivering the car he found for me and giving me a crash course on Irish rules of the road." Tonight is what we've dubbed soul-to-sole night. A group of us that usually includes Jack, Gilly, Meg, Cian, Maureen, Grady, sometimes Niks and her partner, Marisa, and Meg or Jack's sisters and their hubs started a tradition of meeting every few weeks at the Yeats by the Sea Hotel in Waterville to treat ourselves to their life-enhancing Dover sole.

Jack and Gilly have finally been "out" for nearly a month now. They're both relieved their oppressive cloak of secrecy has been lifted. To say scores of fans are in mourning is an understatement. Bobby shared that some intense internet hate cropped up here and there. Sadly, Jack and Gilly had to hire extra private security to deal with the craziness. They even had a fence built around their property in Sneem, with a gate, code required, as an extra precaution. So far, they've not had any press discover the O'Leary home. As nutty as it gets when there are show appearances in Dublin or Belfast, I can't imagine how much worse it would be for them if they were in LA.

Meg hopes when *My Two Loves* begins to air during the brief mid-season break of *The Chieftain's Son*, fans will start to warm to the fact Jack and Gilly are a done deal.

I watch *Work-Bobby* blow out the door. I'll have a glass of wine waiting for him at dinner. He's become more and more pissy after his True Time meetings. I thought he was going to bite the head off one of the TT execs at a table read last week. He's been losing weight too, and the man has no leeway to drop poundage and still be healthy.

"Better have whiskey waiting for that one at dinner," says Jack.

Jimmy and Mary say their goodbyes as I shrug into my hoodie. "You've noticed he's a bit on edge?"

Jack and Gilly make identical *humph* sounds. "That's putting a cocktail dress on a goat," says Jack.

Gilly fixes her ponytail. "He's been insufferable in the writer's room."

I frown. "I think he needs marriage counseling with True Time. I've got a great therapist."

Jack pats my shoulder. "Not to worry. I saw the same pattern on my sitcom, *Randy in 3B*. Once the show catches, there's a honeymoon period, and then it's down to the job of sustaining what makes the show a hit. Lots of pressure there."

I appreciate Jack's analysis and confidence that this tension is a normal part of series growing pains. I wish it was enough to knock out my own fatigue at weathering Bobby's dark moods.

The O'Learys head out. "See you at soul-to-sole night," says Jack.

As I watch them leave, an overwhelming urge to go to Bobby's office pings at me. Maybe if I sit in his eyeline during the meet, it'll have a calming effect on him. True Time won't know I'm there. Later, I'd be a better source of helping him sift through the aggravations of his meeting if I'm privy to its content.

I make my way through the warren of The Clan until I get to Bobby's office. Through the glass wall, I see his attention is locked on the screen. He nods, gesturing wildly with a smile on his face. This is awesome. For once it appears his interaction with True Time isn't going south. He smacks the desk, looking satisfied.

Slowly, I back away before he catches me. No support needed. Bobby Provost looks like he's in for the win. My phone buzzes as I practically dance down the hall. I'm surprised when it isn't Bobby already sharing some positives. It's Patrick, waiting in the car park with my newly acquired vehicle. He scored me a silver mini two door resale from a pal of his who works for a rent-a-car company. Best of all, it's automatic. No stick shift for this woman.

Nothing stops me from imitating Bobby's upbeat scamper as I head out front to meet my new little car.

I thought Bobby would beat me to the restaurant. Our group is small tonight, just Cian, Meg, and Niks. Jack and Gilly begged off because of an early call tomorrow for Jack. Maureen and Grady had to zip down to Offaly to her parent's house for a consult on rentals and new landscaping for the backyard where their wedding reception is taking place.

"I'm here for one drink and then room service with Marisa," says Niks, flicking her wine glass with a perfect French-tipped fingernail. She taps her lips. "Too much kissing with Jack today. Wears me thick."

"Wears you thin," corrects Meg at Niks's botched idiom.

"Or wears you out," adds Cian. "There are choices here."

"I have a question," says Niks. "What does *climb that like a tree* mean?"

Cian almost spits out his old fashioned.

I raise my hand. "I know. I know. Pick me."

Niks stretches her arm. "I pick Elodie."

I tap a finger against my cheek. "Can I have some context first?"

Niks grabs her cell and scrolls. "Social media person called @*Jackisfine* says..." She reads from the screen. "Are you stupid for breaking up with your hot man? I would climb that like a tree."

Meg snatches the phone from Niks's hand to scrutinize the post. "I told you to stop reading this garbage. We're handling your social until the backlash dies down."

I lean in to Niks. "It means you may have to jump a bit to reach the tall person you want to get sexy with."

She chews her lip. "Jack is tall. Cian is tall. Bobby is tall. Lots of tree climbing here, yes?"

Her insinuation raises a laugh from us.

Niks finishes her wine. "Tell Bobby I cried and cried because he was too late." She makes the rounds of cheek kisses and saunters out of the restaurant.

Bobby's wine waits untouched on the table while we remaining three polish off the morsels on the charcuterie board.

Meg's phone pings, and she reads the alert. "Well, here's a fine way to end the evening."

"Did we all get a bonus?"

Cian snorts. "From True Time? You live in a magical world."

He ought to know. Cian Malley, who now goes by Cian O'Malley, his real not Hollywood adopted name, has major PR chops. He stewarded True Time's *Star's Shadow* to supersonic hit territory before he walked away to open a marketing firm with Meg here in Kerry. Despite their cordial beginning, he and Bobby have bonded lately since Cian's been a valuable sounding board for True Time travails.

Meg shoves her phone at me. "You've just garnered an excellent mention from a top shelf source. It's rare for comments about the production design. Most fools have no idea what goes into creating the worlds they see. Well done, Elodie."

We've only leaked glimpses of my season three designs. "Oooo, gimme." I read how I've escalated the vision Jeff Palmer introduced. "It's settled. My superhero name is *The Escalator*."

They laugh, and Cian steals a glance at his watch.

I wag a finger at him. "I see you looking, and no, Bobby hasn't texted." I snatch his waiting wine and take a sip now that mine is empty. I'm not supposed to drink on my meds, but I cheat. "You snooze, you lose," I say to Bobby's empty seat before setting the glass next to my plate. "We should order. I'm sure some brightly colored problem sucked up his attention. It doesn't mean the rest of us should starve."

"Actually," says Meg. "I overdid the donuts today and missed my swim." She nods to the remaining two olives on the charcuterie board. "I'm fine to call this dinner."

"Ditto," says Cian, flashing his handsome man smile. "Are you cool with us hitting the road, Elodie?"

I hold the back of my hand to my forehead and feign distress in my best southern accent. "Whatever shall I do? Soul-to-sole night is ruined." The joke doesn't land so I wave them off. "Head out. Skipping tonight will help prevent the dreaded Dover sole burn out."

They stand. "See you tomorrow then," says Meg and slaps Euros on the table.

I score a cheek peck from Cian. His well-manicured stubble tickles my skin.

His bicep is in range, so I give in a squeeze. "Sole you later." This time they do laugh and the ribbon of strain running through the evening from Bobby's absence eases slightly.

I check my cell again. Now it's getting weird. Bobby getting hung up or having to cancel plans isn't off, but not cutting me in on the source of his delay is. I intend to sip his wine and wait another five or ten minutes before texting him. If he's close, I'll order so he can walk right into the delight of a perfectly plated, flaky sole to replace the stress of his day.

Before I can tap on our text thread, the long-awaited message pops up.

Meet me outside.

What now? I get to typing.

I've got wine and an eager waiter on hold in here.

I look toward the grand archway between the restaurant and the hotel lobby, expecting Bobby to come loping through. I only see guests who can't wait to snag our mostly abandoned table for six, milling around.

Please, El. Just come out.

My jittery fingers manage a thumbs up emoji. What the hell is going on? This is bizarre. I wrestle enough Euros from my wallet to cover what turned into a happy hour instead of dinner and add an indecently large tip so we can show our faces at the Yeats again after shirking our sole responsibilities.

I'm about to leave the table when my gaze catches Bobby's half-full wine glass. I drain it. Something tells me I'm going to need liquid courage for whatever is waiting for me out in the spring night.

I find *Amped-up Bobby* pacing on the sidewalk at the end of the cobbled path that leads to the hotel's entrance. I brace myself for bad news. God, I hope it's not a death or terrible accident. He sees me coming and charges full force. I'm lifted into his arms and swung in circles. My purse flies into the hotel's flower bed. Bobby kisses my neck, my ear, and the skin next to my eye in rapid fire movements before he puts me down to smash his mouth against mine. Static currents sizzle between our lips.

Okay, not what I expected.

To my surprise, he doesn't deepen the kiss, instead he softly breaks away to hold me at arm's length and take me in. It's as if he hasn't seen me in weeks rather than a couple of hours.

His energy is contagious, and I match him grin for grin. "I missed you too."

He crooks an arm through mine and leads me in the direction of a bench next to the hotel, overlooking the ocean. On the way, I stoop to retrieve my purse.

"I have news, El." He gives a gleeful laugh. "A few things. I never thought—I mean it didn't seem right to want…" His fragments break off as he drags us in a sprint toward the bench.

I am absolutely coming apart with conflicting internal blasts of excitement and dread. This brain is not wired for surprises, and I feel a whopper coming on. He drops onto the bench, holding me in his lap, arms locked around me. He's panting from the scoop and run. I'm panting from nervous overload. It's like the collection of moments after climax in lovemaking while conscious thought takes its time to replace all-consuming exquisite sensations.

Bobby releases his death grip on my body to rest his hands of either side of my face. His thumbs softly draw lines to the corners of my lips. "I love you, Elodie Pettipas." His kiss is slow and silky. "I hope you already figured that out, but it deserves to be said out loud."

"You're okay too," I say with a quick rise of one shoulder. I'm pressed against him so I feel the rumble of laughter in his chest. "I kinda love you."

He raises his eyebrows. "Kinda?"

"Kinda very."

Bobby licks his lips. "Wow, kinda very is brand new territory for me. I hope I can live up to it."

"I have every hope," I say before leaning in for another kiss.

He licks my lips. "You taste like wine."

"I taste like your wine. I'm glad you chose the robust red this evening."

"Did I? Robust you say?" He tastes me again, his tongue delving deeper to savor the wine he never drank.

I breathe into his ear because I know it'll rev him from zero to sixty. "You can be late for dinner as often as you want if this is the result. Shall we head down the street to my place to get robuster?" Thank goodness my flat is a mere two blocks away and we've nothing to hide.

He smiles against my mouth. "I don't think that's a word."

I swivel my body to drop my knees on either side of his hips in a saucy straddle. "It should be."

Quick wordplay is Bobby's favorite entre to foreplay, so I don't see it coming when he grabs me by the waist to set me on my feet in front of him and takes both my hands in his. Those jade green eyes sparkle in the globe lights set along the path next to the bench.

"I've got amazing news."

The sensation of slamming on the brakes makes me sway a little. Bobby stands and wraps his arms around me.

"I've been on a virtual meet with LA for the last two hours."

Okay, this could be amazing as in a good thing. I did see his *Happy-Bobby* face before I left The Clan while he was on his video chat. Maybe Dashell Everett has left True Time and his predecessor made a love match with Bobby. Visions of a less energy-sucking production schedule spark hopeful synapses in my brain.

His voice eases me back into the conversation. "You know I turned down the deal with the Stream Up network."

"Yeah." The word *deal* sends a shiver through me. I thought we were through with the topic of deals and offers. He did hold on to the Stream Up proposal longer than the rest, but ultimately it made no sense.

"You're aware they're top of the food chain of streaming services?"

I catch my jaw clench and force myself to relax.

Keep it light, Elodie. He's just sharing the way you asked him to.

I run a thumb over his knuckles in an effort to stay calm. "I believe the term you're looking for is Big Dogs."

"Ha. True Time are dogs. Stream Up is a dragon."

I can't tell if the roar I hear is the surf across the rocky shore or a growl starting in my head. "Dragons aren't real, Bobby."

"This one is. El, they came back out of the blue with a brilliant second offer." He gives my hands a shake and lets go, his pent-up energy busts loose, forcing him to move around. "Development of my original materials and a budget that makes True Time's numbers look like loose change under couch cushions." He reaches his arms to the sky. "And much more creative control."

I'm the polar opposite of his flitting around. My body is frozen on the spot, fingernails digging into my thighs. I start to talk but manage only an exhale of air. Familiar bands of anxiety squeeze my lungs.

Bobby's so caught up with his glee, he doesn't notice I've forgotten to breathe. He plops both hands on my shoulders. "And the best part, Elodie. They want you too. They've got a fantasy show in development that'll let you invent and build worlds, not limit you to recreate what already exists. Of course, you'll be in on any of my projects as well. We can make the move together."

The man who just told me he loves me doesn't seem to know me at all. My voice sounds weak and pitiful. "But recreating is my thing, Bobby."

He drops a series of kisses on the top of my head. "I know. I'm sure you can incorporate that. Stream Up went ga-ga over the portfolio on your website."

I swallow and exhale the stale air in my mouth from holding my breath. My tone is low and measured. "You're not hearing me. My passion is recreating what already existed and giving it a new life, a new visual depth."

He stops shooting moonbeams out of his ass and stills.

"Bobby…" I take a deep breath. "…Did you accept the deal?"

He shakes his head so quickly it's almost comical. "Of course not. I promised not to keep anything from you. It just happened."

The anxiety vise holds firm. There's no point in pouring honey on this shit brick. "You want to take the deal."

He threads his fingers together and locks them behind his head. "They agreed to everything I asked for."

"Including me."

His stress squint appears.

A flash burn in my chest snaps the pressure, and I explode. "You included me in your bargaining without even asking. That is so many levels of fucked up."

He takes a step closer. I counter with one away. "I didn't see this coming, Elodie. I acted on momentum fully intending to bring you in on it before my next move."

"After you threw my future up for grabs." He registers my clenched fists.

"Can't you see I was negotiating for a better situation than we have now?"

I bring those fists to eye level and shake them. "Better? Better than Jack? Better than your writing staff? Better than Meg and Danna and—"

Bobby's never raised his voice to me. He does now. "Better than feeding my spirit piece by piece to True Time as they hack away at the show. Look what they tried to do to Meg last year. Demote her when she does a brilliant job. Every week they squeeze us tighter, dictate more and more that should be my call."

I wish I were taller so I could get in his face more effectively. "Not *the* show, Bobby. Your show. Our show. The show you made a reality for Deidre, Jack, Gilly. *The Chieftain's Son* is your passion." I walk away from him and pull at my hair before whipping back toward him. "How can you even consider abandoning us? You are the glue holding our company together. Bobby Provost is the person who believes in people and makes them shine. That's what you've done for Jack, for Niks, Meg —me."

Bobby's chest heaves as if he's just run the entire Ring of Kerry.

I tone down my anger. Bordering on hysterical is not the way to go here. "I've gutted myself and crawled over jagged rocks to earn the respect of my crew. You expect me to turn my back on everyone? And how will I ever get hired anywhere again when I bail on the show after only working on it for a hot second?"

"That's not an issue. You've already got another job." He huffs. "Damn it, Elodie. You thought you had to crawl. Your team owed you respect from day one, and your self-doubt gave them an opening to give you shit. It drives me fucking crazy you don't have more confidence in yourself when you're one of the most amazing talents I've ever worked with. I see it. Amethyst and Rich Bettencourt see it. Will Tremblay saw it. Stream Up saw it in a red ass second. They don't want you as a bargaining chip to get me. They want you for you."

One phrase slices like a saw, cutting back and forth through a stubborn piece of wood.

I've been driving him *fucking crazy*.

All his encouragement takes on a whole new definition. Instead of trying to understand what makes me tick, he's been trying to smile and kiss it out of me. I've come so close to telling him about my mental health issues. It suffocates me with fear that when I do let people in, they'll see me as fragile or incapable. But here he is, telling me to throw dirt on my wound of self-doubt and get over it. Bobby Provost charges ahead full steam. How could he understand how hard it is for me to even take a first step sometimes, overwhelmed with dread of missteps and conflict due to my fear of inadequacy?

The truth is harder to tell the longer you keep it inside. His one-foot-out-the-door reality forfeits him the chance to hear all of mine. Our relationship gives him the right to hear some of it.

I return to the bench, lean back, and look at the stars. "You know my history. Mom ripped me away from my dad, who let it happen. She was more invested in fantasy love affairs than her kid. I've basically been a vagabond going from job to job, a loner." When Bobby sits next to me, I meet his gaze. "This show, these people, have begun to feel like what I always hoped a family would."

He leans forearms on his knees and studies the horizon. "It functions like a family now, but that's proximity. The show will end."

"In seven years! Or more if Deidre pops out more books."

"Even then, you'll keep in touch with a few people for a while until everyone drifts into new shows, new temporary families. It's the nature of the beast."

"That's the most cynical thing I've ever heard you say. I don't believe you're not going to be lifelong friends with Jack and Gilly."

"There are exceptions."

"It's a betrayal, Bobby. For you to walk away from the show is a broken promise."

A muscle twitches in his jaw. "I'm not betraying you, and Danna is ready to step up as showrunner. Why should I deny her the opportunity?"

I lay a hand on his back. "I know the bastards at True Time are making your life hell, but have you fallen out of love with *The Chieftain's Son*? Because I haven't. This show is my dream, and I'm not ready or willing to wake up."

He twists and grabs my shoulders. "If I take the deal, are you saying you won't come with me?"

My tears turn his face into a blurry mess. "How can I?"

On set, I create castles with plaster and paint. With Bobby, I built one out of joy and partnership. I guess ours isn't strong enough to stand.

Bobby swipes a tear off my cheek with a knuckle. "I'm flying to LA tomorrow night for a quick turnaround to meet with Stream Up. I want you with me. Please El, hear them out, and then we'll make the decision together. Will you do that for me?"

One of the things I admire about Bobby is how driven he is, but if I can't meet him halfway, maybe we're too far apart to ever come together enough to stick.

As if finally sensing what a disaster his news has become, Bobby clutches me to him. "You don't have to answer right now. Think on it tonight or however long you need. You can fly out later and join me. I'm sorry I sprung this on you."

I hold him just as tightly. He's being *Barrel-Ahead-Bobby*. It's who he is and one of the many facets of him I love. The man makes his choices without hemming and hawing. Normally, that's refreshing in my waffly world. Not tonight. Not when this snap call drags me along without warning. Who's got manic impulse issues now?

His voice is raspy and not in a sexy way. "I'm sorry. Let's grab takeaway and go home."

I want to wipe the last half-hour away and rewrite the scenario. I'm loath to acknowledge the delight and relief in his voice the Stream Up deal put there. I do so very much want to grab takeaway and fall asleep in his Hobbit hole with him beside me. I'm on the brink of giving in when one phrase digs hooks deeper in my heart.

It drives me fucking crazy.

I drive him fucking crazy.

Pulling out of his grasp, I flash a weak smile, striving for kind. I don't want to blow him off, but I'm bruised. I need think space.

Fucking crazy.

"I've got an early call. It's best I tuck in at my flat tonight."

He reaches for me but doesn't touch. "Elodie, please don't."

The sadness on his face breaks me as much as the revelation that my insecurity has caused him stress. My urge to comfort rises, but at this moment my brains and emotions are being pulverized in an industrial-grade blender, and I can't follow through.

"Have a safe flight. We'll hash it all out when you get back." With a ridiculously forced wave, I leave Bobby alone with the Atlantic.

CHAPTER 17
ROCK IN THE SEA

A regressive spiral I'm all too familiar with eats me for breakfast after a crap night of non-sleep.

Constant hum trigger: job stress.

Manic spike trigger: the oh so flattering knowledge I drive Bobby fucking crazy.

Emotional disturbance trigger: suffocating dread I've basically set a breakup in motion with the man I'm in love with.

Nagging trigger: keeping my triggers and bipolar disorder a secret.

Bonus trigger: Imposter syndrome

Trigger…Trigger…Trigger.

The result: warring emotions that send a veil of depression descending over me like Eeyore's raincloud making landfall.

My meds usually do wonders to flatten my highs and lows and allow me to function as a rational human being, but there are times my faulty serotonin is completely out of whack—like now. Thank goodness I'm not needed on set today, even though I lied to Bobby about an early call, because I'm unable to absorb a single text or email.

The weeping won't fucking stop.

The effort to get out of bed and call Kevin feels as doable as scaling Everest. All I can do is lie here like one of the stone walls that line Irish roads. I know I should force myself to embrace one of the coping strategies I've learned over the years, but today, sinking into flatline is the only option I seem to manage.

Thus quantifies the love/hate relationship I exist in with my brain chemistry. People who don't constantly fight the dark side really can't understand how powerful it can be. Light sabers are useless when you are your own Vader.

Biology's call finally forces me to peel my lump of a body from between the covers. The puffy purple accents beneath the eyes staring at me from the bathroom mirror are motivation enough to dive back into oblivion, but now that I'm vertical, I summon the fight to stay that way. I've been here before. To keep moving is the first step to claw my way out of the pit. I need to eat. I need to hydrate. I need Bobby.

No, I don't.

I can't.

But I could have him.

No. Elodie, the pleaser, is in danger of giving in to the path that's right for him not me. He'll take too much from me: my show, my belief I'm where I should be, making a mark on *The Chieftain's Son*, and I'll be too big a coward to let him know what he's done.

I pull overalls on over my sleep pants and thermal PJ shirt. Mouthwash will have to do since I've got zero energy to brush my teeth.

Kevin's soothing voice streams through my head. *Positive self-talk, Elodie.*

"Good job getting up." My legs are jelly. "Hang in there. Don't go back to bed." I do a few shuffley laps around my flat and start to feel a little stronger. "You've got this. Leave the womb."

My eyes fall to the cozy sheepskin-lined coat Bobby gave me. It seems hypocritical to wear it when I'm on the verge of ending things with him. Instead, I slip into my show jacket.

"Moving is good. Keep it up." I grab keys and my cross-body bag. Once I make it to the door, all I'm capable of doing is resting my forehead against it. A new supply of tears drips off my chin to the carpet.

Celebrate the small goals, Elodie.

Getting quasi dressed is a small goal. Walking as far as the door is another.

"Open the door."

I do. Next, I close it behind me and lock it. Two more accomplishments. The cold drafts in the hallway against my wet face unnerve me enough to walk to the stairs.

I slap my cheeks. "Downstairs. Across the street. Get a coffee."

The Chieftain's Son company housing has a dorm vibe. There's a desk near the front door. A lovely woman named Beebe is at her post.

"Good morning there, Elodie."

I wave as I rocket across the small reception area and out the door with my head lowered to hide my blotchy, conversation-starter face. "Hiya, Beebe."

She calls something after me with a clear note of concern in her voice, and I add to the list of my short-term goals to bring her donuts for my abrupt, bordering on rude exit.

Across the street at the takeaway coffee window, I recognize actors from this season's Irish clan, grabbing their fix before the shuttle van comes to collect them for the day's shoot. There's no way I'm up for chit chat. Veering left before they catch sight of me, I round the last of the three adjacent company houses and head for the small car park out back. I'm a little shaky as I drop into the driver's seat of my little car and slam the door.

In two three…hold two three…out two three…hold two three.

I box breathe until my body feels more solid and less like a runny egg yolk. My phone vibrates against my chest from its nest in the bib of my overalls. I should answer it in case I need to ward off some set or green-screen disaster. I'll certainly piss one or multiple someones off if I don't answer.

Pile on another trigger: people mad at me.

I pull open the snaps of my jacket and start to reach for the cell but stop.

"Nope."

I sent an email, making it clear I wasn't available today so I need to embrace my unavailability and work through this episode. My mind ping-pongs with pros and cons of answering the call. I've a bevy of super competent assistants and amazing department heads that deserve my full confidence. They'll handle whatever weapon, castle, or animal hide emergency demands attention.

Or it could be Bobby.

Not a conversation I'm capable of right now.

I compromise, vowing to let an hour to pass before I'll peek at the message, because as much as I wish I could detach from everything, that's not me.

"Wow." I impress myself by making a concrete decision. In fact, the mental exercise yanks me a few clicks closer to legit functionality. Closer, but not there. Sinking low in my seat, I close my eyes and take inventory. The mounting pressure of a full-blown anxiety attack has abated. Breathing steady. Weeping dribbled to a stop. My morning dose of anxiety meds kicked in, earning a bucketful of Pettipas points.

I wish I had a horse tethered nearby, but my car will have to do. If only I could whistle and Streaker would bust out of Moose's stable and appear on a hilltop to meet me. Stretching my hands over the steering wheel, I assess their shaking status. Surprisingly steady. I'm a certified mess but not self-destructive. If I thought I wasn't in shape to drive, I'd stay put. Hitting the road in the insane streets of LA would be a no-go, but this is the Ring of Kerry in Ireland on an early weekday morning. A cattle crossing delay is more likely than traffic jams.

I'm pretty sure it's about a twenty-minute, straight shot on the main road from here to Portmagee. I can do this. How lost can I truly get? I'm on an island. Physically lost, not very. Metaphorically lost, that's different territory. I'll take it easy, park by the docks, and grab a coffee where the odds of running into anyone I know are miniscule. Once I'm caffeinated, I'll set my next goal.

I'm deluding myself. I already know my next goal—unpack the nightmare unfolding between Bobby and me.

I drive super slow, ready to pull over at the first sign I'm falling apart again. The mist is calming, just enough to mute the world but not enough to make me nervous on the road. I'm grateful the few cars that charge up behind me zip around without the prolonged LA honk of judgement.

I absorb the visual calm around me and my mood improves in small increments. At Portmagee, there are parking spots right in front of the big restaurant across from the flotilla of moored boats. Early morning in the harbor town personifies those last lazy minutes before you roll out of bed. It's peaceful, a land of half-awake. The fishy smell of the docks assaults my senses, jarring me even further from the remnants of my lingering stupor.

A bell dings as I open the door and head for the takeaway counter along the rear wall of the main dining room. "Large coffee, please."

The grandfatherly man behind the counter squints at my face, which I'm sure still wears signs of the misery sloshing around inside me. "Will you be wanting some whiskey in that coffee?" He leans on his forearm to get closer. "Or some coffee with your whiskey?"

"I choose A, but I really want B."

He grins. "You could choose B, sit awhile, enjoy the best Irish breakfast in Kerry, and contemplate the meaning of life while you sober up."

His cheery brand of teasing does an even better job than my meds to lighten my mood. "Who says I want to sober up?"

He produces a bottle of Jameson from behind the counter and raises his eyebrows. "Brilliant. Shall I pour?"

"As lovely as your suggestion is, I'm driving. I'll make it a point to come back when I can settle in for a spell."

"Brilliant," he says, handing me my coffee and winking.

Ireland, the winking capital of the world.

On the wall behind the counter is a huge photographic poster of Skellig Michael, one of the small islets just off the coast from here. We're scheduled to head over there in early May to map out our shooting locations and a place to stage Jack and Gilly's PR wedding, but I feel a sudden urgency to connect with the islands on this dreamy, hazy morning.

"Can you aim me to where I can book a boat ride to the Skelligs today?"

He shakes his head. "It's early yet for a trip. Nothing runs until May, and even then, it's the Atlantic's decision if you're to go or not."

The disappointment is much more crushing than it should be, given my shaky relationship with functionality.

Obvious concern flashes across the man's face. "Are you all right there?"

My initial response is to keep my garbage to myself, but the crinkles around his eyes are so kind. "Working through some stuff," I say. "But thanks for asking."

He jerks a thumb at the poster. "Best you can do today is head down to the Kerry Cliffs. There's a brilliant lookout spot to take in the Skelligs." He leans over the counter to examine my sneakers. "It's a slippery walk in the fog. Make sure you've got traction on your runners."

Turning, I lift a foot for him to see the bottom of my shoe. Of course I do. I even seek approval from a stranger about the adequacy of my footwear.

"Those'll do." He comes around to my side of the counter and proceeds to tell me how to get to the Kerry Cliffs. "And if you decide today does turn out to be the day for that spot of whiskey, the first shot is on the house." He pats me on the shoulder.

"I will cash in sooner than later." I've almost made it to the door when a rush of humanity rolls in. At least a dozen people dressed in dark colors filter by me. Each stops at the takeaway counter to grab one of the coffees my winky Irish grandpa pours before they congregate in a smaller room off the main dining area around a single banquet table. Their jolly conversations run over one another. I let the chatter wash over me, absorbing the accents and the sense of comradery in the group as if it's an energy drink.

A woman with iron gray hair and a floor-length wool coat catches me watching them and approaches. "Will you be joining us to scatter the ashes then? We've room on the boat."

The invite flusters me. "Thank you, but I didn't know…" I fumble on saying the deceased. It feels like too formal a label for the dear departed in their friendly gathering.

"Old Andy. Used to be the ferryman on the Valentia ferry," she supplies. "I'm sure he'd welcome another prayer to send him up to the big man. You're very welcome to join us."

This second wave of stranger kindness almost breaks me. People who don't know me from a serial killer open their arms to include random me in a major rite of passage. Here come the tears again. "You're so sweet, but I've got to be on my way. I'm sorry for your loss."

She dismisses me with a wave. "None of that now. It was his time. He'll give them a jolly shake up at the pearly gates."

On impulse, I give her a quick hug which she returns with such warmth, I nearly change my mind. "Thank you for the invite."

"Of course, darlin'."

A few tears threaten to spill, but I pull off a weak smile.

"If you change your mind, we'll be on the Valentia ferry at half-ten."

I nod before slipping away. In honor of Old Andy, I make a note to someday soon opt for the Valentia ferry to cross the narrow waterway on the Ring of Kerry instead of the bridge.

When I get to the Kerry Cliffs, the fog does me a favor by mostly burning off so I'll be able to see the islands. After parting with Euros for the fee, I hike the distance to the farthest edge of the railing. I've seen plenty of photos but the sight steals my breath.

There they are—the Skelligs, one larger than the other, steep massive rocks poking out of the sea with tops sharp enough to pierce the clouds. Mist lingers around the peaks, only revealing what the wild Atlantic chooses to share. The surreal pair perfectly conveys the essence of *The Chieftain's Son*, a vibe of traveling through time to reunite with lost love.

I understand why Duagh fled to the haven of Skellig Michael. It looms above the water like a fortress in the sea, daring anyone to breech its rocky coast.

Immovable.

The current group of visitors milling near the terminus of the walkway heads back in the direction of the car park, leaving me alone to pay homage to the Skelligs. Stretching an arm toward the islands, I close my eyes and whisper, "Hello."

Here in this delicate reality that conjures visions of myth and history, reality is naturally one step removed. Staring at the Skelligs, it feels safe to allow Bobby to drift gently into my mind.

That I love him, am in love with him, is not a question. The man who became my friend online and lover in person fills my heart with joy, hope, and a sense of steady confidence I'm just beginning to trust. I've always believed friendship is the core of a relationship. If Bobby and I had never stepped beyond that boundary, he would still be an important part of my life.

But we did, and it felt right.

We're both driven and never settle until we hit the excellence mark in what we set out to achieve. It was easy to fall in love with a version of myself, a version starting to lower the volume on my crippling self-doubt because of this amazing show.

I grip the wet railing. He's fallen for the half-truth of who I am. Standing here a thousand feet above the waves crashing against the Kerry Cliffs, my heart pounds with shame. He deserved my truth, and I've been playing a role. He thinks I'm stronger than I am, thus driving him fucking crazy. My struggle with bipolar disorder and the imposter syndrome it feeds deprived Bobby of my whole heart when he gave me all of his. Now I'm on the brink of running from what we've built and never giving him the chance to know all of me.

I drop my forehead onto my fog-dampened hand. "God, Bobby. This is so damn hard." My tears blend with the mist.

After a few minutes of wallowing, I lay out my mental puzzle pieces. I fought for a sense of belonging on *The Chieftain's Son*, and I've won. The victory gifted me a level of euphoria beyond my expectations. I'm no longer a transient designer, living from one job to the next, accepting endings are inevitable. Yes, *The Chieftain's Son* will end, but not for years. I can build a life here with friends, with colleagues who signed on for the whole journey. Do I wish it included Bobby? Absolutely, but life, at least my life, has never played fair.

The fog rolls farther out toward the horizon, and the Skelligs are etched in sharper relief against the sky. If I choose to build a life with Bobby in California and leave the show, how will I be any different from a rock in the sea that succumbs to the whims of unpredictable wind and tides?

The painful truth isn't hard to define.

I want to stay with the show. Bobby does not.

I understand his happiness index is dinged and scraped by his constant battle with True Time. Naively, I believed his love for the show outweighed his frustration. To be honest, I've watched the struggle drain his creative soul. He's already handed off episodes to other writers I know he was eager to pen himself.

I suck in a ragged breath. It's not just his deep connection with the show I thought was enough to keep him here. I believed our steady, yet passionate relationship was motivation for shoving past True Time's incessant pressures and staying connected with the spirit of *The Chieftain's Son*.

"Oh, Elodie Pettipas, you've told yourself a story that wasn't yours to tell."

A seabird swoops in to perch on the rail nearby, checking out the nutty woman on the edge of a cliff talking to herself. I'll give him something to tell his feathery buds. "It's not enough." He answers my shriek with a shrill cry and takes off.

Sadness born of raw reality, not my anxiety or its partner, depression, sends me into a slump on the walkway, my back braced against the lower rail. Dampness from the concrete seeps into my coat. I'm a mound of pure pathetic here alone at the end of the world. My face tingles from the cold. I shiver and don't even attempt to stop the tears from pouring across my own frozen landscape.

Bobby should not compromise his artistic future to fulfill mine, and I will not reshape my life to fit his.

I can't be a rock in the sea.

CHAPTER 18
AN OCEAN AWAY

I crank the heater in my flat. Bobby's quick Hollywood turnaround stretches into its second week. My stomach grinds at the thought of him in meetings, sketching a future away from *The Chieftain's Son*. He texts me with vague platitudes, and I answer with supportive but noncommittal messages. The time difference we once conquered to come together is now my convenient excuse for creating distance.

My cell buzzes at ten a.m.

Bobby.

It's two a.m. his time. Even though answering has disaster written all over it, I tap the green circle on my phone.

"Hey El. I miss you."

I take a gut breath to shore myself up. "I miss you too." It's not a lie. I burn for him.

"I'm trying to map out a few things on my end. Can I run a schedule by you?"

Damn. I'm sure he's not referring to any map involving geography. I hit speaker and put the cell down on the window seat so I can pulverize the cushions with my fingers. This is it. I told him I'm not going to bail on *The Chieftain's Son*. He's probably ramping up to propose some crazy LA to Ireland plan for us that will break records for frequent flyer miles.

I can almost hear the stress knots bunching along my muscles. It's my fault he's trying to map us out. I've put off a clean ending too long.

Neither of us have broached the subject of Bobby and Elodie uncoupling. It's cowardice on my part and denial on his. I've practiced my breakup speech over and over. I know he deserves to hear it in person, but my appreciation for the strategy of using a breakup text grows by the day. My mother never had any qualms giving her cowboys the heave-ho. Which makes sense since thrill and gratification are her shiny pennies, not longevity. Given her track record, I'm amazed she stayed with my dad long enough for me to happen.

But she never had a Bobby.

My breath stutters in my chest. "I don't think it's a good idea."

Silence on his end.

Don't do this on the phone, Elodie.

I say it before guilt grinds my heart into crumbs. "Bobby, whatever schedule you're figuring out, it's time to take me out of the equation."

More silence, so I forge ahead. "You need to focus on what works for you. When that's clear, everything else will fall into place." Meaning, I won't fit anymore.

He clears his throat. I can't tell if he's choked up or stringing a bow with a verbal arrow to launch at me.

"Everything?"

A car honks on the street below, and I see Gilly waving at me from the window of a silver and blue Renault.

"Bobby, I'm sorry but Gilly's here to pick me up. I'm doing an art lesson in Jack's mom's class this morning." I don't want to convey the tone of a heartless blow-off, so I add. "And it's late. You need to go to bed." Okay, I achieved caring yet noncommittal.

"Fine." There's no goodbye, no warmth in his tone, no more breathing on the line. He ended the call.

Oh shit, did I just break up with him?

Take me out of the equation.

I did.

The decision I made at the Skelligs is now reality. I broke up with Bobby. To my credit, it was a call and not a text. As guilty as I feel, there's also surety that I've given him the clarity he needs on where I stand. He can get on with his life. Still, the coldness of the knife I slashed through our relationship doesn't earn me any Pettipas points.

I rub my eyes and brace myself to face Gilly. On the inside, I fragment. On the outside I fake peppy as we drive to the primary school where Mrs. O'Leary the elder teaches mini-humans.

The kids turn out to be adorable and not half bad with a paintbrush. I teach them some simple techniques for making different types of flowers, and they get totally into it. Maybe there's a budding production designer in the bunch. After I help Jack's mom wipe painty hands, she sends the littles outside to play. Mrs. O'Leary and I clothespin the masterpieces on a string draped across one wall.

"Such a garden of innocence," I say, admiring the work.

"Och, don't let 'em fool ya." She points to a picture near the end. "This little fiend used his fist instead of the brush."

Sure enough, there's a definite green fist print on the paper.

"You're lovely with the kids," says Mrs. O'Leary, patting my arm. "Do you want some of your own?"

Okay, wow. I've just sent the potential father of my future children out to sea in a paper boat. It's a crap time to dig into Elodie's shattered treasure box of dreams and wishes. I attempt to swallow a stitch in my chest. It's not as if I haven't daydreamed about our mini *Work-Bobbies* running around.

"Tough to do in my line of work. Long days, crazy stretches of time not coming up for air. That's not fair to a kid."

She clicks her tongue. "I've heard it before."

Gilly pops into the room with the two dozen donuts she bopped out to grab for the kids while I did the art project. I'd better tell her to duck. Mama O'Leary is in grandma mode.

"And speaking of…" says Jack's mom. As soon as Gilly sets the boxes down, Mrs. O. wraps her in a hug and then lays a hand over Gilly's belly. "How are we today?"

I stare at the hand and realize its cupping a compact but unmistakable bump at the front of Gilly's flouncy dress. She shrugs and flashes me a crinkly smile. Damn, the woman's done a stellar job hiding her stunner of a game changer.

Mrs. O'Leary catches our exchange. "You didn't know then?"

I shake my head. "No, but...wow. This is so cool. How far along are you?"

Gilly smooths her hands over her baby bump. "Almost five months. I swear I just popped last week."

"Oh, and it's going to keep popping, love," chuckles Mrs. O'Leary. She gives me a knowing look. "We all know the size of the daddy."

Gilly kisses her mother-in-law's cheek. "See you at dinner, Mom."

I score a mom hug as well and follow Gilly to the car park in front of the school.

"Surprise," she says throwing her arms up.

"I'll say. Meg is going to have a coronary. We'd better grab a defibrillator on the way to The Clan."

"She already knows."

"And yet, you're still smiling."

Gilly pulls out her scrunchie and redoes her ponytail. "After the initial freak out, she immediately started working on a game plan."

My mind flicks right to Bobby and his game plan of whatever schedule he was cooking up for us. I really wish I could rope Gilly in as a sounding board, but I'm not going to trounce her good news with my tragedy.

We both slide into the car. "Is wardrobe crafting a strategic wedding gown to hide O'Leary junior?"

Gilly sighs. "They're going to have to. I'll probably get stuck with something that looks like the top layer of a wedding cake since we're still two months away from the stupid show pony wedding." She rests her head on the wheel. "Ugh. The thought of a boat ride out to the Skelligs already has me turning green."

"I'm sure you can hitch in one of the helicopters going over."

The color drains from her face. "Even worse. Hopefully I won't be the size of a house by then."

I mimic Mrs. O'Leary. "We all know the size of the daddy."

She rubs her bump. "Don't remind me. And speaking of Jack's giant baby, I have a massive favor to ask you."

"Yes, I will teach your offspring how to draw or ride a horse when the time comes, but fair warning, I'll be shit at any form of babysitting until he or she is old enough to appreciate sarcasm."

"She," Gilly says, beaming bright enough to fill the car with virtual sunlight.

The love in Gilly's voice is so moving, my eyes well up with tears. "I'm over the moon for you and Jack."

She lurches across the car to hug me. "It's amazing to be able to tell someone outside the family besides Meg."

This gushing version of Gilly is new to me. I'm used to snappy and sassy. It's a beautiful shading to add to my new sister/friend. I realize I've just voiced my intention of being here as her daughter grows. It's not that I've waffled on committing to the run of the show, but the bittersweet taste of doing it without Bobby still lingers on my tongue.

"You mentioned a massive favor?"

She gets right to it. "I know you and Bobby were set on joining us in the wife-carrying competition, but is there any way you'd consider stepping in as Jack's partner?"

I squeak. "Me, with Jack."

"Do you think Bobby would be too bummed?" Gilly shrugs one shoulder. "Meg's painting one of her scenarios where you and Jack buddy up to represent *The Chieftain's Son* team. She'll put the kibosh on the inevitable social media trash of you and him being more than good sports teaming up." Gilly chews a fingernail. "There will also be a small crew there to get footage for *My Two Loves*. My post-game interview will be cut in later once we can announce the baby is the reason it was a bad idea for my husband to dangle me upside-down, sprint over hay bales, and through water obstacles."

It's bad Karma to disappoint a pregnant friend. "I'm sure Bobby will agree to do what's best for the show." Which now translates to Bobby won't want anything to do with me, so why not let Jack drag me over the wife-carrying course. It's hard to comment on Bobby's dedication to the show I would once have bet my life on, but now sounds hollow to my heart.

She smiles. "He always does."

"One condition."

Gilly narrows her eyes. "What condition?"

"No way am I doing the Estonian style, upside-down position and sticking my face in your husband's ass."

She giggles. "Not a problem. I can't imagine Bobby allowing you to take that for the team."

I wish she'd stop bringing up his name.

As Gilly starts the car, a loud incoming call chimes through the speakers. *Baby Daddy* flashes across the display. She clicks a button on the steering wheel. "Hi, honey—"

Jack's agitated voice blasts through car, cutting her off. "Somethings turned between Elodie and Bobby. I've just got off the phone with him, and he's a bloody nightmare. I don't know what to say to the poor fool."

My heart lurches. Not only do I drive Bobby fucking crazy, now I've turned him into a bloody nightmare. That's a penalty of ten Pettipas points. Deduct five more for dragging Gilly and Jack into our misery.

I truly believed the steady state of our romance was sustainable, but I never factored in being thousands of miles apart. It shouldn't be so gut-wrenching hard for two people who want to be together to stay together, yet it is.

Gilly's voice is calm. "Jack, I'm here with Elodie, and you're on speaker."

"Holy fuck. Sorry, I'm raving like a madman, Elodie."

Gilly's giving me a raised eyebrow *do you want to elaborate* look.

My gaze locks on the dash display. "Hello, Jack, and congratulations. Your mom spilled the baby beans."

I believe the term for what he does next is *sputter*.

"Don't freak out. I'm not going to run off at the mouth about wee baby O'Leary, and yes, I'll do the wife-carrying thing with you."

The sputter morphs into a grunt. "Grand." He breaths loudly into the phone. It sounds like wind whipping through the car. "I'm not gonna push, but is there anything I can say to Bobby to ease the poor bastard?"

Gilly barks out a loud *Ha*. "You, not pushing? I'll believe it when I see it."

Jack huffs. "I feel like a useless fool talking to him."

Now I've got fucking crazy, bloody nightmare, and useless fool on my scorecard. The callous on my thumb throbs as I spin my ring. "Jack, you can tell him we'll talk when he gets—" I almost say home, but the word sits like clay in my mouth. "Back."

"That'll be right soon. He bunked off with me to call a car to take him to the airport."

Shit. No. It's still the middle of the night, and I've set *Barrell-Ahead-Bobby* running at top speed to get back here. "Jack, please stop him. Convince him cutting his trip short to blast over here right now won't change anything."

Gilly lays a hand on my arm as Jack's voice quiets. "Is it done then with you and him?"

I don't know how to answer without bleeding out in the O'Leary's Renault.

Gilly saves me. "Honey, just call Bobby and tell him Elodie says to stay put until he's finished with his business."

"I'm on it, love. See you at dinner." Another long pause and then— "El—el—ooodie..." He fumbles my name. "If you want company, you're very welcome to dinner at my parents' house tonight."

"Thanks for the offer, Jack. I'm really okay." Such a liar. "Sorry to put you and Gilly in the middle of this."

A low grunt ripples through the speakers. Jack is a very noisy phone guy. "I'm sorry—"

I interrupt. Jack needs to get on the phone to LA. I can't deal with the guilt of being the cause of ruining Bobby's future in addition to screwing up his present. "It's all good, Jack. Please call Bobby." It's so the opposite of good.

Jack and Gilly say quick lovey goodbyes as I drop my head onto my hands.

She rests a warm touch on my hunched back. "I don't know if it helps, but Bobby does go to LA regularly. It's not weird for him to be gone this long."

I think of the cowboys on the ranch, filming a cattle roundup segment. My thoughts are splattered across my brain in desperate need of a roundup. There's still a huge part of me who wants to take back the breakup, but I have to believe I did the right thing. Bobby needs to make decisions for his own path without me as a factor.

Slowly, I turn my head to look at her. "I do want to talk to you, but there's stuff I can't blab about."

"You mean like Bobby considering leaving the show?"

I spring up so fast it knocks her hand away. "You know?"

"Jack and Bobby golf. Think of it as the male equivalent of us getting mani-pedis together." She aims a meaningful look at me. "Bobby looped Jack in on Stream Up's interest."

I lean my head against the window, the relief of shedding part of our prickly secret trickles through me. "If he leaves the show, he wants me to go with him."

"That's not fair."

I gawk, shocked at her reaction. I fully anticipated this half of the most in-love couple in Ireland to go rabid Cupid on my ass, not agree with me.

"Well, it's not," she says, gripping the steering wheel. Gilly cuts the engine and meets my gaze. "For someone who's barely joined the show, you've made a major impact." She pauses. The battle whether to go further showing across her face.

"Hit me with whatever's swimming around in there," I say, gesturing to her temple.

She gives her head a quick shake. "Okay, I may be breaking a confidence, but I know from Bobby's season two rants that Jeff Palmer was basically a ghost."

I stare at her. "What?"

"Apparently, he did a bang-up job on season one, won his awards, and then delegated to the point of ridiculous. He hated it over here and spent the majority of his time designing from LA. His hip replacement was a convenient excuse to bail." She dances her fingertips across the top curve of the wheel. "My parents thought it was a crime he held on to the show as long as he did. Keep it to yourself, but Bobby was going to start looking for a replacement and let Jeff go once season three was set. His unexpected exit moved up the timeline."

I blink, attempting to take this in. It explains so much. I remember my first gig as an assistant art director on a sitcom where the production designer had so many shows going, we only met once per episode to hash out the sets, and then I had to make them happen. My crew was my lifeline. Was *The Chieftain's Son* one of many commitments for Jeff Palmer, not his everything?

It seems the guy leaving abruptly was a gift, not a detriment to the show. *The Chieftain's Son's* art department must have been forced to mesh and see everything through to fruition with Jeff's minimal investment to maintain the high quality of a show they clearly love. No wonder they resented a new face waltzing in with plans to shake up their independence.

My appreciation for my extraordinary department heads and their dedicated crews crosses the threshold into awe. I cringe, realizing in retrospect what a bad call my strategy to come on strong out of the gate was. Bobby tried to warn me to ease in instead of banging the drum of authority. He should have been straight with me about Jeff. Would that have altered the way I handled things? I was so determined to overcome my own fear of inadequacy, I probably still would have cracked the whip of change too hard.

As showrunner, Bobby had the right to impose on the situation. Instead, he supported and believed in me. He allowed me the space to find a rhythm with the crew which I finally achieved with our team success at the Battle of Waterville. Did he think because they survived with Jeff phoning it in they would be fine with yet another transition if I left? How can I abandon them now when we've become a cohesive unit?

I can't, but does that mean I can let Bobby walk out of my life? Oh my God, this is too much. There are too many dust bunnies in my brain to clean up.

Gilly watches my wheels turn. She startles when I whip my body around in the seat to face her. "Did you and Jack discuss yet what you're going to do when the show ends? Are you and..." I gesture to her belly. "...Your kids going to follow him wherever his career takes him?"

"Absolutely we talked. We had to play the *what if* game. It would be magical thinking to believe there's ever going to be another long-term show here at home like *The Chieftain's Son* for Jack. Temporary separations in our lives are a given. It's the reality of both our careers."

"Did you figure out a solution or table the topic until the end of the show rears its ugly head?"

She gives a half-smile. "We have scenarios. Thank God there's plenty of time to flesh them out. We'll most likely establish homes both here and LA." Hands rest on her belly. "Near grandparents at either end." Her sigh is weary. "If he goes off for prolonged periods to do films or another series, I suspect I'll get very good at efficient packing and wrangling kids on airplanes."

I stare at her bump. "What about times when you can't do that, when you have to be separated because of different jobs or kids' schools?"

"We've committed to each other to make it work even if it's a royal pain. We knew the instability of our careers was part of the deal before we got married."

I stare out the front window at the row of houses across the road and the fields beyond. "And the prospect of upheaval doesn't scare you?"

Gilly leans forward to rest her chin on the wheel. "Make no mistake, it terrifies me." She straightens. "In the sense that any adventure is frightening when you start imagining endless possible outcomes." The corners of her lips lift into a soft smile. "However insane our lives might become, at the end of the day, it's Jack and me. That's a strong enough promise for us to build a life on." Her expression goes serious. "I'm not saying it's the answer for everyone."

"So, Crystal Award-winning screenwriter, if you were writing the script of Bobby and Elodie, one in LA and one in Ireland, how would it go?"

She raises both hands. "Oh, no. I am the last person on the planet to ask for relationship advice." Her laugh is brittle. "Jack is my happy ending, but I waded through plenty of mud to get to him."

Mud.

I fall back through time to my first face-to-face meeting with Bobby on the hilltop, me covered in mud. I'd be lying if I denied that was the moment my heart whispered *I found you* for the first time and meant it. I lay hands over my chest. Beneath my fingers, heartbeats pick up the tune of that whisper.

For a designer who has a palette of endless shades and tints of colors in her arsenal, I haven't looked past black and white, you there and me here, when it comes to Bobby and me. My fingers dip into the bib of my overalls to my phone. Gilly's optimism tempts me to text Bobby to ignore Jack to tell him to come home. By some miracle, my often-faulty impulse control kicks in. It would be cruel to surge forward, give Bobby false hope, only to backtrack if I truly can't handle the emotional slaughter of constantly missing him. For fuck's sake, we work on the same show in the same place, and we have to fight for time together. As tempting as Jack and Gilly's model of flexibility is, who's to say it could work for us?

I collapse against my seat. My regrets and creeping indecision are part of the breakup process. I'm sticking to my path because for once, the most important person I need to please is myself. No matter how much it hurts.

CHAPTER 19
STUNT DOUBLE

The Killarney park stretches a few blocks into the distance before it curves out of sight around a bend. Strings of multi-colored flags outline two lanes of the wife-carrying competition. The outgoing route is blocked by a big-ass log Jack will have to navigate over with me on his back. Since I nixed the face-in-butt style, we've landed on a fireman's carry.

Scaling the log won't be a picnic, but the second half of the obstacle course makes me question why I ever agreed to do this bonkers wife-carrying insanity with anyone. Halfway between the far U-turn at the end of the first lane and the finish line, a huge hole has been dug into the ground and filled with water.

I watched every video on wife carrying I could find. There were many civilized, thick-gauge vinyl-lined water obstacles that looked like the sunken version of above ground pools. For my shot at the event, I get a mud puddle.

"Team t'irty-t'ree," calls the jolly man, standing at the scales.

I look down at the bib pinned to the front of my *The Chieftain's Son* t-shirt.

Thirty-three.

I love being weighed in public about as much as I appreciate the sting of a deep paper cut. The winner gets his "wife's" poundage in beer so a date with the scales in unavoidable. If I'm under the required kilograms, they'll have to attach weights to me. This just gets better and better.

I barely pass muster without needing enhancement and head over to join a particularly boisterous group from the show stationed on the other side of the rope.

"Give his bum a good slap at the go," says Maureen.

"That's my job," says Gilly, elbowing her.

One of the plasterers sidles up next to me. "You sure you don't want a nip before you're off, Miss Boss?" He raises a tiny flask from the breast pocket of his flannel.

The previously cutting nickname is now a warm fuzzy. I lean close to him. "Save some for my impending humiliation."

He guffaws and claps me on the shoulder. While I appreciate the enthusiastic support, there's one face in this group I miss. Jack did catch Bobby in time to keep him from jumping on a plane so his LA excursion continues to drag on.

The text thread between Bobby and me dead-ended that same night. I've been tempted to revive it about once an hour. The certainty he needs to do what he needs to do for him kept me from reaching out at first. Then unfair but lingering anger at him for lighting the fuse that blew us apart got me over the weak moments of calling or texting every time I reread our existing thread from happier times.

Every reconciliation scenario I tortured myself with ends with a big red fail sign. I shouldn't even be trying to imagine fixing what I broke. This is best for both of us. Bobby is a high-octane force, not a home and hearth type like Jack. I don't have the career flexibility Gilly's writing has. My profession can't be done anywhere a laptop can travel. No matter how many times I tried to design a solution, the compromises Gilly and Jack are willing to embrace will never work for us.

All I have a right to wish for is a bit of closure after what in retrospect was my heartless goodbye over a phone call. Bobby Provost deserves better.

There's a roar from the bystanders as two teams blow past us. They are neck and neck, or rather face-in-ass to face-in-ass until they come to the log. The first pair slides right over with nary a blip, which makes sense given the man's massive legs. The second husband attempts a belly-down slip-over that results in him dumping his wife onto the ground on the other side of the dry obstacle.

I've never noticed if Jack's legs are particularly long. Damn, I hope they are. Where is he anyway? I get Meg doesn't want him mobbed, so he'll show right before our racing slot. She's not in the crowd, and the camera crew that had to endure my less-than-elegant interview earlier disappeared as well. They must be tucked away in a private corner of the park getting pre-game footage.

I nudge Gilly. "Where's my ride?"

She looks around but doesn't spot him.

"He'd better not be off tailgating with Guinness and pizza." I cross my arms. "I don't want him losing his balance and dunking my head underwater in the mud bath." Thankfully, Jack is both tall and insanely strong. I'll look like an ant on an elephant across his shoulders. As long as he doesn't slip, my head should remain well above the water line.

There's renewed commotion from the sidelines as one couple creates an impressive splash, toppling over into the brackish water feature.

Cian appears at Gilly's side. "Word on the lawn says the pool is..." He busts out an Irish accent. "Wicked slippery."

"Pool? That's generous." I tighten the strap on my helmet. I'd better establish an *I'm drowning* signal to pound into Jack's flesh.

Before my nerves can extend their fangs, Pat and his wife push their way through the crowd. He gathers me in a hug. "You're going to do the show proud." His eyes snap to the starting line. "There goes Jimmy and his lady."

"Wife up," calls the starter.

The stunt coordinator hoists his wife, Mary, into the Estonian carry and off they go. The pair tears up the course as we holler our lungs out. The couple they're competing against doesn't stand a chance to best them. I swear, there's not a drop of mud on Mary when they finish and come over to collect fist bumps.

The next few rounds are painful to watch as husbands and wives dunk under the chocolate brown water and come up sputtering. My mantra become *less than two minutes, less than two minutes,* which is the estimated time to complete the course. I have to trust Jack to carry me from start to finish without cracking any of my teeth.

Cian lays a hand on my shoulder as he reads a text on his phone. "Meg says it's time to meet Jack near the starting line. I'll walk you over."

I'm buried in well-wishes as we leave our cheering section and skirt the back of the crowd to the on-deck pavilion.

I land a playful punch on Cian's bicep. Oh, another tall, thin specimen hiding solid muscle. "I haven't forgiven you and Meg yet for not suffering through this with me."

Cian has mischievous eye-twinkle down perfectly. "Maybe I can talk her into it once she's officially Mrs. O'Malley."

I bark out a laugh, picturing Meg in one of her pencil skirts and blazers slung across Cian's shoulders. "Forgive me if I don't take that bet."

He guides me around the back of a tent into a semi-circle of trees where Jack, Meg, and the camera crew wait. I suffer through Jack hefting me up several times in different positions, then pretending to drop me while the camera rolls. Meg directs more antics for them to capture before my head starts pounding from the blood rushing between my ears.

Jack sets me on my feet. "What do you say, stand-in wife? Are you ready to give us a go?"

I rub my temples and accept a water bottle from a PA and nod at Jack. "Don't believe your press. Those shoulders are not as comfortable as they look."

The crew trails us over to the starting line. I crook a finger at Jack. He bends to *telling secrets* level. "I'm freaking out my head will get dunked in the mud bath. Warn me and yell 'going down' if you feel yourself slipping."

A wicked smile blooms across his face. "I've seen a few splashes. It hasn't killed anyone yet."

I slap his shoulder. "It's not how I want to be remembered."

"Wife up," yells the starter.

Taking a step back, I spread my legs so Jack is free to step between them and hoist me into the fireman's carry. He slings my body over his shoulders like I'm nothing, but instead of settling, I keep going. A sense of falling makes my head spin for a hot second before I slide onto a very different set of shoulders.

Wiry shoulders I recognize well.

Bobby.

The starting signal blasts, and he starts running.

I'm momentarily stunned first by the surprise hand-off, and then breathing in Bobby's distinctive smell of pencil and fresh sweat to top it off. "What are you doing?" I scream into his ear.

"Putting you back in the equation." Trying to run and talk at the same time makes his words come out in bursts.

I dig fingers into his back. "That's not your call."

We reach the log obstacle. He carries us over easily with his long legs.

"Why do you think it's exclusively your call?"

My head bobs behind his shoulder, making my teeth clack together.

"I get I'm shaking up our world, Elodie, but it is *our* world. You can't pull away and claim it's your world alone."

He slows to take the U-turn.

I'm still shouting at him. "I'm making the choices that work for me." He stumbles and I grunt. "And you."

Muscles flex as he tightens his arms around my leg. "Without hearing me out?"

"I heard you loud and clear. Goodbye *The Chieftain's Son*. Hello, Stream Up."

There are only yards before lake mud. "And I heard you—every word about my loyalty and your loyalty to *The Chieftain's Son*."

"But it didn't matter. You still flew off to LA in search of a True Time-free life."

His chest heaves, heat rolling off his body. "Do you think I'm so pig-headed and selfish that I'd do anything more than investigate our possibilities without considering how it affects you?"

I go limp across his shoulders at the sting in his words. It's not what I think, it's what I fear. The vines of my inadequacies slither around my chest, squeezing.

"You already started making choices for me when you offered me as a bargaining chip in your deal." A sob rises in my throat. "You were so happy when Stream Up wanted you. Don't you understand I have to pull away for you to embrace that happiness because I'm not going to leave the show."

"Damn it, Elodie. You are my happiness. I'm just frustrated you've already decided all the ways our life won't work if things change. What about the ways it can work?"

We're two feet from the slight slope into the water hazard. "How can anything work when I drive you fucking crazy?"

"What?"

Bobby's sneaker hits the edge of the pool. He rocks side to side, searching for balance that never comes. Down we stumble, waist-deep into the soup. When he scrambles to keep my head above water, his footing goes to hell. With a splash, we both land on our bums in the muddy mess.

I try to stand, but Bobby grabs my arm to stop me. "Elodie, that's not true."

The flat of my hand smacks the water, spraying his face with brown dots. "It is. You said my lack of confidence drives you fucking crazy."

He looks stricken. "I meant you are fucking amazing, and it kills me you don't trust your talent."

"I'm never going to completely trust it, Bobby." I knock on the side of my head. "This doesn't work like yours does. My wiring defaults to self-doubt, fear, anxiety, and..." There's no point in holding back anything when you're face-to-face in a mud puddle with the relationship you detonated on the phone. "Bobby, I have bipolar disorder. It's who I am. I'm not going to sugarcoat it. It's a reality I wrestle with every day of my life, a fight to function in the world. You say I'm amazing, and I hear you. I just have trouble inhabiting that perception. I'll always tend toward the negative of your positive. The hesitation to your drive."

There's so much more to say, to explain, but at least I finally shared my truth. God, it's freeing.

He looks stricken, not angry, not offput. "You didn't have to keep this from me."

I shake my head. "I never wanted you to see me as flawed."

He finds my hands in the murky pond and grabs them. "I see...the woman I love."

"You only see what I've let you see."

He pulls me closer. "Then show me more. Show me everything. Give me the chance to know it all, Elodie."

I stare into his eyes and see openness, willingness, and not a hint of the reluctance I've experienced the few times I've shared this truth. My own mother doesn't even know because she'd stamp me with a label. It's unfair the way people decide you are your challenge instead of appreciating you as the person forging through life with that challenge.

"I can't even attempt to give you the chance when you're in another time zone. I'm not resilient, Bobby. I try to be, but it's so damn hard." For the first time, I want to open up completely to someone, and I'm losing him. I've ached to find the courage to tell him since we first got together, but my overwhelming fear of judgment made me keep it from him. Bobby is the one my heart tells me to trust. It's been nudging me all along, but years of practiced hiding kept me silent. When you can get by without spilling your secrets, you do.

He lurches through the water to gather me in his arms. "So don't be resilient, El. Just be you. That's enough."

Bobby's words dare other truths about my struggle with mental health to start peeking through the crack in their dungeon door, wondering if it's safe to break out.

Above us, one of the contest officials in a Day-Glo yellow vest peers over the edge. "Do you need a hand with the missus there, pal?"

I press my lips against Bobby's ear. "I think we may be disqualified."

"Well then," he says, pulling me to standing. "Let's give them a real show." He crushes his lips to mine.

Mud never tasted so good, even if this will be our last kiss. I should push him away, but I can't.

After a couple of slips, we stumble out of the water to free the course for the next set of competitors. Bobby holds tight to my hand as we take the long way around the course to *The Chieftain's Son* group. This in-person breakup is fairer to him, mud and all. As long as we're ripping off bandages…

"Okay Bobby, while I appreciate the kiss, get on with dumping all your bad news on me while I'm already covered in muck."

Bobby pulls me against his side. "I would if I had any."

I gently push him away. "Don't put it off. You took the Stream Up deal, didn't you? You should take the Stream Up deal. You can tell me. I promise to listen and not bolt."

He raises his eyebrows. "You're staying in the equation?"

I swallow hard. "You don't know how much I wish I could." Stress wastes no time crawling up my back muscles. I try to switch off my panic at the major life change Bobby's about to shove in my face. I owe it to him and what we've been to each other to listen.

He grins. "I indulged my fantasy and told True Time exactly what they could do with their inhumanly truncated schedule and ridiculous PR games."

My stomach clenches. "Before or after they fired you?"

"I'd quantify it as an explosion not a firing."

I clutch his arm. "So, you are leaving the show, leaving Ireland." It hits me, despite all my big-girl resolve there was still a bead of hope that Bobby would find the wherewithal to stay with the show. It shrinks until there's no sign of it left. "Did they agree to let Danna step up or are we going to have to deal with mystery meat True Time serves up?"

We as in me and the rest of *The Chieftain's Son* family without Bobby.

"Danna is staying put as my second in command."

I swear the temperature drops twenty degrees on this fine May morning as clouds roll in over the park. My wet and clingy clothes ignite a flurry of shivers.

Bobby pulls me behind a tree out of sight of the course. He twists my shoulders to face him. "I don't know how I'd function without her."

He's taking Danna too? "Damn, Bobby. Was your plan to cannibalize the whole show?"

"Why would I do that when I've built such an extraordinary team?" Has the cold turned everything he says into gibberish. "Elodie, I'm not leaving the show."

Yep, complete gibberish.

"But they fired you. What are you going to do, hide out in the stables and run the show from there?"

"I didn't say fired. I said explosion." He cups my face. "True Time exploded. Stream Up bought them out. There is no more True Time. That's why I had to stay longer, to work through details of the transition."

I lay my hands over his. "But you said Stream Up offered you a new show."

"They did, but since you were dead set against leaving with me, the original plan for the trip was to give them a chance to say their piece so I didn't burn a bridge. They're good people. Creative. Ambitious." A corner of his mouth quirks up. "Well funded. I'm talking big league corporate backing. As soon as I stepped into their conference room, prepared with my thanks but no thanks, down went the blinds and their real agenda of buying True Time exploded."

I shiver again, and he draws me close. "They bait and switched you?"

Bobby rubs my arms to warm me up. "Not exactly. There is the possibility of future projects with them, but because *The Chieftain's Son* is True Time's crown jewel, they wanted a strategy session with me. They couldn't leak anything before I showed up." He wobbles his head. "They'd already wooed the showrunner of *Star's Shadow*, but that show only has one more season left, we've got seven."

"But you were calling me about a schedule." I take a step back. "Damn it, Bobby, you made me believe we were going to be separated. I've been in hell over this."

"I was trying to work out a more reasonable production schedule for *The Chieftain's Son* to propose to Stream Up." He stares at the rolling green lawn of the park. "Okay, truth—you shut me down so fast I was pissed and confused. It threw me into a tailspin. It hurt you weren't happier for me when I shared the Stream Up opportunity that night by the Yeats when you knew I've been in hell over True Time." He runs a hand through his hair, then flicks off a mud chunk. "Elodie, I'm used to ramrodding head on into solutions, since it's only me I've had to consider in the past. I get I was an insensitive ass trying to throw you in the mix without asking when Stream Up reconnected. I acted on impulse because being without you was unthinkable."

"Bobby, the issue is you left me in the dark again. I can't deal with being in the dark because my dark is a fucking blackout."

He reaches for me, but I back away. "Elodie, I told you I was crap at relationships. I should have called you sooner from LA, but by then I knew I'd fucked up so badly, I didn't want to make things any worse until I had all the particulars to share with you."

I ball my hands in fists and press knuckles against my temples. "And I decided we were done because the only information I had to work with was you leaving the show."

He pulls my hands away from my head. "El, I was scared you'd had enough of me and my bullshit moves." His grip tightens. "I can't see an end to us. I don't want to see an end."

For once, I don't even attempt to tame my temper. "Then stop making decisions that affect us without including me. Is that something you're capable of? Because based on your track record of withholding, I'm having serious doubts you can."

His gaze meets mine. "I swear to you, I'll keep trying until I get it right. Please, Elodie, give me a chance."

I grab the front of his shirt. "You stupid man. Of course I knew you were on your last nut with True Time. I saw how happy you were when Stream Up came knocking. I thought what I was doing by letting you go was best for you. I took myself out of the equation because I love you."

Bobby tries to speak, and I lay a muddy finger on his lips. "Can you be *Shut-Up-Bobby* while I finish?" He nods. "I'm also learning to love me. It wrung me inside out to come to the realization I would stay with the show if you left, but that's what was best for me, even if it meant letting you go." I feel tears welling. "Staying together in the insanity of our careers may always mean one of us has to sacrifice. I can live with that if you promise me decisions will be dialogues, not monologues in your head."

"I promise. I swear. I'll walk through fucking fire to prove it."

The gravity of Bobby's news begins to sink in. The idiocy of not trusting him with my mental illness follows right behind it. Keeping things from one another nearly destroyed us, but we don't have to break. This is our chance to take the pieces that flew apart and fit them back together in a better way, a stronger way.

He grips my upper arms. "I will be spending a bit more time in LA to work on developing new properties for Stream Up, but as long as *The Chieftain's Son* lasts, Ireland is my home, our home. Whatever happens after that, we'll figure out together." His expression is pained, waiting for my answer. "Please tell me it's what you want too?"

I thread my fingers into his disgustingly gooey hair and pull his face down until we're nose to nose. "I want you."

Our kiss is a promise, and then it's a need. He backs me against the tree, pressing his body into mine. If we weren't so damn cold and drippy, we'd give Killarney Park something to remember.

Hand in hand, we slog our way around the tree to our people.

"Stream Up agreed to everything I asked for, including a livable schedule, budget increases, and facilities upgrade." He kisses my muddy temple. "How would you like your own 360-degree LED stage?"

I goggle at him. "They don't even have one of those in Belfast."

"Guess folks will be coming to rent ours."

I slip my arm around his back, wanting to be closer. "Are you disappointed by your debut at wife carrying?"

He looks at me from under brows caked with drying flecks of dirt. "I don't consider it my official debut."

"Complications due to mud?"

"Complications due to not having a wife."

As his gaze bores into mine, my heart gallops faster than the couple flying down the first leg of the course. He stops before we hit the edge of the spectators and winds his arms around me. "A complication I'm eager to fix."

"Shh." I can't let him go on.

His eyes open wide. "Did you shush me?"

"You're already doing it again. We just unbroke up. Stop trying to usurp decisions that belong to both of us. Besides, I'd like to take advantage of lots of make-up plunging before we plunge ahead with anything else."

He laughs. "As I hope I've proven, I'm very good at plunging." His hand circles my wrist. "You really don't want to talk about taking things to a new level?"

I kiss his knuckle. "As a matter of fact, I do. I just want one of our big moments to be mud free."

"Fair enough."

We're close enough now for our group to spot us. Gilly and Jack reach us first. I smack him on his Viking deity forearm. "I vow to get my revenge on you for that sneaky hand off."

Jack nods at my hand firmly tucked into Bobby's. "Brilliant. I'll be happy to take my punishment." And surprising me not at all, he winks.

We're quickly swarmed. A camera gets shoved in my face along with a barrage of inane questions. For once, I don't care how stupid I look or sound, as long as Bobby Provost and I don't let go of each other's hand.

CHAPTER 20

SEASON FINALE

G illy squints at the frescoes I've painted into the castle set wall.

"Well, what do you think?"

She slowly shakes her head. "I think they're remarkable."

I shrug. "They won't read clearly on camera, but I'll know they're there."

Gilly tilts her head to the side. "Oh, I'll bet a certain someone will find a way to bring them into frame."

We share a laugh. "I'm sure you're right, Mrs. O'Leary."

Gilly closes her eyes and smiles. She looks like a contented cat. "I will never get tired of hearing that out loud—in public."

When Stream Up swallowed True Time, they also ended the charade of Jack's *come and get me* dateability. Meg deftly handled the press release announcing the truth of the O'Leary's marriage and baby news. The real coup was the way our PR queen vilified True Time for forcing all involved to lie to the fans. Fan outrage at the deception and the toll it took on personal lives is building a nice buzz for Jack and Gilly's *My Two Loves* show. Cinderella has nothing on Gilly's real-life love story.

I pat her belly that's graduated from bump to boulder. A testament to the love she no longer has to hide. "And you two managed to avoid a vomitous boat ride to Skellig Michael."

She runs a finger along one of the frescoes. "I'm damn grateful we didn't go through with that runaway train of a sham wedding."

I bump my shoulder into hers. "Ah, come on. It would have been spectacular."

"Not for this backyard wedding type of girl." She picks up the cat carrier next to her feet, jostling two grumbling tabbies. "Speaking of which. It's time to get Tom and Max home."

"Did they behave during the interview?"

Entertaining For You travelled to The Clan to do a photo spread complete with Gilly, Jack, and their two kitties to illustrate domestic O'Leary bliss.

"The furry hussies did a bang-up job flaunting their feline Jack worship for the camera."

I bend to peek into the carrier. One of the cats, I can't tell them apart, stops washing its face to give me the stink eye. No, that did not just happen. Won't Patrick laugh when I confess his goofy saying about cat eyes and marriage may yet have some basis in truth.

Gilly gives me a one arm hug.

"Do you need help carrying the girls?"

"Nope, it's all the workout I can manage these days. Can't give it up." She waddles a few steps toward the door, then turns back. "Did I mention you look stunning? Knock 'em dead. I want every detail at soul-to-sole night. Bye, El."

"Bye, G." I couldn't ask for a better sister-by-association, and I've also inherited Maureen in the process. Two sisters for the price of one.

The massive sound stage sleeps. The crew has gone home. It's only me, security, and my workaholic lover left occupying The Clan.

I check my watch. Bobby will be here any minute. We've synced our lives for the most part except for his marathon editing sessions or what I've dubbed laundry nights when I take his clothes and mine to wash at my flat.

I shouldn't be surprised Bobby completely immerses himself in learning about bipolar disorder. He's formed a mutual admiration society with Kevin these past few months during our joint therapy sessions. The two have become so thick, sometimes when the three of us are on video chat I wave my hands to remind them I'm part of the convo. It takes getting used to, accepting that I deserve these two worthwhile human beings. I'm working on it.

Truthfully, life is kinda wonderful. I do my best not to feel like I'm playing at a successful relationship and will be found out soon. Now whenever doubts creep in, I tell Bobby, and we work on it. He doesn't talk at me or write off my worries as overreactions. We navigate his issues and my issues together. For years, I've maintained a career and got to where I am on a massive hit show despite my mental stumbling blocks, but having someone to share both my triumphs and fears with is a whole new level of living.

I hear the door at the far end of the sound stage bang shut. Attempting to scurry halfway up the stairs of the castle set doesn't go great since I have to gather buttercup's skirts in one hand and brace myself against the faux stone wall with the other. It took some searching in wardrobe storage, but I managed to find the bright yellow dress that stopped Bobby's heart once before. I roost in a dark section of the stairs where the work lights don't reach.

"El?"

"I'm in the Rock of Cashel," I call through an arrow loop into the cavernous sound stage. We're close to the end of shooting on this set before we transform it into the digs for next season's chieftain. The season wrap is fast approaching as well, and then a blessed but short hiatus for us all, thanks to Stream Up's revised production schedule.

From my perch in the shadows, I watch *Work-Bobby* turn the corner at the edge of the set at full steam. He scans the ground level for me, but I'm high enough to be out of his eyeline.

"Elodie, where—" His voice cuts off as he reaches the two frescoes I added to the set, inspired by the ones we saw at Coolderry Castle. I've made a few improvements. In my castle, the chieftain and his honey are dressed in their period finery, holding hands as they survey their domain.

Bobby stares, then runs a finger down the paintings.

"Remind you of anyone you know?"

His head snaps up, searching until he finds me on the stairs. "It's us."

That's my cue. Slowly, like a proper chieftess, I descend the stairs. When I step into the light, I hear his sharp intake of breath.

Bobby walks to the bottom of the stairs, gazing up at me with a look of adoration to satisfy any chieftain's lady. His voice is pitched low. "I do love that dress."

I stop when we are eye to eye and manage a half-curtsy. "I do love you, Robert Benjamin Provost."

He moves as close as he can get with a couple of stairs still between us and holds out a hand to help me to the floor. "Dear one, my heart is filled with the glory of your beauty."

It's pretty cool to have a writer as a boyfriend. You get some very fancy phrases.

I take his hand but hold my position. "Do you want to know how much I love you?"

His lips curl into a half smile. "What currency are you suggesting to quantify your love, Euros, gold bars, plunging?"

"Time."

"How much time?"

I smile back. "A lifetime."

He climbs the first step, his gaze locked to mine. "It's yours."

I set my hands on his shoulders. "Will you spend that lifetime being my husband?"

His hands grip my waist. "Only if we get to keep this dress."

"I think it can be arranged. I know the guy in charge." I lean into him, and he swings me down to the ground.

"I am aching to marry you, Elodie Pettipas." His lips find mine and show no mercy. When he backs me into the set wall, I say a silent thank you to the carpenters and plasters that built it strong enough to withstand a thorough plunging. Bobby rucks up my skirts, moaning into my mouth when he realizes I'm naked and naughty underneath.

"This is unprofessional," he says, tasting the skin along my collarbone.

"Not as unprofessional as…" I pop one breast over buttercup's neckline.

Bobby's teeth accept the offering as his hands continue to meet the challenge of finding me under the skirts. The way his fingers manage to skim across my most sensitive parts before they succumb to skirt interference sets me on fire. With a huff, he loses the battle of buttercup and lowers me to the ground. "I'm a total failure at castle ravishing 101."

I laugh and drop my head against his chest, while my fingers tease the bulge in his khakis. "I know a certain fitting area with a very soft carpet."

Fiancé-Bobby sweeps me into his arms. We fly through the hallways toward wardrobe at a speed that would put any wife-carrying couple to shame.

EPILOGUE
UNDER THE HAWTHORN TREE

Bobby and I stand with our soul-to-sole group along with Rich and Amethyst Bettencourt, Jack's parents, and his sister, Bonnie's, family upon the hilltop near the studio under a hawthorn tree. No one can argue now that magic does exist on the tiny rise. Gilly and Jack became engaged here, and I first met my darling Bobby on this very spot.

Jack ties a small pewter Christening spoon to the branches of the hawthorn to join the other ribbons and offerings at this purported gateway into the realm of the fae. He whispers a wish to the faeries for his baby girl, who coos in the arms of her godfather, my beloved fiancé. Her godmother, Deidre, drops a kiss on the infant's forehead. Sun breaks through the clouds to set the layer of soft strawberry-colored down on the baby's tiny head ablaze.

Bobby surrenders his bundle into her father's arms and returns to my side, wrapping an arm around me. His lips graze my ear. "My goddaughter deserves a playmate."

Next to us, Cian stands behind Meg, his arms wrapped around her growing waistline.

I smile up at the future father of my babies, the Irish babies we plan to start making here during the run of *The Chieftain's Son.* "Someone beat us to it."

My thumb rubs against the beautiful jade and topaz engagement ring we had made at a local jeweler here in Kerry, twirling it around my finger not with nerves, but with contentment. A lovely peace settles over me with visions of Bobby, babies, and *The Chieftain's Son* painting my future.

I look around our circle and see all the different colored threads that bind a family together—love, blood, shared creative goals, and most of all appreciation you're in each other's lives. A certain bipolar, off-kilter kid from a movie ranch in Wyoming is so grateful to belong here.

Jack and Gilly hold their beautiful child together and speak a blessing in unison.

"May your heart ever shine with love, our dearest Nieve Deidre O'Leary."

Thank you for reading! Did you enjoy? Please add your review because nothing helps an author more and encourages readers to take a chance on a book than a review.

And don't miss more in the Behind the Scenes series coming this fall! Until then read more from Leslie O'Sullivan with PINK GUITARS AND FALLING STARS. Turn the page for a sneak peek!

Also be sure to sign up for the City Owl Press newsletter to receive notice of all book releases!

SNEAK PEEK OF PINK GUITARS AND FALLING STARS

You only get one parachute. There's no point packing two for a B.A.S.E. jump since you'll be pavement art before the second chute blossoms.

"Justin!"

Startled by a bellow from my jump leader/uncle, Timmer MacKenzie, my toe jerks to a stop half an inch above the trigger pedal of my launcher. Is his gray matter shredded, distracting me during a safety check? There's no chute on my back. One accidental tap on the business end of this launcher, and I'll be eye to eye with the flock of seagulls patrolling the Hollywood skies. I retreat onto the non-ballistic end of my perch. Peering over the edge of the Rampion Records Tower, I analyze the antics of the wind.

"Join us," Unc calls, teeth clenched in a P.R. smile. He hosts a cluster of reporters near the center of the circular roof. "Meet the rising star of the Slinging Seven."

Their faces morph into a collective portrait of panic as I leap more dramatically than necessary from launcher to the terra firma of the rooftop. After a salute to the Hollywood sign, a photo op my uncle will appreciate, I join the party. Pre-jump interviews are not my happy place, but keeping a smile on Timmer's face is essential. He leads our B.A.S.E. jump troop, giving the green light for my carcass to launch off skyscrapers, bridges, and cliffs in a wing suit.

"This Rampion Records Tower may rival Mount Olympus for acceptable jump altitude," Timmer tells the press jam sandwich. "Even so, I believe in enhancing the safety zone for my lads."

I sweep an arm across the roof. "Thus, the launchers."

"Your latest exhibitions of low altitude B.A.S.E. jumps have raised serious concerns," says a fresh-out-of-journalism-school reporter. He rocks a Channel Six pin on the lapel of a blazer clearly tailored for someone else. We get his type all the time: low man on the news roster, usually stuck with covering mudslides or C-list celebrity screw-ups.

I grunt at the question. Timmer's a walking archive of aerodynamics. His B.A.S.E. jump designs adhere to a superhuman canon of safety. Even Unc can't control the wreath of clouds descending on the tower. Humidity makes trickier conditions. My bangs congeal into a sweaty clump. Twenty-three is too young to die when you have plans, and I have plans.

"To you, B.A.S.E. jumping is an extreme sport. To me, it's a science." Timmer slings an arm around my shoulder. "Would I risk my own nephew's life?"

A grandfatherly dude slides square-framed sunglasses to the end of a nose in serious need of a good hair plucking. "Come on, Mr. MacKenzie, that kid can't be eighteen."

I wince at the familiar speculation my youthful image always dredges up. Satan's roadies have prepped a new circle of hell for Timmer's perpetuation of the lie about me being eighteen. My B.A.S.E. jumping talents at twenty-three are PDG – pretty damn great—but a fresh out of high-school dude rocking my moves is prodigy wonder boy territory, great P.R. fodder.

I keep my lip zipped over the deception. I'm not going to lie, it does not suck being a prodigy wonder boy.

Unc spins me to display the product emblems plastered all over my banana-colored wing suit. "Endorsements like these don't come from launching children into the sky. Justin jumps one-hundred percent legally."

The reporter's skepticism settles at the edges of his mouth. Metallic coating on his sunglasses turn my gray eyes silver as I catch my reflection. The gloaming breeze plucks strands of my tawny mane free from the generous layer of product I always apply before a jump. I'll have to retame those suckers to restore my roguishly hot vibe instead of the young and soft look Timmer prefers. I'd give my right nut to have a growth spurt on the spot. Sadly, thanks to MacKenzie short man genes, there probably aren't any in my future.

A gust of wind blows the press a tiptoe closer to the curved edge of the roof. Timmer and I hold our ground with matching "no big thing" expressions.

A babe in a raspberry-colored lady suit pushes toward me, eyes bulging with concern. Twitchy fingers alight on my shoulder. Next to my banana wingsuit, we're a fruit salad. Here comes the *concerned auntie* vibe.

"Justin, why take risks B.A.S.E. jumping with the Slinging Seven Troupe even for someone as enchanting as Zeli?"

I bite back a groan at the mention of the pop queen.

"Is glorifying her platinum record worth your life?"

Truth rumbles in my throat. *Yes, ma'am, B.A.S.E. jumping is worth the moon. It got me to Hollywood, the land of my music dreams. Dreams that will free me from Timmer's whims so I can make my own destiny.*

Timmer's glare scorches a hole in my suit, cueing the trained monkey answer he expects.

I open my arms to the clouds. "Who doesn't want to fly?" Every person on this roof does. I see it in the way their eyes brighten.

My stomach loops into a knot. Unc may piss himself when his prize canary asks to go AWOL. I've jumped off everything Timmer asked of me on our jiggy pathway around the country to make it here. My gaze drifts to the Hollywood Sign as I press toes into the roof of Rampion Records, the touchstone by which all music greatness is measured.

Tonight, this bird will fly off the Rampion Tower. Tomorrow, I dive into the audition for Rampion's annual singing competition, The Summer Number One. It's the U.S. Open of music, amateurs vs. pros, where Rampion Records dangles a chance for nobodies like me to go mic to mic with their current stable of rock stars. According to the Rampion P.R. machine – *Even the little people in this world have a shot at the Summer Number One dream.* This ammie is going to kick some serious pro ass and score a Rampion Records contract. I've got everything I need for the audition: demo tracks, my guitar, ass-hugging black jeans, and a sexy aviator jacket.

For the last five years, in every crappy rent-a-room the Slinging Seven have crashed, I've done dozens of online music courses. I study. I practice. I'm ready.

Unc laughs at one of the reporters he's chatting up, and I see Ma's smile here on the rooftop. Our signature MacKenzie smile packs serious wattage. I should know, I've busted it out often enough to sway, play, and dazzle females of the species.

Once I grab the top spot in the Summer Number One, my pile of gold for winning will be enough to snag my own digs here in L.A., the last place I remember Ma smiling. The cold burn of loneliness flares when I think of her and wonder if she's safe.

Clouds thicken as I watch the sun dip into the Pacific Ocean. I ignore a stitch of concern at the base of my neck as the jump difficulty ticks up a notch and think in my language of future Justin merch.

T-shirt moment: Music Dreams Sucker Punch Death.

Channel Six pushes in front of his colleagues. "Justin, does Zeli have a lock on the top pro spot in the Summer Number One?"

Lady Suit bumps her shoulder into mine. "Is Zeli your dream girl?"

My lips twist into a frown. Zeli is my nightmare.

Timmer digs his fist into my back, my cue to fix my pissy face. I manage to upgrade to a grimace dressed as a smile. By their winks and snickers, the reporters take my tension as embarrassment. I'd like to water cannon them all off the roof. I'm entitled to a dream girl, but it will never be the plastic diva with her bubblegum diluted pop crap. That chickadee is an affront to everything I love about music.

Unc hasn't run out of bluster. "It's an honor for the Slinging Seven to be part of Zeli's platinum record celebration."

My temple throbs. I'm more than half nuts to risk a concrete sandwich for that over-hyped female commodity with a pink guitar.

Don't stop now. Keep reading with your copy of <u>PINK GUITARS AND</u>
<u>FALLING STARS</u>

And find more from Leslie O'Sullivan at
www.leslieosullivanwrites.com

Want even more from Leslie O'Sullivan? Read PINK GUITARS AND FALLING STARS and be sure to check out all the details on her website at www.leslieosullivanwrites.com

Zeli's signature pop diva sound and image are nothing short of magical —literally. Her fame comes with hidden costs, a curse that could ruin her voice forever.

Aspiring indie musician, Justin MacKenzie, is determined to kick it to the top of the Rampion Records' Summer Number One professional vs. amateur singing competition.

The favorite to beat in the annual televised contest is none other than the label's smoking hot superstar, Zeli, whose crazy extensions flow the length of a football field. Those ridiculous extensions, coupled with her bubblegum brand of pop, are an affront to everything Justin loves about music until a stolen kiss blazes into a romantic encounter.

Once inside Zeli's world, Justin discovers things are not as they seem. In their quest to allow the real Zeli, to step into the spotlight, the pair must confront the mysterious force behind the dazzle of Rampion's success. If these star-crossed lovers can't rally their own magic to defeat the darkness, they will lose everything—including each other.

Please sign up for the City Owl Press newsletter for chances to win special subscriber-only contests and giveaways as well as receiving information on upcoming releases and special excerpts.

All reviews are **welcome** and **appreciated**. Please consider leaving one on your favorite social media and book buying sites.

For books in the world of romance and speculative fiction that embody Innovation, Creativity, and Affordability, check out City Owl Press at www.cityowlpress.com.

ACKNOWLEDGMENTS

Thank you to all the readers who've come on this journey with me to peek into the offstage fun in the "Behind the Scenes" series. I'm going to miss these characters, my virtual work family. I've adored revisiting the world of TV that was a well-loved part of my life. Shout out to everyone on "It's Garry Shandling's Show" and "The Boys (1989)," moments in time I'll always cherish.

Big hugs to Booktokers, Bookstagrammers, book bloggers and all the other book besties online who share their love of books for all the world to see. Extra hugs to the member of my Advanced Reading Team, "A Company of Readers," for their enthusiasm and support. If you want to join the ARC team party with us, you'll find the link here.

Much gratitude to Theresa Cole and Lisa Green, two superstar editors who believed in this series and made it a reality. I'm beyond grateful to the amazing folks at City Owl Press for their stellar and patient support. My stories couldn't wish for a better home.

Love to my always-there-for-me family and friends. You make this journey a blast.

Finally, thank you, *go raibh maith agat,* Ireland for being the magical land of inspiration filled with super sweet and fun-loving people and the best damn Guinness stew on the planet.

ABOUT THE AUTHOR

LESLIE O'SULLIVAN is the award-winning author of the adult romantasy *Rockin' Fairy Tales* series of fairy tale retellings set against the backdrop of a fictional Hollywood music scene and the contemporary romantic comedy series, *Behind the Scenes,* that peeks into the off-camera sizzle of a wildly popular Irish television drama. She's a UCLA Bruin with a BA and MFA from their Department of Theater where she also taught for years on the design faculty. Her tenure in the world of television was as the assistant art director on "It's Garry Shandling's Show." Leslie loves to indulge her fangirl side at Cons.

www.leslieosullivanwrites.com

f facebook.com/leslie.osullivanauthor
⊙ instagram.com/leslieosullivanwrites
𝕏 x.com/LeslieSulliRose
♪ tiktok.com/@leslieosullivanwrites

About the Publisher

City Owl Press is a cutting edge indie publishing company, bringing the world of romance and speculative fiction to discerning readers.

Escape Your World. Get Lost in Ours!

www.cityowlpress.com

facebook.com/YourCityOwlPress
x.com/cityowlpress
instagram.com/cityowlbooks
pinterest.com/cityowlpress

www.ingramcontent.com/pod-product-compliance
Lightning Source LLC
Chambersburg PA
CBHW020834260626
47169CB00003B/984